THE CHRONOTOPE

Time travel and brothels; unusual visitors from different eras, dimensions and realities; human zoos maintained by curious aliens who like to watch; private eyes who are zombies; leafy-green literary collaborators; moral steampunk issues; a dreamer at the edge of the solar system; a new life at the outskirts of the heart, soul, and reality; a last meal at the end of the world; an astronaut who has gone insane; an otherworldly observer that goes homicidal; and the conspiracies of chrono-assassins—these are the fantastical topics found in the sixteen stories from Michael Hemmingson's first collection of speculative fiction. Page-turners each one of them, these "what if" tales add new twists to classic themes of wonder.

Borgo Press Books by MICHAEL HEMMINGSON

THE
CHRONOTOPE

AND OTHER
SPECULATIVE FICTIONS

MICHAEL

HEMMINGSON

THE BORGO PRESS

MMXIII

THE CHRONOTOPE

FIRST EDITION

Published by Wildside Press LLC

www.wildsidebooks.com

CONTENTS

CONSEQUENCES OF STEAM

I.

Ellis Chamberlain is a stocky and powerful man who, when walking into a room, draws all attention to him—perhaps because of his flamboyant clothing, a nineteenth-century tuxedo with a top hat and white cane and a cape, giving him the appearance of a dapper gent from antiquity or a ostentatious stage magician; or perhaps it's the fact that he is one of the richest men in Nevada, holder of proprietary time manipulation technology, and owner of the state's four ChronoBrothels that renders an air of awe around him.

"All men are whores, and so are all women," is one of his favorite mottoes, "and whoredom being the oldest profession in human history, why deny this truth—why not embrace and become one with your inner whore? Defy conventions, I say! Sabers, gentlemen, sabers! To arms, and let us fornicate through time!"

No one knows more about history and prostitution than Ellis Chamberlain, sometimes referred to in the media as The Pimp of Time, "the man who will sell your great-great-great-grand-mother's virtue for the right price," an accusation he does not deny.

"I have had clients wanting to sleep with ancient ancestors," he says, "and I've provided them with that particular kink. They used to say, 'Whatever floats your anti-grav'—and who am I to judge another person's passion?"

* * * * * * *

"If I had never met Wilson Wilcox, my current timeline would be completely different," Chamberlain says, sitting at the bar in the Reno ChronoBrothel, or Time Lust #2. "I'd be still selling real estate on the moon, or I'd be a politician—what's the difference when both hock moldy green cheese?"

He met Wilson Wilcox when they were both freshman sharing a dorm room at MIT. This was no chance encounter, according to Chamberlain. "Before then, when we were just tots, on the same street. But we weren't playmates then, we didn't even know about each other. At the sweet sixteen birthday party of this lovely creature I wanted to—get to know better (and I did, too)—I happened to cross paths with young Wilson and someone said, 'Hey, you two come from the same pod,' and we talked about the pod and sex and science. Next came college, and we went to the same institution. I was majoring in international finance and he was a nose beak in quantum physics, and it was all Russian gibberish to me until he said, one day, he says, 'I believe I can open a portal between temporal dimensions.' That is, *time travel*, but only going backwards, never into the future, because the future doesn't exist."

* * * * * * *

Chamberlain reminisces: "I'm a history buff, focused on the economic changes of decades, examining the patterns of commerce, so the theme of a different era per each floor was my initial idea. With Wilson's time technology, we came up with magic, something the sex industry has never seen before—and you know they say that the sex industry is always the first to adopt any new technology. Think about it: it's the oldest profession of all, going back to the cavemen times, so who could resist sampling prostitutes throughout history? You want a whore from Biblical times, we can do that; from the time of Marie-Antoinette, no problem; or ancient Greece to pre-colonial Mexico to Victorian England. Try a harlot from the Wild West or a beer *frau* from nineteenth-century Germany!

"The question now is: which would you like to experience for yourself? All in the name of research, of course. Which you must do, sir. You can't write an article about the ChronoBrothels without hopping down the line and having some fun. Sabers!"

II.

May 16, 1806
London, England

My Dear Rosemary,

I am writing to you to narrate a most strange occurrence that happened last night while I engaged in my weekly group dining, in the company of friends and colleagues whose names I will only attribute initials to: K., V., A., W., S., and Q. We were entertained with a wonderfully magnificent and flabbergasting story by a man who called himself The Time Traveler.

The Time Traveler was a handsome gent who wore the clothing of our era, yet he did not seem comfortable in the attire, as if he were wearing alien skin. He told us to call him 'The Time Traveler,' stating that his actual name would mean nothing to us.

There were seven of us at the table. We had just finished dinner in the back room of the inn, and were enjoying brandy and cigars and telling ribald jokes when this fellow approached us. He said not a word, and sat down at our table without an invitation. He looked around at each one of us with his pale blue eyes, and we glanced at him with the same curiosity. He produced a cigar, a brand that I had never seen or smelled before. He struck a match. 'I would like to tell you a story,' said he.

'We love stories,' said S., 'but we do not know you. Rather bold to place yourself to our company without telling us, at least, your name.'

'I am truly sorry,' said he, 'but I do not have the time for pleasantries.' He laughed. 'How ironic. Here I am, a time traveler, and I have no time to spare.'

'Did you say "time traveler"?' inquired K.

'Indeed: it is who I am and the name I will go by.'

'And where, or whence, do you hail from, sir?'

"The United States. What you know as the colonies. I come from the future, the year 2106. Exactly three hundred years from now.'

That was worthy of a laugh from all of us. 'Preposterous!' 'Impossible!' 'Insane!'

The Time Traveler puffed his cigar. 'Please, gentlemen, hear my story before passing judgment.'

We agreed to listen to him. I asked if he would care for some brandy and he replied, 'Yes, most kind of you. Thank you.' I poured him a glass of the fine brown liquid and he told us the following:

'As I stated, I am from 2106. I am what you call a Hunter. I hunt those who break the laws of time travel, who go back and change the course of history, thus altering the timeline and the lives of our ancestors, with dire impact on the future. The individual I seek—we shall call him The Journalist, for that was his occupation. He was on assignment to write a feature article on the ChronoBrothels in Nevada. I will try to explain this in a way you can understand. I trust you gentlemen know what a brothel is, correct?'

'An outlandish question!' said W.

'Of course we do!' said S.

'I meant no offense,' said The Time Traveler. 'There are ten ChronoBrothels from my era; six are in Nevada, the others are in France, Florida, New Zealand, and Japan. Yes, these places still exist hundreds of years from now. The ChronoBrothels are enormous structures, one hundred stories tall, one hundred floors of different eras for sexual gratification.'

'You are making no sense, sir,' I piped in.

'Each floor is a portal into a different century, millennium, decade...you go to one floor, you will enter a corresponding brothel in, say, feudal China, or Denmark in the early twentieth century, or a harem in the Ottoman Empire. There had never been a breach before, a breach that would drastically alter the shape of history. It was, no pun intended, only a matter of time before it happened. And The Journalist was the man who committed this act. The first, I should note, as there have been others since, creating my occupation.

'The Journalist told the proprietor of the establishment— Mr. Chamberlain, my boss—that he wished to visit a brothel in London in the year 1769. The Journalist went to that floor in the ChronoB and he never came back. At first no one knew what he had done, because the entire history of earth had changed. It so happened that a customer who was in ancient Sumeria returned with his memories intact of a history no one else recalled. That person was—*is*—me. I know this may not make sense to you gentlemen, so I will get right down to it: The Journalist introduced to the British Empire certain concepts of steam-based technology that powered airships, naval vessels, and weapons of mass destruction; a technology that aided England in defeating the American Revolution and maintaining control of the colonies—the result eradicating many major events that would follow, such as the American Civil War, the Spanish Civil War, World Wars One and Two, the Jihads Uprising....'

'Pardon me,' said Q., 'did you say *steam-based* technology?'

'Yes.'

'We have that now.'

'You should not. It was introduced into this timeline one hundred years before it was meant to.'

'Thus creating an alternate timeline,' said V.

The Time Traveler stared at V. for a long moment, and the energy in the air was quite uncomfortable. The Time Traveler stated: 'Exactly. A *completely* different future history.'

'If all those wars were avoided,' said V., 'would not that be a good thing?'

'Stopping any war is good for mankind,' said A.

'Not if the end result are wars more horrible,' said the Time Traveler. 'To stop the power-hungry monarchy of the England of the nineteenth century, France developed, or will, the atomic bomb in 1887, rushing forth a time of massive nuclear warfare, nearly destroying all of our race. By 1890, there was, or will be, a total of five thousand human beings left, living underground.'

'All because of steam technology?' asked K.

'Yes. The consequences of innovation.'

'This is completely insane and absurd!' cried Q. 'The Empire *losing* the colonies? That would have been *impossible.*'

'I assure you,' the Time Traveler replied, 'it was once a true course.'

'I refuse to accept that those uneducated, uncouth colonial barbarians could defeat Her Majesty's armies,' said A.

We all agreed and toasted the Empire. The Time Traveler did not join us.

'We must know, sir,' said V. rather slowly, 'why are you here narrating this tale of impossible wonder?'

The Time Traveler glared at V. and stated: 'Oh, you know *why*, Mr. Vance.'

We all turned to V. in unison. Vance? That was not the name we knew him by.

I hope, dear sister, you are still reading attentively and not laughing, deciding that your older brother has been composing a humorous false letter or has fallen ill to hallucination. I assure you: I am quite sincerely serious about what I heard this man declare, and what was about to transpire.

V. and the Time Traveler continued to stare at one another.

'Well, that certainly *is* quite the adventure story,' said W., breaking the tension at the table.

'Gentlemen,' said V., 'I regret to inform you that everything you have heard from our visitor is true. To the best of my knowledge, that is. I am the Journalist our friend speaks of; and

I come from the future just as he. However, I was not aware that my actions had such negative repercussions on history. My initial intention was merely to get away from the life I once had. I was not happy in the twenty-second century, I had lost people I loved and my heart was broken. I did not go to the ChronoB with the intention of escaping into the past. It was only when I *went* back to 1769, and spoke with the young lady in my company, that I decided the eighteenth century would be a better era to live. The Empire was at its height of power; morality was decent, and I was then, as I am now, a true British citizen at heart. When I went back, and it seemed to me no one was going to come for me, I settled down to a new life. In fact, I married the young trollop in the brothel; you all know my wife, Christine, and that is her secret past. We had a child. I wanted a better United Kingdom for my family, so I drew up designs I had seen before in libraries, technology I remembered from my college days: designs for airships, battleships, tanks, troop transports, and mechanical armor suits, all operated on the single concept of steam power from coal. It was the best available technology to acquire, albeit too soon.

'Yes, gentlemen,' V. continued, his head down in shame, 'it would appear I am a temporal criminal. Millions have perished as a result of one single act by me, and a desire to create a better world. Instead, I fashioned one that was—or will be—worse.'

'It took a lot of energy and effort to finally locate you,' said the Time Traveler.

'I did not want to be found,' said V., 'yet here you are. You have me. What is next?'

'Will you resist arrest?'

'No at all.'

'Arrest?!' said K., a retired barrister. 'On what ground, on what authority? I demand to see your constable badge and a writ for such a detainment!'

'It is quite all right, my friend,' said V., standing up from the table, 'this gentlemen has the authority to take me...back to whence I came...so I can face judgment.'

'Say here,' protested W. to the Time Traveler, 'what will happen to him?'

'History will be shifted back to its proper course,' responded the Time Traveler.

K. inquired: 'How do you know the future history our friend here created by his actions is not, in fact, the more proper history, and the one you know is wrong?'

The Time Traveler did not offer an answer.

What happened next, dear sister, neither my colleagues nor I were prepared for. V. walked toward the Time Traveler and the two men stood side by side. The Time Traveler did something with his belt and I saw some odd lights emit from his body and....

I am not quite sure how to convey this other than to write: *V. and the Time Traveler vanished right before our eyes!*

I swear on the graves of our parents that this is what happened!

It has indeed crossed my mind—and the minds of the others—that this was all an elaborate hoax concocted by V. for some nefarious amusement. Magicians can do wonders today with smoke and mirrors, and the vanishing act could have been contrived via the magical arts.

The more I ponder on this, the more I believe it to be so, and soon V. will return to our weekly gatherings and confess to his trickery. To think that the colonies did *not* persevere and there was never a United States is indeed an absurd notion!

If you have had a laugh from this letter, it is my sincere desire that it was a good chortle.

I remain, as always,

Your Loving Brother,

Prescott Wells

III.

Seventeen-year-old Christine Williams waited in her chambers for the next customer, who would be coming from the "portal" rather than downstairs. She never quite understood what this portal thing was, beyond the doors of the closet, and Mr. Chamberlain, the man who owned the brothel, told her not think about these things too much. One matter was for sure: the customers who came from the portal were better dressed and smelled nicer and treated her more kindly than the inebriated, rough "gentlemen" of London.

The customer who emerged from the portal was a tall man with a beard, wearing an odd body-hugging black fabric.

Christine sat up from the bed, letting her robe fall so the customer could get a good view of her body.

He wasn't interested in her body.

—Some other time, my dear, he said with an accent, a curious accent, and one she could not place. Maybe he was from Australia?

He seemed familiar, though.

—Have we been together before, sir? she asked him.

He seemed nervous, glancing around, as if someone were chasing him.

—I know you from somewhere, said Christine.

—What? No, no—yes, yes. We—I know you too.

She stood up, closing the robe around her nakedness.

—My skin, it tingles, she said.

—I have to go.

—No! Please, I do not understand this....

She ran to the customer, this stranger whom she felt like she had known all her life.

He held her and kissed her on the forehead.

—A form of *déjà-vu*, it seems, he said.

—I do not understand, she said.

—Goddamn time paradoxes. I'm sorry, Christine, but I must

go now.

—How do you know my name?

—I will come back for you, I promise. It is, what? 1869, is that the year? What is the month?

—March, she said.

—I will come back for you by September, after I complete my—well, there are some things I must attend to. We have a child to enjoy, you and I. And this time I will get it right.

He started for the door. She grabbed his arm.

—How do you know my name? Why do I feel like I have known you all my life?

—Listen, my dear, can you do something for me? he asked.

—Anything.

—If another man comes out of the portal searching for me....

—*Another* man? said Christine.

—Tell him not to worry. Tell him…there will be no consequences of steam this time. Will you tell him that?

She nodded and he gave her another kiss and left the chambers, not through the portal but out the door where England awaited him.

—March-April, 2011
Tijuana, México

BROTHERS

I.

"Listen," I say into the microphone, "Jack, listen to me," and I lower my voice, "Jack, I know you're listening to me up there, I know this is piping into the cockpit or whatever you call it on the shuttle. They tell me you have not cut off communication; they tell me you're listening but you're not responding. This madness has to stop, Jack. This is all just crazy, you know? *You have to know this.* You can't just blackmail the government into stopping a war. Listen, Jack, do this for me: just respond. You owe me, for what they've put me through. They came in the middle of the night, these men in black suits and sunglasses— what a cliché—these men in black in black government sedans came by at three in the morning and they didn't even knock, they didn't ring the bell, they just busted into my home, waking the kids up, scaring Janice—my second wife, Janice, I know you only met her twice—scaring her, and the kids, scaring us all. To hell with rights and the Constitution and Amendment and courtesy, they just broke in and woke me up and said: 'You have to talk to your brother; he's gone off the ranch.' 'National Security,' they said. 'A matter of global crises,' they said. They wouldn't tell me *what exactly* you did until I got here at this government installation, this place underground somewhere. And here I am, in this room, this little room, and I know they are listening, I know the mirror is two-way and they are watching me. I think they think I may have been in on it with you, that I knew what you had planned, because we are brothers. To that I say: 'Am I my brother's keeper?' I mean, we have barely spoken the past year, ever since you joined the space program, ever since you trained for this mission, whatever it is, like it was a big secret. 'National security.' I know nothing, nothing other than what they have told me and what they have told me doesn't sound good, Jack. Listen: this madness has to stop."

II.

"Gentleman: I have done all that I can," I say. "I don't know what else to do. Tell me and I will try. I'll do what my country asks. I don't know my brother as well as you think."

III.

"I don't know my brother as well as you think," I say to the government psychologist.

We sit at a metal table, facing each other. The room is cold and empty except for the table and chairs. He wears a gray suit and blue tie. He may not be a psychologist. He says he is. I have no other choice but to believe what they tell me.

The psychologist asks: "When he was a child, when you two were growing up, was Colonel Kornbluth violent?"

"I'm not sure what you mean. What does that mean, exactly?"

"Did he torture insects, animals? Did he beat other kids up for fun? Did he beat you up?"

"He was a gentle kid, as far as I'm concerned," I say. "He believed in fairness, in justice. One time a bully two years older than me picked on me, that's the one who beat me up, this bully gave me a black eye. Jack went after the bully. Jack held the bully down and told me to punch him in the eye. 'A black eye for a black eye,' he said. I hit the bully. It made me feel good. The bully cried, he begged for mercy, begged forgiveness. I felt good. I learned a lesson, I think, about bullies: that they're all cowards really."

"Have there been any issues with his wife," asks the psychologist, "Gretchen Kornbluth?"

I don't answer right away. What should I say? Saying little as possible is often best. I say, "None that I know of."

The psychologist clears his throat. "Didn't you have an *affair* with her? Your sister-in-law? *Your own brother's wife?*"

"Excuse me?"

Matter-of-fact: "The affair." In fact.

"Affair," I say.

"Don't deny it."

I can't. Goddamn it: "How do you know these things?"

"What did Mrs. Kornbluth say about her husband?" he asks. "When you were with her, before or after you committed the act...."

"Pillow talk?"

"Call it what you wish."

"I need to get out of here," I tell him, "I need some air, some sunlight. This madness has to stop. *Let me out of here.*"

I stand. He reaches and touches my arm. I sit down.

He says, "In due time."

"What do you want to know?"

"What did Mrs. Kornbluth confide to you about her husband?"

I tell him: "The affair was short, a mistake, it didn't last long, and it was two years ago."

"What did you two discuss?"

"We didn't talk much."

"That's hard to believe."

"I'm telling the truth. We *fucked*. We didn't *talk*," I say.

"How do you think we learned of the affair?" the psychologist asks. "Colonel Kornbluth told us, in the psych evaluation before he was picked for the mission. He knew, sir. Your brother *knows* what you *did* with his wife."

IV.

They replay the video transmission Jack sent twenty-four hours ago: he looks so calm and serene as he says, "Listen. This message is to go straight to the President of the United States. I have murdered my crewmates. This is correct, gentlemen: I killed the pilot and the man who was to press the button. I'm on the button now. This mission is an error—this impending war is foolish and I will stop it. The missile with the warheads that was targeted at the enemy's capitol is now targeted at Washington, D.C. If the President does not recall the Navy and sign the proposed peace treaty within seventy-two hours, I will press the button and the government will see what it is like to nuke a city over petty indifferences. You will see what it is like to slaughter innocent civilians: children, women, the homeless, people who have nothing to do with politics. The clock is ticking, gentlemen."

V.

"Jack, listen, this madness has to stop."

VI.

Gretchen: oh, Gretchen, they have brought Gretchen in. Beautiful Gretchen: my brother's trophy wife, a wife fitting for an astronaut: tall, blonde, chiseled features, perfect teeth, perfect breasts, long legs. Smith College, former teenage beauty queen, law degree.

We are in the cold empty room together, sitting at the metal table. We're alone but I know they are watching and listening.

"I tried to talk to him," I say.

"Me too."

"They...?"

"...had us both trying to reach him," she says, "and who

knows whom else."

"What do you think?"

"Think?" she says. "What am I *supposed* to think? I don't *have* any thoughts on this. I don't have an *opinion*. I'm nobody, we both are, nobodies in this big game. Who are we? *Nobodies*."

"They know," I say.

"Of course," Gretchen says.

"Jack knows."

"I told him."

Pause.

"Why?"

She says: "I had to come clean."

"Jesus Christ."

She says: "Do you know what he said?"

"I don't."

She says: "'I don't care.' That's what he said. 'At least you kept it in the family,' he said."

I laugh.

She asks: "You find that funny?"

"How else am I *supposed* to 'find' it?" I say. "How am I supposed to react to something like that?" I ask.

She laughs too. We both have a good laugh. We hope that those who are listening and watching also laugh.

VII.

The bed they provide is stiff and uncomfortable. Nevertheless, I need sleep; I have been up nearly twenty hours. In have slept on harder surfaces in the past: the ground, the street.

The clock is ticking.

Every three hours my brother transmits a message: "Forty-two hours left." "Thirty-nine hours left." "Thirty-six." "Thirty-three," he says, "a pivotal year for any man, the most significant year of Jesus. Thirty hours left," etc.

Sleep and dream: sex with Gretchen and the sex is as good as

I remember it was between us. Gretchen enjoys the rough treatment: slap across the face, biting the nipples, smack on the ass, leaving a handprint embedded into white creamy flesh. "Jack has always fucked like a pussy," she says in the dream (like she said in real life), "but you fuck like a caveman and that's what I like. *Pull my hair, punch me, stick it my ass....*"

I wake up. I have a hard-on, what they call a "quality erection" for men my age who have problems with tumescence without pharmaceutical aid. A dark figure stands by my bed. It moves near me. It's Jack. He holds his space helmet in his hand, but he's naked. He gets into bed with me and grabs my cock and takes it in his mouth—

I wake up. *A dream within a dream.* I still have an erection. Why would I dream of such a thing about my brother? A dark figure stands by my bed. It moves near me. It's Gretchen. She's not naked. She wears the same clothes. She gets into bed with me but she does not grab my cock. She snuggles next to me.

"They let me in here," she whispers; "they wanted me to come in here for some reason."

"I'm dreaming."

"We're all dreaming."

"Don't get philosophical on me, you bitch," I say, "you goddamn bitch, this is *my* dream and you *won't* talk shit to me."

Shocked: "What did you say?"

"Bitch."

"You're half-asleep," she says, "you don't mean that."

"I mean it, bitch," I say, "you cheating bitch, sleeping with me all that time and then calling it off because you felt 'guilty.' Fuck your guilt."

"Fuck it all," she says, closing her eyes.

I get on top of her.

"Go ahead and slam me," she says, "fuck it, go ahead, just fuck it."

VIII.

A dark figure stands by my bed, looking down at me. I expect it to be Gretchen. It is my wife, Janice, my second wife. "How could you," she says, "how could you with your sister-in-law? Isn't that incest?"

IX.

"Twelve hours left for your answer," Colonel Jack Kornbluth announces.

X.

"Fuck it," Gretchen says, "just say fuck it at times like these. Do you understand me?"

"Yes," I say.

I know I'm still dreaming. She gets up and goes into the bathroom. When she comes out, she has changed. She's a man. At first I think it is my brother. This man is naked. He does not have a helmet. The naked man is I. I get into bed with myself. "Time to fuck," he/I say(s). This is interesting, I think, as this *doppelgänger* buggers me. What would Freud or Lacan make of such a dream?

XI.

"Listen, Jack," I say into the microphone, "listen to me: this madness has to stop."

He replies, finally: "I agree."

"Fuck it," I say.

"Okay," he says. "Fuck me, why not."

I reflect on the dream.

"That's it," I say, "that's what it's all about."

"What?"

"Do it," I say.

XII.

Eleven hours later, he presses the button. "Fuck it," he says, and that's the last words the world hears from Colonel Jack Kornbluth.

XIII.

Gretchen holds me close. I'm still inside her. "We did it," she whispers into my ear, nibbling on the lobe; "we showed the bastards. *We did it*. Everything worked as planned...."

XIV.

"You tricked us," the psychologist says, coming into the room with several armed soldiers. One takes the microphone from me. "Goddamn you," he says, "you tricked us."
"Fuck me," I say, before the world burns.

XV.

I remove the simulation goggles and sit up. From the look on the NASA psychologist's face, I know I have flunked this portion of the test. *Badly*. I'll never make it as an astronaut. "You tricked us," the psychologist says, "and that will never work, not for this mission," My wife, Gretchen, is going to be disappointed. So will my whole family, especially my younger brother, who has always looked up to me. I love my brother; I even forgave him for what he did.

—September, 2009
San Diego

MORE ALLISONS THAN I KNOW WHAT TO DO WITH

I.

I didn't intend to murder Allison Benning twice; she was having a flashback of something that happened in Afghanistan or Iraq and she went crazy on me; it was a heat-of-the-moment action, and I believe it could be classified as self-defense. You would have to know the full story, which I am prepared to tell.

I met Allison seven weeks ago at my friend Wendy's birthday party. She had just turned thirty and was ambiguous about this milestone age. "So many candles on the cake," she laughed sarcastically, but I could hear her thoughts: *I haven't accomplished enough yet, I haven't done enough yet, I haven't put my mark on the world.* I knew because I had the same thoughts, five months ago, when I turned thirty-three.

Allison was the sister of one of Wendy's friends. She claimed she was dragged to this party, her sister insisted she get out and meet new people. She had just returned from two tours in the Middle East, stationed both in Afghanistan and Iraq. She was Army.

I was taken with her. She was tall, fit, with piercing blue eyes and a pointed jaw. Blonde hair pulled back in a tail. She had the best posture I had ever seen on a woman, and I knew that was the Army. She was twenty-seven.

She gave me her number and I played the rules and waited three days to call her. "Took your time, Mr. Thompson," she said. She agreed to meet me for dinner that night.

We had Italian in a small cozy joint I knew in West Hollywood. I told her I was a screen and TV writer, that I had two independent films under my belt and had sold a pilot that never made it test on the air.

"They paid you for it," she said, "but it was never shown?"

"Paid well," I said; "that's the nature of the business."

"Tell me. I have no idea how it works."

I was more than pleased to talk about my world. "Every year the networks and cables buy, say, 80-100 TV ideas. You go in and pitch the idea, write a three-to-four-page proposal, what they call a leave behind. If the execs like it, they buy it, you write the pilot before Christmas. Over the holidays, these execs read the 80-100 pilots they bought anywhere from $50-100,000 each, and decide which ones to go forward with and shoot the test pilot. Which will be, say, eighteen or twenty. These get shot, using non-union actors, and go through meetings, and more meetings, and focus groups, and more meetings, then focus groups, then screenings by Madison Avenue suits, and more meetings. The ad guys determine what kind of ads they may sell to match a show, based on what they think the mass public out there wants to watch when they sit in from of the glass teat. Perhaps eight or ten of these will get lucky, the pilot re-shot with union actors, a few known faces and names, and then aired. Numbers of viewers and audience reaction are analyzed. Of those eight or ten, one or two will make it to a full season and go on to season two."

"How far did yours go?"

"Focus groups. Two million spent, down the drain."

"Seems like a waste of money."

"Like I said, nature of the business."

"I don't know why my sister wanted to get into the business. She's a costumer, like your friend Wendy, but she really wants to be a producer of some sort. Doesn't everyone want to be in the entertainment biz here in L.A.?"

"Of course."

"Not me."

"I bet you have some great stories of your Army service that would make a good show," I said, my head going to story production and life exploitation.

"Not really," she said with a smile. "I saw no action. I was behind the scenes."

"You're still a hero."

"Oh, *please*," she laughed, "do you really think a line like that will get me into bed?"

She was in my bed on the third date, like the rules dictate. She liked it vigorous and rough, the way I suspected a soldier would.

"Hold me until I sleep," she said.

She didn't sleep well. She tossed, turned, and hit me in the face, and screamed out a set of numbers that didn't make sense.

"I'm sorry," she told me.

"It's okay."

"I lied when I said I didn't see any action," she said. "I was in some pretty hairy battles and lost some close friends in my unit. I was taken hostage for three days by insurgents and a Delta Team rescued us."

"Wow," was all I could say.

"I can see it in your eyes."

"My eyes?"

"You're writing a pilot for a TV show."

She had me.

"That's all right," she said. "It *might* make an interesting program."

I kept seeing her. I enjoyed the rough sex, bruises and scratches and bitten lips. Each time we got together, she opened up more, felt comfortable enough to tell me about seeing her friends killed when they drove over improvised explosive devices or their HumVees were hit with RPGs. She told me how many enemy combatants she had shot and killed, and how they had roughed her up while she was a prisoner, and came close to being gang-raped if the Deltas had not burst in.

"I'm thinking of enlisting for a third tour," she said. "My sister will freak out, but I'm serious."

"Why? After all that happened...."

"Because it's *real* over there," she said seriously. "Is it 'real' here in Los Angeles? Hollywood? It's all make-believe; it's all bullshit illusion, people living fantasies and virtual lives. I don't want that. I grew up here, I know that life, and it's not for me. I don't know what I want, but I never felt more alive in war than I ever have. Here, it is all 'reel'—spelled like the spool is moving pictures."

Yet three weeks later, she informed me that she was now having second thoughts about reenlisting because she was officially in love with my sorry dreamer's ass. I didn't know how to respond to that; you never do when someone says, "I love you," and you do not love them back. "No need to answer, TV boy," she said, fingers on my lower lip, "what I feel has nothing to do with what you feel, and I can wait." Wait for what? I was fond of her, she was great to talk to and have sex with, but I had only known her for seven weeks and I was more occupied with getting a staff writer's job on a new hit science-fiction show than getting involved; if I landed the job, I wouldn't have the free time to see her as I did as an unemployed writer.

Then we had our first big fight. It was about a camping trip she and her sister had planned, a week in Big Bear; her sister was bringing her fiancé and Allison wanted to know if I would join them.

"A week?" I said. "A weekend, maybe, but Allison, I'm sorry, I can't do a *whole week* out of the city."

She wasn't pleased with my response. "Why not?"

"I can be called into a meeting last minute," I told her. "I have pitches out there, I'm up for this staff position. I have to be in the city."

"Company town," she said with distaste.

"You know how it is. Look, I'll go two days, Saturday and Sunday...."

"And leave me alone with my sister and her future husband?"

"The best I can do."

"Is it because of what I said?" she asked. "Confessing I love you?"

"What? No."

"I can see it in your eyes."

"See *what?*"

"I don't expect you to love me back yet, but I expect you not to lie to me and pull *bullshit!*"

"Allison," I said, and then I got it: her flattened palm into my nose. I felt the blood flow. I don't know what happened; it was in her eyes: she was not the same person, she was a mad woman, or a soldier, and she had a serious intent to hurt me. She used whatever hand-to-hand combat training she had been given and did some serious damage to my body, hiding her hands and feet, kicking and punching and chopping and screaming, calling me every name in the book. *"Kidnap and torture me?!?"* she yelled, and I felt a rib crack as I went to the ground. She was not here in Los Angeles; she was somewhere back in the Middle East, reliving a moment of violence, and I was not the guy she was dating, but an insurgent who had to be taken down.

And down I went.

II.

I woke up in my bed and every inch of my body hurt, like Godzilla had stepped on me a few times, treating me like Little Tokyo. She must have put me in bed after she knocked me out. I could hear her in the living room, pacing about, talking to herself.

I reached under the bed, where I kept a .38 snub nose in a shoebox for intruders. There are a lot of criminals in Los Angeles. I checked the chamber and made sure the six rounds were there. I had been on the firing range, and my Dad had taught me how to shoot.

I limped to the living room, wondering if she had broken my

foot. Determination and self-preservation kept me moving.

She stopped pacing when she saw me. "Oh, God, Brad," she said. "I'm so sorry what I did. I don't know what happened—I snapped, and...."

She saw the gun I was pointing at her.

"Brad?"

"Get out of my apartment," I said as calmly as I could.

"I don't understand."

"Get out of my home, and get the hell out of my life, *you psychopathic bitch.*"

Her eyes became hard. "You don't know what you're saying."

"I don't know what happened to you," I said, "but you're *nuts*, and I want nothing of it. *Look what you did to me.*"

She stepped forward. "I can explain."

I didn't give her a chance. I fired three times, all in her chest.

III.

I poured myself three shots of vodka. I wasn't aware of the pain in my body now that I had a dead body to contend with.

I considered what to do. Call the cops? Would they believe me? Soldier goes crazy, uses the karate chops, I had to shoot her. Or would I get fifteen years for manslaughter? I had plans, dreams, schemes. Even if the D.A. agreed it was self-defense, the scandal would ruin me; no studio wanted to hire a writer who'd shot a woman, justified or not.

I used to surf in Malibu when I first moved to Los Angeles. I still had two boards, and two surfboard bags. Allison fit into of the bags; I had to bend her body some, using gloves on my hand; I got her in there, zipped the bag up, carried the bag over my shoulder down to the garage and placed her in the trunk.

No one saw me.

I had no idea what I would say if anyone did.

IV.

I drove toward Malibu. It was past midnight. I kept to the speed limit. I stopped off at a canyon on the way. No one was on the road. I parked, opened the trunk, and dumped her body into the canyon.

Driving home, I went through my story for when Wendy reported to the cops her sister was missing more than twenty-four hours.

"I was expecting her to come by," I would say, "and she never did.

"No, everything was going great.

"We panned a weekend trip with her sister and fiancé.

"I'm really worried about her.

"Did you ask the Army? Maybe she went back...."

And when someone found the body...?

I couldn't think that far.

V.

I slept for two days; then met my agent for lunch. He had a meeting set up for me with Harold Croker, head of a new cable station looking for quality material. "Get your best pitches ready," said agent. Normally, I would have been excited, but the only thing on my mind was Allison Bennings' body: when they would find it, what I would say when the cops came around.

But there were no cops for now, and what I found strange was that Wendy had not called or come around asking where her sister was.

I found out why when I got home.

Allison was there.

She was cooking dinner, some sort of stuffed bell pepper. She had opened a bottle of wine.

"Bet you didn't know I was an *awe*some cook," she said. "I thought I'd make us something special for our two-month anniversary."

She looked fine: no gunshot wounds, no bruises from being tossed into a canyon. She was more chipper than she usually was, the Allison I had known. It was obvious I had no idea who this woman was. I killed her again when she slept, after we had made curious tender love, no rough stuff. I took a pillow, put it over her face, pulled the trigger twice. I used the second surf-board bag and did the same as before: bundled her into it, took her to the canyon, tossed her down. "Let's see you climb back up with two bullets in your brain," I muttered into the darkness of the earth.

VI.

The next day she called and asked if I had a sleeping bag for our trip to Big Bear. "I have an extra, and a tent, if you need it. I'll come by at seven, okay? I have a surprise for you. I want to cook you dinner. Well I guess it won't be a surprise now, huh? See you then, Brad. Love ya!"

I didn't even contemplate how weird this was getting. All I knew was that I was going to get it right; I was going to kill her for good this time. I would put six bullets into her body, then reload the pistol and put six more into her carcass. I would chop off her head and bury it in the desert and put her body in a different canyon.

It was five o'clock and I heard someone opening the door to my apartment. She had gotten in before; she must have made a copy of my key. Why was she here early? No matter, I would kill her now rather than later.

A middle-aged man with a bald head, wearing a military uniform, stood at the opened door and smiled at me.

"Hello, Mr. Thompson."

I pointed the gun at him.

"No need for that, Mr. Thompson."

Someone was behind me. Before I could turn, I felt a needle

pierce my neck and my knees gave way, I felt like jelly and I laughed at the man's bald head and asked, "Where did all your hair go?"

VII.

I came to sitting on the living room couch, still smiling. The man in the uniform sat across from me, and another bald man, twice the size and half the age as the uniform guy, and wearing a dark sweater and black jeans, stood to the right of me, a syringe in his hand. He was waiting.

"How do you feel, Mr. Thompson?" asked the man in the uniform.

"Strangely, pretty good. This is some happy drug you gave me." I felt calm, at ease, wanted to giggle.

"We gave you something to relax you, and so that your mind will be more receptive to what I am about to say."

"Lay it on me, General Feel Good," I said and giggled.

"That would be Colonel, son," he said, serious. "You murdered one of our operatives, two units destroyed, in fact. Allison seemed to be happy dating you. So what happened? Are you a serial killer and our file on you was all wrong?"

"*She's* the nutcase," I said. "She snapped on me, acting like she was back in the Middle East and I was the enemy. She beat the crap out of me. I thought she was going to snap for good and do me in, so I protected myself."

"Hmm. What triggered her 'alter'?"

"Her what?"

"What made her violent?"

"We had an argument. Nothing big, but she wigged out."

"She's a trained killer. A weapon."

"And I was sleeping with her," I said, finding it funny.

"Here's the situation, son: Allison Benning was created by me and my team. We took a young enlistee and played with the wetware and made us what they call a 'super soldier.' But losing such a unit, all that money and time and training put in, well, we had to ensure the weapon would remain intact should something unfortunate happen. So we cloned her, her and many others. Whenever one unit is terminated, a new one is automatically switched on. The memories of the dead one get transferred to the new one. I won't go into all the details of this technology because you'd need a clearance I couldn't get, and you wouldn't understand it. Hell, I barely do myself. All I know is that you killed two Allison units and they were replaced. We can't afford you killing a third, the one heading over here at seven."

"I almost believe you," I said.

"You got any other explanation why the woman you murdered keeps coming back?"

"Y'got me there. Say," I giggled, "aren't you telling me top secret stuff? You're not going to kill me now, or wipe my memory are you?"

"What good would that do? You became part of an experiment, Mr. Thompson. We wanted to see if our super soldiers could reintegrate themselves back into society. After all the programming, training, and experience, could the originals or copies return to their old lives, or become civilians? We were pleased about the relationship, and that she had fallen in love, because it looked like it would be a success: she would return to civilian life, but always be ready to go on a mission if we needed her...or her clone.

"So, instead of terminating your function, Mr. Thompson, I want to make you a deal you cannot refuse, and the drugs we put in you should make the deal sound feasible and sweet, You will continue your relationship with Allison Benning, You will refrain from any arguments that will trigger her alter—the super soldier, as it were. You will make her *happy*, marry her perhaps, have children."

"That's asking a lot," I said. "Am I supposed to do it as a patriotic duty?"

"Not at all; we will give you something in return. Something that you desire more than anything else."

"Yeah? What? Strawberry ice cream? 'Cause I'd sure love me some right now." Giggles, giggles, ha, ha. What the hell had they given me?

"In a few days you have a meeting with Harold Croker, a powerful new player in Tinsel Town, and one of ours. On your desk you will find a proposal for a new TV show. A TV show that will get the green light and be a hit. A TV show that will make you rich and allow you to create more TV shows down the line—an important executive producer and showrunner, with his beautiful wife Allison at his side."

"And if I reject that life?"

"We erase you. Your choice." He nodded at the other bald man in the suit, who moved to inject me in the neck with the syringe.

VIII.

I found myself sitting at the table with Allison, eating the linguini and baked potato she had prepared.

"Well?" she said.

"It's wonderful," I said.

"A woman who can cook! A soldier and a chef," she said, grabbing my hand.

"A keeper," I heard myself saying, groggy and stifling one last giggle.

IX.

The pages on my desk were quite curious, and something I might have thought up myself: a group of soldiers who believe the government enhanced them in a secret program band together to learn the truth, and help others in need along the way. They were called the Idyllwild Group.

What the hell. I took it and pitched it to Croker along with three of my ideas. I thought it was a good pitch meeting. My agent called ten minutes after I left Croker's office on Wiltshire and Santa Monica, as I was about to get on the freeway and return to Allison, who was waiting for me, our camping gear packed.

"You certainly made an impression, Brad," said the agent. "Croker wants to buy *The Idyllwild Group* right off, and for half a million. Can you believe that? Hey, what is this storyline anyway? You never drove it past me. Never mind, he wants to go for it and get it on the fast track for his Fall season line-up. This could be big, buddy. You were on your A-game and it paid off. Now go out and celebrate."

Yeah, I could go along with this life change, and everything else in the deal.

I felt damn patriotic.

X.

Allison and I finished packing and headed to Big Bear with her sister and fiancé, who also happened to be in the Army, and bore a strong resemblance to the fellow in the black jeans who had injected me with the wonder drugs. But he wasn't bald, and that toupee was impressive. I took it in stride. They had to keep an eye on the merchandise.

It was going to be a nice week, I knew it; and maybe a nice life. Sure, I could marry this soldier girl, and if I ever got tired of her, and decided to kill her again, she would simply come back to me, bright shiny new.

I would have more Allisons than I'd ever know what to do with.

—November, 2012
Tijuana, México

SIX DAYS APART

I.

They appeared six days apart from one another. That wasn't too bad; they were told the uncontrollable variables could be anywhere from ten seconds to ten months, and in the early days of the Transmigration, couples who went together could be separated up to ten years—one had to wait a long time for a partner to show up.

Bethany and Gabriel Morton did not arrive in the same cities, either. Bethany appeared, naked, in the middle of a busy beachside intersection in San Diego, California, while Gabriel appeared, equally nude, in the living room of a large house in West Hollywood.

II.

Cars swerved, avoiding Bethany. People on the sidewalk stopped and gawked like they had never seen a naked woman appear out of mid-air. The twenty-first century is a strange place, thought Bethany. She inhaled the stale air and looked up at the bright blue sky. It was a warm southern California day.

The police arrived. One officer put his jacket around her, covering her body, which she found a bit amusing.

III.

Gabriel popped into a home where a family was watching television: a husband and wife and two teenage daughters who giggled and pointed at Gabriel's genitals and muscles.

The adult woman screamed. The man went to a closet and removed a shotgun and pointed it at Gabriel.

"Please," said Gabriel, "I mean you no harm."

"You're trespassing and intruding," the man said. "Who do you think you are?"

"I apologize greatly."

"He's a real live *time traveler*, Daddy!" one of the teenage girls said.

"Is that true?" the man asked the sudden intruder.

"Yes," Gabriel said. "I'm a transmigrator."

"You future people have *no* sense of decorum," the man said with distaste, lowering the shotgun. "You show up anywhere you want without a stitch of clothes."

"Again, I apologize," said Gabriel.

"Dear," the man said to his trembling wife, "go get one of my dress shirts and a pair of slacks. We're about the same size, him and me."

She nodded and left the room, her body still shaking from the surprise.

"For Pete's sake," the man said, pointing the shotgun at Gabriel's crotch, "cover yourself, sir; show some modesty— you're standing in front of my little girls."

"Oh, it's *okay*, Daddy," one teenage daughter said, rolling her eyes. "Like I've never seen...." She stopped, as if letting her father know too much about what she has or has not seen in her fourteen years was a good idea.

"He's *hot*," said the other, who was fifteen.

They giggled and admired Gabriel's form and parts.

"Enough of that," the father said.

The wife returned with some clothes; she handed them

outward, not looking at the naked man as her daughters were. Gabriel quickly dressed.

"Thank you," he said, and he was indeed grateful (mostly that the man had not shot him on sight, which Gabriel heard had happened on occasion).

"Daddy, do you know what this *means?*" one of the girls said. "We're going to be *famous!* We bagged us a *time traveler.*"

"And *rich*," the other girl said.

"Thank you for the clothes," Gabriel said again.

"You need to meet my brother," the man said, thinking and nodding his head. "Yes, my brother Harold—he'll know what to do with you. He deals with these sorts of situations."

IV.

Gabriel had appeared first; he didn't know that his wife, Bethany, was six days behind him. When Bethany did show up in the middle of a street, she was taken to a police substation and her custody quickly switched over to government agent types in dark suits, who whisked her off to a Federal building downtown San Diego.

She was placed in a cold, bare room with silver walls and monitor cameras in all four corners. She had been given blue jeans and a green t-shirt to wear. No one said anything to her. They provided her food and water (or milk/soda, if she liked). They told her to wait.

Within an hour, a smartly dressed woman who was perhaps fifty years old walked in, holding a notepad and a file folder. She was shorter than Bethany.

Bethany had been pacing back and forth in the room; she was not concerned with her situation, she was worried about her husband and where he was.

"Please, sit down," the woman said.

The two sat at the metal table in the room.

The woman looked at the uneaten food. "Not hungry?"

"No."

"Have you been treated well?"

"Yes."

"No abuse?"

"I don't know what you mean."

"Sometimes when female transmigrations appear naked in public, especially one as attractive and young as yourself...they are taken advantage of."

"No. That did not happen. I have not been molested."

The woman opened the file folder. "All right then. Almost got run over there, eh? Some travelers have appeared in the middle of the ocean or in the air, so yours is no great horror story. Can I have your name?"

"Bethany Morton."

"What year are you from?"

"You call it 2533."

"Your age?"

"Twenty-eight cycles."

"Married?"

"Yes."

"Did you travel with your husband?"

"Yes."

"Where is he?"

"I do not know."

"His name?"

"Gabriel Morton."

"I'll check the database and see if we have him yet...or not."

"That is kind of you."

"No kindness involved. Do you think we *like* having people from the future pop up out of nowhere? The world is crowded enough."

"Not like mine."

"How many people are there in 2533?"

"Thirty billion."

The woman shook her head. "That's incredible."

"You have spoken to other transmigrators?" Bethany asked.

"A few."

"Then you know why."

"The chance to get away from an overpopulated world, I know, I've heard it all, I know the sales talk you folks were given by the people who run the time machines."

"Not machine," Bethany said. "Organics, metaphysics; *desire* is how...."

The woman held up her hand. "Spare me the quantum pataphysics. I've never understood future technology. But there are colleagues of mine who want to know all about it and they will ask you a million questions."

"I was told the authorities might detain me."

"Indeed."

"Am I a prisoner?"

"Not at all."

"But I'm not free to go?"

"Not right now."

V.

Harold Morris was a Hollywood agent, a big Hollywood agent, and he thought his brother, Dan, was bullshitting him when he said a time traveler showed up in his living room.

"Bullshit," Harold said.

"I have him here, come over and see," his brother said on the phone.

"If this is true...."

"I figured you'd know what to do."

"Oh," Harold said, smiling, "I know *exactly* what to do."

He left his office on Wiltshire and Santa Monica Boulevards and drove to his brother's house, fifteen minutes away. The man who called himself Gabriel sat on the couch, a cup of coffee in his hand.

"This is amazing," Gabriel said, drinking. "Wonderful."

"You don't have coffee in the future?" Harold asked.

"No."

He introduced himself to Gabriel, sitting across from him. His brother's wife and kids stood nearby, watching and listening. His brother sat next to him, shotgun in hand.

"You don't need the weapon, Dan," he said.

"I feel better with it near, right now."

"You afraid he'll run, along with your chance to cash in?"

"You could say that."

"Mr. Morton," Harold Morris said, "you're about to have your fifteen minutes."

"I am?" said Gabriel.

"I'm going to make you famous, my brother rich, and I'll take 15% of everything—all merchandizing, any technological wonders you know about that could become of use, and your life story for a movie of the week. You will have status, wealth, and half the women in the world will want to take you to bed."

The teenage girls giggled.

"Including my jailbait nieces," Harold added.

"Then I will shoot him," Dan said.

"I am married," Gabriel said.

"Don't listen to my brother," Harold said. "He won't kill his lottery ticket. Now, the government offers one million dollars for turning in a traveler who has not appeared in public. There's that route. A better route is to exploit all possible revenue outlets— TV, print, radio, Internet. Exclusives, one-on-one interviews; an intimate look at the future. How does this sound so far?"

Gabriel sipped the coffee. "I don't understand."

"No worries. You will."

VI.

The woman's name was Grace, "Agent Beryl Grace," she said. Bethany started to feel comfortable in her presence when she realized that the woman was here to help her, not threaten. She had been told the authorities of this era were suspicious and paranoid, and were not exactly hospitable to travelers from the future.

Agent Grace had a flat screen television monitor brought in.

"This was on a talk show last night," Agent Grace said. She turned on the TV with a remote device in her hand.

On the screen: Gabriel. Her Gabriel.

Bethany's heart raced. She tried not to show a reaction.

Gabriel was wearing a light gray suit with a white tie and white shoes. He was talking to a man behind an oak wood desk; this man had a deep tan and silver hair.

"I love having peeps from the future come on," the man said.

"Thank you for having me."

"So how long have you been in the twenty-first century now?"

"Six days," said Gabriel.

Audience applause.

"Six days," said the man, "same amount of time that it took God to make the world."

"So they say."

More applause.

Agent Grace paused the image with the remote device: Gabriel smiling at the camera.

"Is this your husband?" the agent asked.

Bethany was quiet.

"We need to know the truth."

"Yes," Bethany said, "that is my husband."

"Gabriel."

"That's him."

"He arrived six days before you."

"That seems to be the case."

"We didn't get to him first," Agent Grace said with some dismay in her voice. "He's out there in public. He's making trouble."

"Trouble?" Bethany said.

"It's—not good," and Agent Grace pressed the remote and Gabriel's interview continued. Gabriel talked about an overcrowded future, war, famine, disease, despair, and how much he loved his wife, Bethany, and how they dreamed of a better life in the past where they could be happy and free of stress.

"Touching, touching," said the interviewer. "So where is your wife?"

"I'm not sure if she has arrived yet or not. If she has, I do not know where she is."

"The government could have her tucked away somewhere. They do that with you peeps. They like to keep a leash on you, all hushy-hush and on the Q.T."

"That is what I am afraid of," Gabriel said.

"Is *that* freedom?" To the audience: "I ask, is it freedom to travel back in time only to be a prisoner of the government?"

From the audience: "NO!"

Boos.

"If your wife is being held," the man said, "what would you like to say to her, Gabriel?"

Gabriel looked at the camera. The camera closed in on him. Gabriel never sounded more sincere: "Bethany, I love you, and we will be together again, I promise, I will wait for you and never stop looking for you."

Applause.

The TV went black.

"Am I a prisoner?" Bethany asked.

"Of course not," Agent Grace said.

"Can I walk out of here and leave?"

Agent Grace did not respond.

Bethany stood. She walked to the gray metal door. She placed her hand on the handle. "It's locked."

"For your protection."

"I'd like to leave this place."

"I'm afraid you cannot right now."

"Why?"

"For your protection."

"From who?"

"There are people out there...who would like to use you, to

get information. People like the ones using your husband for propaganda, smearing the government's name and intentions."

"So I am a prisoner."

"You are a *guest*."

"I want to speak to my husband. I want to contact him. I want him to know that I am here and I am all right and safe. Can I do this?"

"Not at the moment."

"Why?"

"It is not feasible."

"He doesn't know...."

"We have treated you kindly, fairly."

"You have no right."

"Yes, we do."

"How do you justify holding me here against my will?"

"You were naked in public—that's an offense. Public indecency. You can be charged for that."

"Then 'charge' me, and let me go."

"That...is not feasible."

"You have no right!" Bethany slammed her palms on the door.

Agent Grace said, "You are detained as an 'enemy combatant.'"

"I don't know what that means."

"You present a threat."

"How can I threaten? How am I an 'enemy'?"

Agent Grace cleared her throat. "You represent the future."

"The future is an enemy?"

"In a manner of speaking."

"The future is a threat?"

"Very much so."

VII.

Harold Morris said, "According to my sources, which cost a pretty penny, the feds have her."

"Is this certain?" Gabriel asked.

"Nothing in this world is certain except time travelers and taxes." Morris laughed. The two were sitting on the deck of a Malibu house. The house belonged to an actor Morris represented, presently on location in Africa for a film, glad to let the new time traveler stay as a guest.

Below, on the Malibu beach, a dozen paparazzi with cameras were taking photos of Gabriel and his agent lounging on the deck and drinking sodas from the can.

Morris said, "A naked woman was reported to have appeared in San Diego a week and a half ago. The cops nabbed her. She has long blonde hair."

"Bethany."

"Most likely."

"How can they do this?"

"Because they have guns and power. That doesn't mean we have to sit back and take it quietly. We will work up a campaign for her release. We will get the country—the world—on your side. There will be protests, emails glutting the White House servers. Free commercials. Bumper stickers: 'Free Bethany Now.' There will be a documentary, a book deal, and who knows, the guy who owns this place will play you in the film."

"This will work?" Gabriel asked.

"Kid," Morris said with a smile, "that kind of media *always works.*"

VIII.

Agent Grace no longer visited her. Now it was a man, "you may call me Carl," who wore soft color suits and always had a pleasant, but suspicious, smile. He told her they needed to know information; if she gave them information, she would be transferred to the Traveler Reorientation Center in Prescott, Arizona.

"What is that?" Bethany asked.

"It's where many transmigrators go," he said. "They adjust to the twenty-first century; we determine aptitude and skills, we find you jobs and relocate you, and you become contributing members of society."

She nodded; she'd been told to expect this. "What do you want to know?"

"The biggest item on the list is transmigration technology."

"There is no technology; there is only the desire and the need."

"What does that mean?"

"If you want me to tell you how to make a time machine, I have no knowledge. If you want me to tell you how the physics work, I have no knowledge. I had a need, and I had a desire, to take the backwards step with my husband, and we did."

"How long did the people of your time have this—ability?"

"As long as I remember."

"Since you were a child?"

"I first heard of transmigrating when I had...nine or ten years."

"Do you know how many people have been sent back so far?"

"How would I? Don't you know?"

"We assume many have gotten past us."

"The ones you 'catch,' if that's the word...."

"Detain."

"Have any—died in custody?"

"Have you been treated cruelly?" Carl asked.

"Not physically."

"Please elaborate."

"You're keeping me from my husband, the man I need and love," she said. "That's a form of mental torture and duress. You dangle freedom in front of me if I tell you information that I do not have or know. If I knew how transmigration worked, I would tell you; if I knew how the machines were put together, I would draw a diagram for you. I can tell you how many people died of disease and starvation before I left," she said softly; "I can tell you how many committed suicide in my home city alone."

"That's not very comforting."

"Maybe you can change the future."

"Can one?" Carl said. "Change the past, change the future—aren't there laws?"

"What laws?"

"God's laws."

"I have no idea. All I want is to see my husband."

"That will occur soon."

"Are you just saying that?"

"Your husband," Carl said, "and the people behind him are responsible for a lot of attention on your behalf. I expect the order for your release to come in the next forty-eight hours."

"You're lying," she said.

"Or my superiors are lying to me. We live in a world of lies. You could be lying, about everything: the future, time travel, your true motives."

"So we don't trust each other," Bethany said.

Carl smiled. "Who does?"

IX.

Gabriel was amazed how the entire world sympathized with his cause and the plight of Bethany. The White House was bombarded with emails, faxes, and old-fashioned carrier letters demanding that Bethany Morton be released. The White House denied any knowledge of such a woman, who did not exist in any database. There were protests in front of the Federal Building in San Diego, where it was believed she was held, and other Federal structures across the country, demanding the release of not only Bethany but any other time traveler. The topic was the main focus on numerous radio, TV, and internet talk shows. Op-Ed pieces were published, letters to the editor; one young woman in Seattle poured gasoline on her body and set herself on fire "in solidarity with Bethany." So many loved her, Gabriel mused, and no one knew what she looked like.

Then the phone call came.

It was Harold Morris: "We have her."

"Have...?"

"They let your wife go."

X.

It happened so fast. They came for her—men in green uniforms, one in a suit. "Time to go." They placed a blindfold on her. She was escorted to a vehicle. She was told to get in. She sat and waited for anything. The vehicle drove for half an hour and stopped. She was told to get out. One of them placed something in her hand.

The vehicle drove away. Bethany pulled off the blindfold. The light hurt her eyes—the sun was coming up, it was morning. She'd been left next to a telephone booth on a long, empty stretch of road. Mountains in the background.

In her hand was currency: four five-dollar bills.

She looked at the phone. She knew it was a communication device but she didn't know how to use it.

She was wearing what she wore in the government holding facility: jeans and t-shirt.

She walked down the road.

She was thirsty.

A small yellow car approached her, like a bee. She waved at it.

The car pulled over. Two young women in halter tops were inside.

"You need help?" one of them asked.

"Yes."

"Why you out here in the middle of nothing, honey?" said the second one.

"My name is Bethany Morton," Bethany said.

The two girls looked at each other and squealed and giggled. Their bodies jumped up and down in the car seats.

"Are you kidding?!"

"No way!"

"You shittin' us?"

"Omigawd!"

"This is so—awesome possum!"

"I need…," Bethany started to say.

"Oh we *know* what you need!" they said, and: "Your hubby is a hunk!"

She sat in the back of the small car and they drove. The young women were excited, talking about how famous they were going to be: *they found the time traveler the whole world was talking about.*

"Your husband is going to have the best day!" said the young woman who was driving.

"Do you know Gabriel?" Bethany asked.

"Everyone knows who Gabriel Morton is!"

What an odd world, Bethany thought, wondering if these people truly deserved what was in store for them.

XI.

Their reunion was broadcast for the whole world to see— Gabriel and Bethany running to one another and embracing. There were cheers from the crowd watching. There wasn't a dry eye in any household in America, or Europe, or Japan.

"Cha-*ching,*" said Harold Morris, as he watched, and calculated all the story rights deals to be made.

XII.

Three weeks later.

Gabriel and Beth settled into their new home in Walnut

Creek, a suburb outside San Francisco. Their home had been purchased with the money from the various book, film, audio, and digital rights their agent, Mr. Morris, had made.

Their story was now old news, as other time travelers were showing up, and those whisked away by police or government agents were now the focus of the "time traveler rights" awareness groups.

One morning, Gabriel and Beth were paid a visit by a woman. The woman was familiar: known as Beryl Grace, but also known by another name they would not speak.

They invited Grace inside. Bethany made some tea. They sat and talked.

"You did good," Grace told Bethany. "You kept to the script."

"Thank you."

"All is going well."

"And these people believe it," Gabriel said, smiling. "They think we're travelers from the future."

"They believe because they want to believe," Grace said. "They think the future is horrible; they think they can change that."

"They have no idea," Gabriel said, shaking his head, "where we're really from."

"They're naïve," Bethany said. "I almost have second thoughts."

Grace shot a look, became stern. "You have a *mission*, soldier; do not forget your pledge."

"Of course. I am…sorry."

Silence followed.

"I miss the home world already," Gabriel said, easing the tension. "When do we begin the invasion?"

"In three months, when the final teams have arrived," Grace said. "More soldiers are being sent every day, now that we have spent years infiltrating all the correct government infrastructures."

"They think their future is set," Gabriel said, and laughed; "they haven't a clue what is coming!"

The three stood and saluted in the fashion of their world, their culture, their military.

"Victory," Grace said.

"Conquest," Gabriel said.

"Enslavement," Bethany muttered.

—July-August, 2010
San Diego

TRAILER PARK TRASH

I.

Lenore knocked on the door. Robert let her inside the trailer. He thought, at first, it was Maryann, even though they had agreed not to see each other until receiving an answer from the Keepers regarding their request.

Lenore was dressed in tight black jeans and a blue halter that revealed her midriff and ample bosom. No bra, she never wore a bra, her nipples visibly erect under the fabric of the blue halter. High-heel pumps, too, the cheap kind you used to get for $10 at a Wal-Mart or Rite Aid.

She waltzed in and kissed him and grabbed his crotch and said, "Let's feel that thing get nice and hard, baby."

Gently, he pushed her away. "What are you doing here, Lenore?"

"Why, *Robert*, would you ask just a silly question?" She kissed him again.

"Lenore."

"Yes, darlin'?"

"I can't. We can't."

"They ain't watchin'," she whispered. "You can usually feel 'em watchin', their bug-eyes and eye stalks and whatever else; like the ones with just one giant eye—*eww*." She shuddered.

"It's not that."

"What's your trip, baby?"

"I requested marriage, you know," he said, "with Maryann

Combs."

"Hockey puck," said Lenore. "Do you really think the Keepers will grant such a request? The Watchers like to see us promiscuous and wild, not married and borin'; that's what they think a trailer park is: one big fricken orgy. And that's what we give them. You may wanna marry that trollop, but it ain't gonna happen."

"It's happened before."

"Yeah, and *where* are they? They ain't *here*."

"Relocated."

"You think? *Truly?*" She sighed, shook her head. "Your innocence is what makes you so damn sexy." She was two years younger than Robert: twenty-five. He didn't remind her. He also didn't tell her that Maryann was pregnant, a factor that the Keepers would have to consider, an element that was necessary for marriage.

Her kisses and touching and the smell of her cheap perfume, and her smeared lipstick after kissing, was hard to resist... always was....

"*That's* my Robby-boo," she said with a smile.

"I don't wanna feel guilty," he said.

"You think Maryann is bein' chaste in the wait? I happen to *know* she's been over to see Bill Morgan and—"

"*Stop,*" he said. The only way to stop her talking, to tell him things that would drive him mad with jealousy, was to kiss her. So he kissed her. And he removed her halter and kissed her breasts, the pink nipples, kissed down to her flat white belly....

And so on...so sex happened...he had no idea if there was an audience, if the Watchers were there for today's entertainment, and he didn't care. He'd long since cared about strange and odd aliens observing human being mating habits.

II.

Robert Smyth had no idea how long he'd been a denizen of the trailer park. He stopped keeping track of time after the second year. He'd arrived when he was nineteen—that is, he'd been taken from earth, from the actual trailer park that was home, and found himself in this new park: same Airstream he'd been living in since he was seventeen, different world. He was twenty-seven now, so he supposed he had been here eight years.

Time was pointless. The sky was always gray, starless. Some speculated they were in a dome, and outside the dome were the Keepers, who kept them, and the Watchers, who observed their lives. Now and then you might get a glimpse of a Watcher: beings tall and short, multi-eyed, one-eyed, even a creature that seemed to nothing but a *floating eye*. As for the Keepers, they were green or brown and had scales and reminded Robert of alligators standing upright. They all looked the same to him; they all wore the same black tunics and smelled the same and were the same height.

There had been talk of other domes: the city, suburbia, the country, the mountains, the prison, the jungle—all the possible human habitations from earth. Robert had no reason to not believe this, and it made sense. Humans did the same at zoos with animals from all over, like the polar bear: re-created icy tundra for people to look at them in a simulacrum of their natural environment.

The food was decent, there was no rent to pay, no police officers to tell you what to do. And there was plenty of sex, as expected in a trailer park populated by white trash former Americans. The Keepers encouraged sexual activity, and the Watchers watched with curiosity, like watching those old reality game shows where people ate live exotic insects or drank horse urine to win points and obtain the prize.

III.

And then Maryann was in his life. She was a new arrival to the park and Robert was the first to greet her, to have sex with her. She was tall and thin and had straight black hair that fell down to her shoulders. She eventually had sex with the other men here but she came to him often, and he came to her often, and soon enough they fell in love, and she said she was pregnant, and they agreed that marriage was the best idea, so they put in an application of matrimony through the proper Keeper channels.

The pregnancy was intentional, of course; they had discussed marriage before that happened.

"They won't be happy if I 'forget' to take my birth control," Maryann said.

"They can't deny us marriage otherwise," Robert said.

"What if they make me get rid of it?"

"That has never happened, unless there's a defect in the fetus."

"You've 'heard' of this?"

"Yeah."

"No proof?"

"They welcome new humans," Robert said, "just not a lot of them. They're not interested in humans growing up here; they want a simulation of earth life. But they understand the value of procreation."

"I want a baby," Maryann, who was twenty-two, said.

"Then let's make one," he said, and they did.

IV.

He went to sleep with Lenore in his bed, after several exhausting hours of coitus, and woke up in a cold gray metallic room, naked on a bed. Standing around him were three Keepers, each holding a clipboard of some sort. He had only been taken in his sleep three times: once from earth, twice when he was sick with the flu.

He wasn't sick, though. "Why am I here?"

"Your request has been denied," one said in strained English, a language that was not easy for them to speak.

He sat up. "What? Why? She's pregnant!"

"The fetus does not contain your genetic code," the second Keeper said.

"Impossible," Robert said. "I'm the father."

"Conducted systematic tests," said the third; "as suspected, you are sterile. You cannot sire infants."

"No," he said, "no, I don't believe you. Then how did Maryann...?"

He knew the answer before they told him:

"The father is another man in the park. William Morgan. The tests are conclusive. If Maryann Butler wishes to marry, it would be with William Morgan."

"Bullshit," Robert said. *"Bullshit."*

The Keepers left the room and Maryann, naked, walked in.

She was timid, embarrassed. She even tried to cover her breasts and loins. There were Watchers watching, of course— how could they miss the chance to observe human pain, betrayal, and shock? To see first-hand a man confront a woman about....

"We had agreed only us, during the time," Robert said.

"I know, I'm sorry," Maryann said. "But one night Bill knocked on the door...and...and I couldn't help myself...and it was takin' so long for us...*months*...six months and *nuttin*...and now they tell me y'been shootin' blanks. It all makes sense."

She made her way toward him. He held up a hand, stopped her.

"Y'all hate me?" she asked.

"Will you marry Bill now?"

"No. I *don't* love him. He was just a *lay*."

"But the baby...."

"He don't need to know. I don't have to tell him."

"They will probably tell him."

"The hell with the Keepers," she said. "And the hell with gettin' hitched. We can raise the baby as we are. And they can watch. The hell with them." She looked around and held up her hands, each with the middle finger exposed. "You hear that, you creepy-crawlies? To hell with all y'all!"

"Go away," Robert said.

"What?"

"Leave me alone."

"You hate me?"

"No," he said. "Just go away."

"Bobby...."

"Go away!"

"Where? There's nowhere to go!"

V.

The first thing he did, when returned to the park, was pay a visit to Bill Morgan. Morgan was about his height and size, and thirty-three. He wore his hair in an awful mullet, and his moustache long.

"Hey, buddy," Morgan said, "wanna beer?"

Robert was not here for beer. He was here to fight. He punched Morgan straight in the nose. Morgan stumbled back, leaning against his trailer. His nose was bleeding. He was shocked, and then he smiled.

"'Bout Maryann, ain't it?" he said.

"You bastard."

"Hey, man, you know how it is here, how they want it."

"I'll kill you."

"You don't want my baby to grow up without a father, now do ya?" He grinned and wiped away some blood. "Yep, they told me. That's why I'm celebratin'." He held up his beer can, then tossed it at Robert.

The fight was on. Members of the park came out of their trailers to watch. And the Watchers were watching. Robert had a feeling they hoped this would happen: to see some actual human violence. So be it. Robert would give it to them.

The fight lasted five minutes, but to Robert it felt like five hours. There was a lot of punching and biting and blood. Bones were broken, ribs were cracked. Robert got Morgan into a head-lock and smashed the man's skull into the trailer a dozen times until Morgan's skull caved in and brains oozed out of his ears and his body went limp.

Robert stepped away from the lifeless body of Bill Morgan, breathing hard, bleeding badly, his entire body in terrible human pain.

The audience of park denizens cheered. The winner! The Watchers were also making strange chirping and whistling sounds of approval.

VI.

There were no earth laws here. He would not be tried and convicted for homicide. Morgan's body was disposed of. Robert went to sleep that night, and when he woke up, all his wounds were healed. The Keepers always kept their humans in top condition.

Maryann was gone, though. Her trailer and her body were missing. He wondered if that was his punishment, or because she was pregnant without a biological father. A few days later, one of the park denizens told Robert he heard some Keepers—the ones that removed her—mention the city. Robert hoped she would have a better life in the tall buildings and the posh apartments; certainly better than this trailer park and all the trash that resided here.

Every woman in the park wanted to have sex with him now: he was the virile alpha male who had won rank by murder. Plus, he was sterile and no woman had to worry about birth control with him, so he was doubly desirable. But Robert just wasn't interested. He considered celibacy.

I will be a monk, he thought.

VII.

Celibacy was impossible, especially on Orgy Day. It seemed to come around early this time. Perhaps there was a special delegation of Watchers. The Keepers pumped a powerful aphrodisiac into the air system, which caused a person to become delirious with desire. It was pure Bacchanalia: everyone stripped off their clothes and danced madly about the park. Couples began to fornicate, and others would join in until there were masses of ten, eleven, fourteen bodies daisy-chained in crazy fucking. There went Robert's notion of monkdom. He could not help himself and joined in, taking every woman—and sometimes a man—that he could.

There was a new body among the masses of the lustfully insane. She reminded him of Maryann: same body, same hair, but her breasts were smaller and her eyes were more spaced apart. She seemed to enjoy the sexual antics more than other women, taking on half a dozen men at the same time, one being Robert.

VIII.

After Orgy Day, Robert paid her a visit. She said her name was Nancy and she was eighteen years old. She had been taken from earth a few days ago and was just starting to comprehend and accept this new life. She said she'd been living in trailer parks since she was six.

"Is it always crazy like that?" she asked. "All that sex?"

"Not out in the open, with everyone, that's rare," he said, "but it happens."

"Wow. Well, it *was* fun."

"Fun, yes," he said.

"Does anyone ever fall in love here?" she asked.

"It's not wise," he told her, "but yes."

"I'd like to fall in love someday," she said. "I ain't never have...."

"It might happen."

"Wanna beer?"

"Sure."

She got two beer cans from her fridge. They opened the cans and toasted: "To trailer park life, may it always be a shocker!"

"I'm assuming you wanna spend the night," she said.

"You assume correctly, m'lady," he replied.

"That's cool with me," she said. "You're *hot*," she said, and then they did what the Watchers hoped they'd do.

—June, 2010
Borrego Springs, California

OF PROMS, TIME, AND ALIENS

I.

I thought I saw a glowing disk in the sky, driving home.

Actually I *did*, I saw it. I stopped the car and got out and looked at it. Other people also stopped their cars. Then it took off into the sky.

I drove home, a bit numb; not because of the sighting, but the memory it brought back.

My girlfriend, Anne, was home. She didn't look happy. I told her about the disk.

"I met someone," she said.

"I see," I said.

"I could be in love," she said.

"I understand," I said.

"We discussed this before, right? Am I right?" she said. "We discussed this. If either of us ever had an affair with someone else, we'd talk about it. I should've mentioned it sooner, I know. I didn't think it meant anything at first. Now...it's becoming something."

"What's his name?" I asked.

"You don't know him. His name is Bill."

"Bill," I said. "A solid name. I said I saw something."

"You're not bothered?"

"Only by my memories," I said. "Sometimes I wonder how accurate they are."

She had an incredulous look on her face. "I could be leaving you!"

"I know."

"David," she said.

"Yes?"

"If we'd gotten married," she said, and said no more.

II.

I'd skipped my ten-year high school reunion. My folks had passed along the information, the invitation, the request for a small bio from me. I wrote back, *David Stephens is alive and well.* I couldn't go; I hadn't become everything I'd set out to be. In fact, I'd become nothing. I was unemployed, my acting career was going nowhere: three failed sitcoms, a lot of bad plays, never the roles I really wanted, the roles I knew I could do. I didn't want to see people I once knew; I didn't want to see my former best friend, Mark, or my former girlfriend, Ginny, or the girl I really loved, Helen. If she was still on this planet.

I was trying to remember the senior prom, and what really happened. It hadn't actually come to mind until I saw the UFO; you see, the night of the prom I had *seen* a UFO—I think—and I think I saw Helen board the ship, telling me her real place was with her people.

Or was this a dream? Prom night, thirteen years ago, and I can only recall patches—the rented tux, Ginny's dress, the limo, the hillside party, the drinking, Helen's green dress, Ginny's pregnant belly.

I've had dreams, over the years, that I was having sex with Helen; just as I've had dreams that I was reunited with Ginny and we were having sex as well. Sometimes I think about these dreams and wonder if they were *not* dreams, if they were really misplaced moments in my life that I've conveniently discarded.

I went to see Craig, a psychotherapist friend of mine.

III.

"Hypnotize you?" Craig said.

"Yeah," I said. "That's what I want you to do."

"I'm not sure it'd be a good idea," he said.

"This is just between you and me. I'm not a patient. I'm your friend."

"That's the problem. You'll go from being my friend to being my patient."

"I have to know," I said.

"If you saw a UFO thirteen years ago?"

"I saw one three nights ago," I said. "I may have seen one thirteen years ago."

"Did you see aliens?" he asked.

"No," I said.

"I have a number of patients who claim to be abductees," Craig said.

"I wasn't abducted," I said. "And what do you think about these other patients of yours? Are they crazy?"

"Something is going on," Craig said. "Okay, look. We'll set a time for next week. Until then, I want you to concentrate on your memories. We may not have to use hypnosis. If we do, we do. But for the next week, just think back. Focus on details. Try to map out the night in question, anything and everything you can recall. From the moment you woke up, until the moment the night ended."

IV.

I tried, and I was afraid. I was alone, trying, and I was afraid. I'd come home and Anne wouldn't be there. Some nights she'd be home, some she wouldn't. She was with that person she talked about. Bill—the solid name. What had I done wrong?—all my life, what had I done wrong? This is why I didn't like to dwell on the past: I always rediscovered my blunders and overanalyzed them.

I was going with Ginny my last two years in high school. I had pursued her; she wasn't interested at first, then something happened, then we were boyfriend and girlfriend. I didn't know what I was doing, she didn't know what she was doing. We were making it up as we went along. We were kids. We were in love. (I *think* we were in love.) Yes, we were in love, as kids like us could be in love; but I wanted more. I didn't know what "more" was. There was something missing. I think she felt it.

We lost our virginity together.

She had a horrible mother, a tyrant of a mother, like one of those wicked witch anti-mothers from children's fantasies; the bad antagonist you must do battle with and overcome. Ginny and I certainly did battle with her. Her mother, whom we called The Monster, hated me. She thought I was a bad choice of a boyfriend, and maybe I was; my parents were no one special, I didn't have a job or a car, and my only interest in the future was acting. I wanted to be an actor.

The Monster often hit Ginny in the face. "Hit her back," I suggested once.

"She would murder me," Ginny said.

"Like kill you?"

"Once, there was this news item on TV," Ginny said. "About a woman who stabbed her son to death. The Monster said, 'I bet he drove her to it.'"

Two or three times a week, The Monster would ask questions like: "Did you fuck him yet?" and "Are you pregnant yet?"

Ginny answered in the negative; sex was our secret.

Sex was a secret in high school, as well as fuel for gossip— who's having sex with who, which teachers have had sex with their students, what wild thing happened one drunken night. The first item of gossip I'd heard about Helen was that she was drinking tequila in a car with two boys (this was at the movies), and she performed various oral sexual acts with both of them. When I looked at Helen, I couldn't believe this tale of debauched drunkenness; Helen was quiet and demure, with pale skin and pale blonde hair and gold-rimmed glasses. She dressed in skirt suits and fine dresses, and held herself—when she sat, when she walked—like royalty.

It was halfway through senior year that I was convinced I was in love with Helen. And I didn't even really know her! She sat near me in my Spanish and Political History classes, and sometimes we talked (her soft, bird-like voice). I started to have dreams about her, which translated into daytime fantasies. The worst of it all was that I spent my time, then, with Ginny, when I really wished to be with Helen. And then Ginny got pregnant, and I really wanted to be with Helen; I escaped into my fantasies with Helen. Perhaps I just wanted to escape.

V.

When Ginny told me she knew she was pregnant, I went, "Oh." Oh—oh, I don't know. I didn't want to think about it. We didn't talk about it. We went on like it wasn't true. But it was there—her sickness, her body changes. She was six weeks gone. I was hoping it would go away. I thought about Helen a lot more, I created worlds of the future for us. She came to me in my dreams. She said, in my dreams, Helen said, "Open your eyes, Stephen." "They're open," I replied, *they are!"*

VI.

I didn't want to go to the senior prom, which to me was scenes of horror and destruction in that movie, *Carrie.* You know, Sissy Spacek, the meek telekinetic, thought she was the sad little girl whose dreams had all come true, the lout turned to princess, only to find out it was all a practical joke. So what does she do? She kills everyone. (I had a fantasy of Ginny getting those powers and doing to The Monster what Carrie did to her evil mother.)

Ginny wanted to go to the prom, and my mother wanted us to go. My mother took me to be fitted for a tux rental; I thought I looked rather well in it, standing before the mirror, turning sideways, then spinning forward, my hand out like a gun, the James Bond theme running through my mind, the way impressionable young men dream of being heroes. My mother even rented a dress for Ginny, because The Monster certainly wasn't going to lift a finger for this event. I don't know what my mother was thinking, about Ginny and me. Did she think we were going to get married? What would my mother say if she knew Ginny was pregnant? The whole time I kept thinking these things—especially when she took me to get my finger fitted for a class ring. What would my mother say if she knew she were going to be a grandmother?

Perhaps she would've been happy.

I wasn't happy.

I was scared as all hell.

VII.

Anne came home.

"Hello," I said.

"Hi," she said. She wouldn't look at me.

"Home tonight?" I asked.

"You want dinner?" she said. "I was thinking of making dinner."

I joined her in the kitchen. She was starting to make spaghetti.

"I want a quiet night," she said. Something was wrong, I could tell by her voice.

"What?"

"Don't ask me about Bill."

"I won't. I wasn't going to."

"Oh," she said. "How've you been?"

"Did you go to your senior prom?" I asked.

"What?"

"Prom," I said.

"Of course," she said, thinking. "Of course." She stirred the noodles.

"Who'd you go with?"

"Hank," she said.

"Another solid name," I said.

"Please," she said.

"Meat sauce tonight?"

"All we have is marinara."

"Did you love Hank?" I asked.

"No, no," she said. "He was a *jock*. Football. Someone to go with. He asked me, I said yes. He was a good lay, too. Now that I think about it. A good hard fuck."

VIII.

"So, wait," Anne said as we ate dinner, "you were with Ginny, but you didn't want to be with Ginny."

"No."

"You wanted this Helen."

"I think so."

"You said you loved Ginny."

"I loved her," I said. "Yes, I loved her very much."

"But you loved Helen."

"No."

"You were afraid," Anne said. "Ginny was knocked up, you couldn't deal with it, so you had eyes on Helen."

"That's what I've been saying."

"Geez," Anne said, drinking red wine.

"It was a shitty thing."

"You were a kid."

"It was still shitty."

"What happened to Ginny?" Anne asked.

"She's married, as far as I know," I said. "Two kids. She became a Born-Again Christian."

"I hate it when that happens. What about Helen?"

"I don't know."

"Wait. Ginny has two kids?"

"Last I heard."

"One isn't yours?"

"No," I said. I realized that for all the time Anne and I had lived together, she didn't know me. I didn't know her. We'd never really talked about our pasts, like this.

"What happened to your kid? She was pregnant."

"Well," I said, "we didn't have it."

IX.

"Just relax," Craig said.

"I'm relaxed," I said. I was sitting in a deep, plush, comfortable armchair in his office. He stared at me with his abysmal blue eyes.

"Just relax," he said, "and listen to my voice."

I don't know how he did it—I don't want to know—but I went under. It's a funny thing. First you think: I'm not really hypnotized, I'm aware of everything. Then you realize something is different: you have total access to the past, and it's happening right before you. You're going through the motions like you're back there again, you're that age. You can feel it, you can smell it.

"Senior prom, thirteen years ago," Craig said.

"Ginny and I are in the living room of my parents' house," I said. "My mother is excited. She's taking all kinds of pictures. I'm in my James Bond penguin suit and Ginny is in her dress. I keep looking at her stomach, I keep thinking about the life that's growing in there. I'm afraid. How the hell will I tell them? Will they understand? They'll understand, of course; it happens. But I'll have responsibilities. I'm not ready for this. I don't want this."

"Focus on Ginny's face."

"She's glowing. She's smiling."

"What happens next?"

"While no one's looking, my father shakes my hand and says, 'Have fun, kid.' He has slipped a one hundred dollar bill into my hand. I'm surprised. He was against renting the limo. He's been drinking, I see. I want to be drunk. I'll get drunk later on, I know."

"Let's move to the prom itself."

X.

A hotel ballroom near the beach. It was a nice feeling, arriving in a limo, when few couples here had a limo. There was food, and Ginny and I had food. There was dancing, and Ginny and I danced. There was a photographer taking photos of all the couples, and Ginny and I stood in the line and we got our photos taken: she sitting in a chair, me standing beside her, one arm around her shoulder, one hand taking her hand.

I saw Helen. She'd come stag, apparently, with several other girls. How could she not have a date? I wondered. She was exquisite in her green dress, black gloves that came to her elbows. She wasn't wearing her glasses, and her blonde hair was bunched up, strands falling over her forehead and eyes. I think Ginny saw me looking at her—she cleared her throat. I forced myself not to look at Helen.

Something felt empty in me. Something felt wrong. I was in the wrong Universe. This wasn't the way things were supposed to happen, I wasn't intended to graduate high school and go straight into fatherhood, maybe even marriage.

I looked at Ginny, and for a brief moment, I felt resentment.

I wanted to say something to her, but tonight was certainly not the night.

I was scared.

Ginny and I danced a slow dance. We returned to our table. I was trying to be sly, my eye seeking out Helen—she danced with a few guys, but mostly remained with her friends.

Mark joined us. Mark was my best friend. He was a tall, overweight guy who was into a lot of the things I was: acting, literature, rock music. We had a good connection. We'd spent many nights driving around in his car, looking for adventures that never came to us.

Mark had also come stag, with a couple of other guys.

Mark tried to get dates, but it never happened.

His tux didn't quite fit him, either.

Mark was full of talk, and he was talking to Ginny, which distracted her enough for me to watch Helen's movements.

What the hell was I doing? This was the senior prom! I was supposed to be having fun....

"Mind if I dance with your date?" Mark said to me, that usual hint of sarcasm in his voice.

"Not at all, sir," said I.

So Ginny danced with Mark—it was a funny sight: Ginny was five-two, Mark was six-three.

Helen was looking at me. She had a drink in her hand, and she was looking my way. I didn't know what to do. She waved. I waved back. Then I looked away.

What the hell was I doing? I should've gone over there, I should've asked her for a dance. Helen was in two of my classes, right, she sat next to me, right—so Ginny would understand.

Ginny and Mark returned.

"Dance with me?" Ginny said.

"Yes," I said, standing up.

"Me and my big clumsy feet," Mark said.

XI.

I used the hundred dollar bill to get a motel room. Ginny and I had gotten a motel room a few times—it was an exciting teenage thing to do. We drove around in the limo until our time was up. "You're the quietest couple I've had in a while," he said, "usually proms are pretty wild." I tipped him twenty bucks at the motel.

"We *are* quiet," Ginny said when we went into our room.

"We're getting old," I said. "This is scary."

We undressed and got into bed.

"Senior prom," Ginny said. "Do you want to make love?"

My hand was on her slightly protruding belly. "I don't know."

"I'm not in the mood. I will if you want to."

"I'm not in the mood," I said.

"Okay."

"Oh God."

"Oh God is right."

"We're talking like some kind of old married couple," I said.

"We're comfortable," she said, hugging me.

There were knocks at the door.

"Mark?" Ginny said.

"Probably," I said.

I got dressed and let Mark it. Ginny pulled the covers to her chin.

"Old man," Mark said, like he was reading my mind. "I come to whisk you away for an adventure. The both of you."

"No adventures for me," Ginny said. "Sleep is for me."

I looked at Ginny.

"Go ahead," she told me. Her eyes said it was all right.

I did need to get away from this scene.

Mark and I left and got into his car. There was plenty of booze on the floor. I picked up a bottle of Jim Beam and took a good swig.

"You're getting boring," Mark said.

"Fuck you. Where we going?"

"Everyone's headed to Presidio Park."

"And that's where we're off to?"

"You bet," Mark said, revving the engine. "It's the end of our lives tonight! Ha! Hey, you think I might get laid up there?"

XII.

"Presidio Park is on top of this small mountain," I said under hypnosis. "It's basically the big party hangout—people gather and party until the cops come and tell them to leave. The cops aren't going to come tonight, not on this special night. Even cops have hearts sometimes. So Mark and I are there, drinking, and there's all these kids from school, and from other schools too. There's a lot of loud music. It is here that I saw the UFO."

"You see it now?" Craig asked.

"Not now, no. I see Helen. I'm stunned. She's still in her green dress, and those gloves. She's alone, drinking a beer. I know this is my one and only chance. I can't blow it. I grab a bottle of tequila from Mark's car and tell him I have to meet my destiny. Can you believe that? I actually say that. 'Destiny!' But I'm already drunk. 'Oh fine,' Mark says, 'just leave me all alone.' 'Bitch,' I say to him. 'Double-bitch,' he says to me."

"Tell me about the sky."

"It's a very clear night, a lot of stars out."

"Tell me about Helen."

"God, she's gorgeous. She sees me coming her away, and she smiles. Her teeth are perfect and white."

XIII.

"Hey there," Helen said, "hello."

I wanted to tell her she was the most perfect woman in the world; I wanted to tell her she was the invader of my dreams.

"Hi," I said.

"Nice tequila bottle," she said.

"Yes," I said, "yes, it is."

I took a drink. She was just looking at me. "Would you like some?" I said.

"Sure." She tossed her beer away, took the bottle, and took a good long swig.

"So," I said, looking at all the people here.

"Where's Ginny?" she asked.

"Not here."

"Oh."

"She's not—"

"It's okay."

"What?"

We looked at one another. What the hell was going on here?

"I know this *spot*," she said. "Do you want to go?"

Oh, yes I did.

XIV.

"She takes my hand," I said to Craig. "My hand is in her small hand, and we're leaving the general party area. She seems to know where she's going. She knows this place well. I've only been up here a few times. She's been up here many times. She's gotten fucked-up up here, I know, she's been drunk and smoked pot and maybe even had sex with a few guys. Then she says something to me which scares me. Like she's reading my mind. She says, 'Yes, I've been up here many times.' We're on the other side of the park, alone, and it's dark, and we can see almost all of the city—at least this part of the city on this side. Helen and I sit under a tree, and we drink from the tequila bottle."

XV.

"It's nice here," I said to her.

"Put your arm around me," Helen said.

I did.

She leaned into me. "That's nice."

"Yeah," I said.

"I know," she said. "I've seen it in your eyes. I've felt you looking at me."

"What?"

"I know," she said, and kissed me.

I was nervous.

"Are you okay?" she asked.

"Yeah," I said.

"I'm being abrupt," she said.

I kissed her. It was a long kiss. She stopped me.

"I know what you want, David," she said.

"You think I'm bad," I said. "Here I am, with you here, and I have a girlfriend—"

"And she's pregnant," Helen said.

"What?"

She smiled. "Come on."

"How'd—how'd you know?"

"Girls know," she laughed. "And I'm psychic."

"Oh," I said.

We were silent, and both took drinks from the bottle.

"I've seen her sick in the bathroom," Helen said. "I've seen her eating crackers. It's so obvious."

"Oh," I said, and drank.

"You're not ready," she said.

"No."

"It sucks."

"It does."

"I like you."

"You should've been my prom date," I said suddenly.

"No," she said, "no. And," she said, "you don't love me."

"I do love you."

"No."

"You've been in my dreams," I said.

"I know," she said. "because you keep *thinking* about me. I feel your thoughts. So I go into your dreams."

We drank.

I laughed. "Are you a witch?"

"You're getting drunk."

"You're not?"

"Not yet."

"Get drunk with me."

"I will."

"And?"

"And?"

"And," I said.

"You want to screw me," Helen said. "That's all you really want."

XVI.

"And?" Craig said.

I was silent, which prompted him.

"We're kissing," I said. "Man, are we kissing. Her lipstick is all over me, and her perfume. I'm grabbing at her tits and she's rubbing my cock. I try to unzip her dress, from the back. Then something funny happens. Helen pushes me away, she has this weird look on her face. I ask her what's wrong. She says, 'There is much you don't understand.' She doesn't seem drunk anymore. She says, 'Look up at the sky.' I look. And I see it. My God, I see it!"

"The UFO?"

"YES! It's right there, hovering near us. Well—not at first. At first, it's just this glowing dot in the sky, moving strangely. Then it gets bigger, coming toward us. Then it is there. Huge. Disk-shaped. Flying saucer, but really just a lot of glowing light. I look at Helen and she's smiling. 'I have to go,' she says, 'do you want to go with me?'

"The light is intense, too intense. It hurts my eyes. I scream. I'm scared. NO! NO! THIS ISN'T WHAT I WANT!"

I screamed.

"David," Craig said, "you're coming out from the memory on the count of three—one, two, three!" He clapped his hands.

I caught my breath. "Shit."

XVII.

"Shit," Anne said, "you're bullshitting me."

"No," I said, "I remember now."

"So there's this UFO there, and she what?"

"Yeah," I say, "and she tells me, 'I have to go home now, I have to return to my people.' I'm like, 'What?' and Helen says, 'I was hoping we'd have a moment, but my people are calling me back.' The next thing I know, she's standing under the ship, and this beam of light comes down, engulfing her, and she disappears."

"And?"

"And then I watch the UFO fly away."

"And?"

"I don't know," I said. "I remember walking back to the party. The cops were there, dispersing people. Mark grabbed me and said, 'Let's go!' In the car, he said, 'Where the hell did you take off to?' I said, 'I don't know.' And I really didn't. I was in a daze. Mark thought I was drunk off my ass."

"And Ginny was at the motel room."

"Yes."

XVIII.

Ginny wasn't in bed. The bathroom door was closed, and I heard her crying. The door was locked.

"Ginny," I said.

"Go away," she said.

"Let me in," I said.

"No," she said, crying.

"LET ME IN!"

She opened the door. She was a mess. She pointed to the toilet. There was blood everywhere.

"It's gone," she said.

XIX.

Anne and I washed the dinner dishes together.

"She had a miscarriage," Anne said.

"Yeah," I said.

"How'd you feel?"

"I don't know. Remorse, in a way. It was our baby. But also relief. I wasn't going to be a father. I didn't have to tell my parents anything. Responsibility was gone. I was free. I looked into Ginny's eyes and I saw the same, but I also saw a mother who'd lost a child. I think I aged five years in that single moment."

"You were too young. You weren't ready, either of you. Think of what your life, your life and her life, would be like right now."

"Sometimes I think about it," I said.

"So what happens next in the story?"

"What happens next," I said, my hands covered in soap suds. "We still lived a secret life. We couldn't tell anyone, and I called an ambulance to take her to the hospital. They cleaned her out. Prom night was over. She started to go to church a few weeks later. She said God was telling us something. She became Born-Again. She wanted me to join. I wasn't into Jesus and sin. We broke up, I guess. She met a guy in church, he got her pregnant. They got married. I went to state college."

"Helen?"

"Never saw or talked to her again."

"She went back to her planet," Anne laughed.

"Sure."

"Sorry."

Anne and I went to the bedroom. We undressed, and got into bed.

"Senior prom," Anne said. "I went with a jack whose only interest was to shove himself up my cunt. Do you want to make love?"

My hand was on the wiry pubic hair of her sex. "I don't know."

"I'm not in the mood. I will if you want to."

"I'm not in the mood," I said.

"Okay."

"Oh God," I laughed.

"Oh God is right."

"We're talking like some kind of old married couple," I laughed.

"We're comfortable," she said, hugging me.

We made love anyway.

"What about," I started to say.

"What?" she said.

"Nothing."

"Tell me."

"No."

"Tell me, dammit."

"Solid Bill," I said.

"There is no Bill no more," she said softly.

XX.

I drove up to Presidio Park the next night. It was mid-week and there were a few high school kids drinking beer and hanging out. I parked my car, and started walking to the place Helen took me to thirteen years ago. I hadn't been up here since. I had a small bottle of tequila in my jacket. I found the tree Helen and I had sat under, and I sat. The tree looked the same, if memory serve me. Memory was my nemesis, this I knew. So I drank. I tried to think of Helen's kisses, her skin, the way she smelled, the way her tits felt. I knew those sensations during my hypnosis sensation, but I couldn't grasp them now. I could only think of the way Ginny felt, tasted, and smelled. I looked at the city. The sky was mostly clear, a few clouds. Lots of stars, as always. I imagined one star coming alive, and getting bigger, and coming near me. It's a ship. And Helen gets out. "Hello, old friend," she says, all dressed up in a silver suit.

I finished the bottle.

None of it ever happened, of course. It was just a way to escape.

I needed to get more in tune with reality.

Walking back to my car, I passed a young couple heading for my tree. I smiled at them. The boy looked away, the girl smiled back—bashfully. I was just some old geek to them, I'm sure.

I got into my car, and drove home.

From the sky, a flying, glowing disk appeared, and hovered for a moment over my car, and flew away.

I got out, and watched it.

I went to the flower store. They were just about to close. I bought a bouquet of tulips and sunflowers. I hate roses. Ginny loved roses. I remember, once, seeing Helen walking to a class, holding a sunflower someone had given her.

Anne was watching TV when I got home. A game show.

"We're in the wrong universe, David," she said.

"These are yours, please," I said.

She took the flowers, and she kissed me.

—May, 1998
San Diego

SOMETHING WEIRD HAPPENED ON THE WAY BACK FROM BORREGO SPRINGS

OR, BUD THE MOTHMAN IN LOVE

I.

When the UFO passed over me, my entire sense of reality took a good crack in the jaw by the gnarly-knuckled fist of Fate.

I was driving from the desert, a two-hour trip back into the city, being unfaithful to my wife—with a woman from my past.

I'd been seeing Katie five months now; twice a week I went out to her desert home, spending the day with her, sometimes even the night—if it seemed right, if circumstances permitted. I was an investigative reporter for San Diego's largest newspaper, and the excuse of an assignment or research allotted me time for extramarital activity.

I'm not sure if my wife, Sheila, cared. Our marriage had been falling apart for some time; and was, I knew now, a mistake from the beginning.

I didn't know how to get out.

I'd been unfaithful to her before: the impromptu one-night stand, the occasional married friend who also wanted a mutual break from the spouse. I didn't doubt Sheila had done the same...I didn't blame her if she did.

I didn't care.

Katie was different. I knew her from before, another life; she wasn't a lover, she was my first wife's best friend.

I was driving back from the Anza-Borrego desert, from a little town called Borrego Springs, heading into San Diego, not sure what reality was anymore, when reality got weird.

The UFO was big, black, and triangular, the way some of these UFOs tend to be.

II.

"Just tell me," I said to Katie, before I left, "and I'll do it."

She smiled, pushing her curly blonde hair from her eyes. All she wore was a long beige skirt. Her breasts pressed into me. "Tell you what?"

"Tell me to leave Sheila," I said.

"I'm not going to tell you to do anything. If you want to leave her, leave her. That's a decision you have to make on your own."

"Don't you want me to leave her?"

"I want you to do what you feel you want to do," adding: "and need to do."

"It doesn't bother you that I'm married?" I asked.

"No," she said.

We were lapsing into a conversation we'd had many times, as lovers tend to do. I just didn't understand her position. And I told her this, too.

She sighed, and slipped a t-shirt on. "I've been in a lot of relationships, Neil. Good, bad, beautiful, and ugly. What do we have? We have the good and the beautiful. We love each other. You're in a bad marriage. Being here with me is good for you. And it's good for me. I was celibate for three years out here, all alone. But do you really think if you got a divorce and came out here more often things would remain so nice and wonderful? One of the reasons it works is because we see each other twice a week, under a time constraint, so we're always missing each other, and every moment is...." She smiled. She didn't have to go on.

"I'll still only come out twice a week," I told her.

"No, it'll be more often. You'll spend several nights, maybe a whole week, maybe two weeks. At first, it'll be great. But then...."

"Then?"

"I really need a lot of private time and space," Katie said. "You haven't seen my bad side."

"You don't have a bad side."

"Oh yes I do," she said, seriously.

"I'm just confused," I said.

"I know," she said. "So am I. That's part of it."

"Part of 'it'?"

Shrug, and, "Everything."

"Maybe it's the mid-life crisis thing on the horizon," I said. "I'll be forty soon."

"Me too."

I hate these moments. I said, "Guess I should go."

She held out her arms. I went to her. We kissed.

Katie said, "Then again, I could be wrong, and we might be able to spend life together in bliss, forever in an embrace."

"See you Thursday," I said.

"Thursday," she said.

III.

It was a moonless, star-filled night. My car went dead. The black triangle was about fifty feet above the ground. I got out and looked at it. It was several hundred feet long. It didn't make a sound. I'd heard about flying aircraft such as this, like on the Art Bell show. I'd read about them here and there, even through faxes that came into the newspaper offices late at night, often small towns with a great number of witnesses, outlandish stories that always disappeared.

I told myself it was a stealth military craft. There were secret bases out here in the desert, the military had them everywhere. I never doubted sighting stories, there were just too many; but I also knew our military was testing a whole lot of goodies it didn't want to make public.

The black triangle disappeared.

One moment it was there, the next it was gone. *Poof.* So long.

A greenish-purplish ripple followed, like a jagged line in the sky, small at first, getting larger, coming toward me.

The ground below me rippled as well, like waves, like a silent earthquake. I lost my balance. I saw my car shaking.

Then it stopped.

Everything was quiet.

The stars twinkled, etc.

I felt sick. I was dizzy; my stomach was twisting in on itself. I thought I was going to vomit. I tried. I didn't.

I sat there on the ground for a minute.

I got up, went back to my car; didn't know if it would start. It did.

I slowly started driving away, back on course for home.

Ten minutes later, I retrieved my cell phone from the glove compartment and called Katie. "You won't believe what just happened to me."

"Neil? I can't talk right now."

"What?"

"I just can't."

"You *want* to hear this," I said.

"Neil, I *cannot* talk...."

"What's going on?"

"Call me tomorrow."

"When?"

"Whenever," she said, and, "sorry," and hung up.

I saw what looked like a hitchhiker up ahead. It was. It wasn't quite human, either. It wore a shabby suit, and stood on two legs, but had a long green tail and three elongated heads three times the size of a human being's head; each head had three eyes and three mouths with rows of shiny sharp teeth, like something out of a wild Saturday cartoon. It held out a very long arm with a very long thumb and was staring intently as I drove by.

I drove by fast and delirious.

I saw it again a mile up. Or another creature like it. Better suit, same appearance.

"HEY," all nine mouths of the three heads yelled, "GIVE ME A LIFT!"

"Right," I said.

My iPhone rang. I hoped it was Katie. "Yeah."

A robotic-sounding male voice said: "Take this advice: do not talk about what you just saw."

"What's that?"

"Do not think about it, do not utter a word, pretend it was all a dream."

"Who is this?"

"Listen and be smart," the robotic voice said, "do not talk about what you just saw, to anyone. You called your girlfriend, you were going to tell her. Do not do that again."

"Yeah," I said, "and *what* did I just see?"

I passed another thumbing three-head, three eyed, three-mouthed, now wearing an Armani.

"Do not play games," said the voice.

"Who the hell is this?" I demanded.

The line went dead.

An octopus-looking thing was standing on several tentacles in the middle of the road. I slammed on the brakes. It sprouted wings and flew over my car.

IV.

The rest of the drive was uneventful.

I got home at eleven-forty-five. Sheila was in bed, watching *The Tonight Show*. Jay Leno was telling some bad jokes and smiling his big-chinned smile. I thought if he had three heads and three mouths, he might look like those hitchers.

Sheila and I said hello to one another.

As I always did when returning from Katie and the desert, I took a shower—I guess to get Katie's smell off me, or maybe to feel clean when returning to my other life, this married life.

I got into bed.

Sheila stared at the TV.

"I don't know what reality is anymore," I blurted out, looking at Jay Leno.

Sheila did something surprising. She reached over and kissed me. It was a deep kiss, an erotic kiss, helped by her hand reaching down to my crotch.

It didn't help enough. I wasn't into it.

"Bastard," Sheila said, turning away from me.

She knew. I should've said, "Let's just get a divorce and make this clean." Instead, I lay there silently. Sheila went to sleep. I turned off the TV. I listened to her light snoring. I looked out the bedroom window, at the stars.

The stars just aren't the same in the city as they are in the desert.

V.

"Do you ever think about Jenny?" Katie had asked me once, maybe twice.

"All the time," I'd told her. "Not as much as I used to, like ten years ago. But a day doesn't go by when I don't think about her one way or the other"—like seeing someone walking down the street that had straight black hair like she did, like smelling something that reminded me of a smell she liked—a food, a perfume, a body...her body.

Katie'd said, once or twice or maybe even more, "I always think about her."

"Of course"—they'd grown up together, had been best friends.

Katie'd said, "Sometimes I wonder what she'd feel, about the two of us being together now."

"Are we together?"

"You know what I mean."

"I wonder about that too," I'd said.

"She'd be happy, I believe this," Katie'd said, once, twice.

"Yes," I'd said, but I was uncertain.

"She would, because when we're together, it's almost like magic."

"Almost?"

"We're *almost* there," Katie'd said.

VI.

Sheila was gone in the morning. She was at work. She was a public defender; work started early in the morning for her.

I called Katie. She didn't answer. She didn't have an answering machine or voicemail, neither of which she believed in.

"If you're meant to get in touch with me," she always said, "you will."

VII,

Getting dressed, I recalled a dream from last night. There was something, somebody, at my window. The window was open. The stars were very bright and all that. This person at my window was large and grayish in color—human-like, with a lot of muscles, and wings and glowing red eyes.

"What do you want?" I asked.

"Not you," it said in a whisper: "I want her."

It pointed a long-nailed finger at Sheila.

"You want my wife?" I asked.

"You do not," it said.

VIII.

Tried calling Katie again. Nothing. I tried Sheila fifteen minutes later. It was eleven-thirty. She answered.

"Something weird happened last night," I said.

"Yeah," she said, "tell me about it," and hung up.

I decided I should go into work, not call in sick like I had been doing a lot of lately.

Outside, leaning against my car, was a six-foot-five man with very pale skin. He was extremely thin. He wore a shiny black suit with a thin black tie, a button-down shirt, shades, and a black fedora.

He spoke with that robotic voice from yesterday's call: "Did I not advise you not to talk about what you saw?"

"Eh?" I said, and: "That was you, eh?"

"Of course it was me!" he yelled; not much emotion in its robotic nature, however.

"I didn't say anything," I said.

"Come with me please."

"No."

"Come with me please," he said, and pointed to a black sedan parked across the street, tinted windows.

My curiosity got the best of me. I wanted to know where this would go, and what this was about.

I went with him.

"Do you have a name?" I asked.

"No," he said.

"You're just one of those mysterious Men in Black, right?"

There were three of them. One behind the wheel, one riding shotgun. They all looked exactly the same, like clones. I sat in back with the first one. The car drove away, wandering around the neighborhood streets.

My MiB said, "here we are."

"What's the deal?"

"I gave you a warning last night. But you have been trying

to call your girlfriend, with the intent of talking about what you saw. And you called your estranged wife, wanting to talk to her as well. She is unhappy with you, as you are unhappy with her. Do you know that she has not, in fact, been unfaithful to you, as you have been? That will soon change."

I asked, "How do you know so much about me?"

He replied, "I am resourceful."

"Okay, I get it," I said. "Last night I saw a test flight of some secret aircraft. That's what this is about, right? I saw the black triangle; you don't want me to talk about it."

"The airship is not our concern," he told me. "It's what started this. It's what you saw on the road."

"The weird creatures?"

"They might take offense to that description."

"Those were hallucinations," I said.

"That is a good start," the MiB said. "Think of them as… bad dreams. Think of me as a bad dream. This ride, this car, this whole conversation. File it away as a bad dream before it becomes an ugly nightmare. We're here, we want to go back; we don't need complications. It is the nature of colliding realities." He leaned into me. "What's that saying? 'Mum's the word.'"

The car stopped.

"You may get out."

I got out. The sedan drove away. I looked around; maybe half a mile walk back home. I had a nauseating feeling, like I did last night, and heard what sounded like the crack of a whip. I turned around. The black sedan wasn't anywhere in sight.

IX.

I got married to Jenny when we were both twenty-five. Katie was always around, being my wife's best friend, and I never thought that one day I would be in love with Katie. I never thought that one day Jenny would die, either.

X.

I must've fallen asleep at my desk—this is what I was telling myself when I found myself in the middle of the dream, or vision, or whatever it was.

I was standing in front of my apartment building. The sun was setting; a fog was coming in. I had a sense of dread. Something was wrong, something not quite right. My bones hurt. A voice in my head was saying: *Don't go inside.*

I went inside.

The apartment was dark. I knew Sheila was here. I could almost smell her. I could *hear* her. Soft moans coming from the bedroom. I didn't turn on any lights and I'm not sure why. The fog seemed to be coming into the apartment. I walked down the hall to the bedroom. The hall seemed longer than usual, the kind of clichéd distortion you'd expect in a dream/vision like this. Sheila's moans were increasing in frequency and loudness.

I opened the bedroom door, half-expecting it to be locked, half-determined to bust it open if it were.

The room was dark and filled with fog. The window was open, but it was very warm. The smell of sex was as thick as the fog. Sheila was naked on the bed, lying on her stomach; her rear-end arched high, meeting the thrusts of the figure that was fucking her.

The thing molesting my wife was the gray, red-eyed, winged-man from my previous dream. I caught a glimpse of its oddly-shaped penis going into her, as I moved closer, and said,

"Sheila?"

They both looked at me. Sheila's hair was damp, in her eyes; her whole body was covered in sweat. The creature's wings expanded, and I got a good look at them: yellow-spotted like a moth's. In fact, his face was like a moth, fuzzy and gray. His eyes seemed redder than last time.

"Neil," Sheila said, "I'm in ecstasy,"

"Go away," the mothman told me.

I snapped out of the dream, the vision, the state, and stood there, well aware that this was quite real. I *was* in the room, the fog was still here, the mothman was still on top of her.

"LEAVE," it said, rising up on its legs to confront me.

"Don't hurt him," Sheila said to her lover.

I ran.

XI.

My car was outside. I didn't know how I got here, I didn't remember driving here, leaving work, nothing. I called Katie.

"Neil, I can't talk right now."

"Don't give me that, don't *even* give me that," I said. "I *need* to talk to you!"

A pause, and then: "Come out here."

XII.

A plethora—maybe circus is the word—of oddities were trying to hitch a ride on my way to Borrego Springs. They didn't start showing up until I'd gotten out of Ramona and reached San Ysabel, taking Highway S2 to S22 into the desert. The thing with three heads and three mouths and eyes and the good suits started first; next came some amalgamations of squids and birds; monkeys and dragons; fish and giraffes. It was like some mad scientist was going haywire on genetic splicing. The closer I got to Borrego, the more adamant and aggressive they became—yelling at me, calling me names, trying to jump in front of my car. I wasn't going to stop. I'd plow through them all. I wished I had a gun; I knew I would not hesitate to fire upon any of these monsters. They wanted to frighten me away, I realized, and while I was scared, I was also determined. I found it strange how easily I accepted all this. I knew it had to do with the black triangle I saw in the sky. I knew the answers were in Borrego, with Katie.

XIII.

She was sitting serenely on her couch, in a long, dark skirt and blouse, petting some strange cat-sized creature that was sitting demurely in her lap. But it wasn't a cat, more like a small lion, with a goat's head sticking out of its back and a snake for a tail.

"Something incredible is happening," she said.

"Tell me about it," I said, sitting cautiously next to her. The thing in her lap looked up at me with three eyes. "What is that?" I asked, rather calmly.

"Generally known as a chimera, if I know my mythical beasts. She's quite harmless. She's a baby chimera, actually. I don't know if she breathes fire, so let's not provoke her."

I heard a car pull up outside, a door open.

Next came several angry knocks.

"Who could that be?" Katie said, not like she really cared.

The familiar metallic voice of my persistent MiB said: "Open up right now!"

"Neil," Katie said.

"It's okay," I told her.

I opened the door. There stood my MiB. Before he could talk, I punched him in the face. He stepped back. I punched him again. His shades broke, his eyes popped out, green jelly started coming out of his ears. Then springs came out of his head, and he fell down. I started kicking him.

Katie, holding her chimera, said, "Neil, stop, that's *not* necessary."

"I'm sick of this jerk!" I kicked him some more. Springs popped out all along his body, with loud *twangs*!

"He was only following the attitude of the image he's in."

I stopped, breathing hard. "Say what?!"

The other two identical black-clad goons came out of the sedan. I was ready for them. I wondered what I'd do if they pulled out weapons. They ignored me; they picked up their fallen companion, took him back to the vehicle, and drove away.

"I knew it," I said. "Their threats are empty."

XIV.

"This is what I think happened," Katie said.

We settled back in her house; she'd seen the UFO as well, it'd passed over Borrego, and the same rippling aftershock followed.

"I don't know if that UFO was ours or someone else's, but it kept disappearing and reappearing. I think it was traveling interdimensionally. Maybe it was having problems. I believe it tore open a hole between dimensions—ours and others—and a few inhabitants of those other realms came through here.

"Think about it," she went on. "In the past, people have reported visitations by mysterious Men in Black making all kinds of threats, after seeing a UFO. Just like those three that were at the door."

"You didn't seem at all shocked or surprised about it," I said.

"Not after what I've been seeing around here lately," Katie said, petting the chimera in her lap—first the lion's head, then the goat's head, then the snake head on the end of the tail. "This sleepy little town has been a madhouse of all kinds of creatures of our collective dreams."

"Dreams," I said.

"Yes. These things we have been seeing—they are entities of another reality—a reality we can't even comprehend—taking the shape and form of the things of our myths and nightmares. All my life, I studied about how to enter other dimensions and realities, but I could never do it. Yet there was always the warning: prepare yourself. Many who have gone to other realities have come back insane. The other reality was too much to comprehend, to understand; it didn't conform to this reality.

"I believe the residents of whatever other realities were opened up don't have shape and form or mass like we know and understand. By the same token, this reality we know doesn't make a damn bit of sense to them. They try making sense of it, or becoming part of it, by reaching into our minds and taking forms...of images in our subconscious."

I asked, "Why not just take human shape?"

"Maybe they don't understand something that tangible."

The door opened, and a woman walked in. She was wearing jeans and a heavy jacket. She looked just as I remembered her— her hair, her make-up, her smile.

"There's something else, too," Katie said, softly.

I stood up. "Jenny."

"I had a nice walk," Jenny said.

"Jenny," I said, "what the...?"

"The dead walked through the reality rip as well," Katie said.

XV.

Jenny wanted to talk with me outside. We took a paranormal stroll into the dark desert night.

"I can't get enough of breathing air again," she said. She stopped me. She hugged me. "I missed you," she confessed.

"You're alive," I said.

"For now."

"I don't understand."

"Does it matter?"

"I don't—don't know what to do."

"Do you have to do anything?" she said.

"I don't know what to feel," I said.

She took my hand. "Feel joy."

We walked in silence.

"What's it like on the other side?" I asked her.

"I don't remember," she said. "I remember being alive, we were married, and then I died, and now I'm here."

"Almost ten years later."

"Yes," she said.

"I have so many things to tell you. To ask you. To...."

"Hush," she said, stopping again. She put two fingers to my lips. "I know you remarried, I know you're having sex with Katie. It's okay. It doesn't mean anything to me."

"You're not the Jenny I knew," I said.

"Of course I'm not," she said. "I've been dead for a decade. It can change a person."

"Why'd you do it?" I wanted to know. "I've always wanted to ask that. Why did you shoot yourself?"

She made a face. She said, "I wasn't happy with life. Maybe I seemed happy on the outside, but on the inside.…"

I stepped away from her. "You're not Jenny. She didn't kill herself. She died of cancer. Who *are* you?"

She, it, smiled. "Someone who enjoyed pretending to be her for a moment."

This fake Jenny changed shape before my eyes. She became a thirty-foot snake. I was ready to die, for anything. The snake stuck its tail in its mouth and rolled away into the night.

XVI.

Katie had a beer opened for me when I got back, and one for herself.

"That wasn't Jenny!" I said.

"I suspected," she said. "I wasn't sure."

"I need to sit down."

We sat down together on the couch. I sipped my beer.

"Hold me," I said to her.

Katie held out her arms. I pressed my face against into her breasts.

"All my life I searched for the mystical and the mysterious," Katie said, running her hands through my hair. "That's why I moved out here to Borrego. There's an energy here. It was either Sedona or Borrego, and I picked this desert. I knew it would come to me one day, it would knock on my door when I least expected it. And I also knew I probably wouldn't be prepared, I wouldn't know what to do." She paused. "And I didn't. I've been as flabbergasted as you, as everyone else who's been touched by the other reality."

"Hey," I said, sitting up. "Where's your pet?"

"I don't know. It vanished not long after you left with—with—her.... It vanished. I don't think it's coming back. I think the rip in reality is mending itself."

"Then all this craziness will stop?"

Did I sound too hopeful, like a child?

"Perhaps. But it's changed us as well. So does it ever really stop?"

"I need to go back into the city," I said.

"I know," she said.

XVII.

I didn't leave immediately. I stayed with Katie until dawn, until she was asleep, with her dreams.

As I drove up the mountain to leave the desert, an old man with elongated features was riding a bicycle up with me. He wore red shorts. His skin was a weird tint of orange, his body bony and muscular. He looked like he was a hundred years old. I tried to get away from him. He maintained his speed alongside me.

"Hey there!" he said.

"Hello," I said.

"Amazing, isn't it?"

"What's that?"

"That I can keep up with you," he said.

I picked up the speed, tires screeching around every sharp corner. He was still beside me.

"You see?" he said.

"It *is* pretty amazing," I said.

"It's like I have superhuman strength," he said.

"Maybe that's because you're not a human," I said.

"You make a good point," he said.

"Look, what do you want?" I asked.

"Nothing really."

I shrugged. Let him do what he wanted to do. I ignored him. At some point, I'm not sure when, he wasn't alongside me anymore.

XVIII.

Sheila and the mothman were lounging around naked in the living room, drinking coffee and eating bagels and watching the news on TV.

"Hello, Neil," Sheila said, without a hint of embarrassment or shame.

"Good morning," the mothman said.

I sat across from them. "Do you have a name?"

"Call me Bud," he said. He laughed: a strong, confident chuckle.

"This is going to be hard to explain," Sheila said to me.

"No, it won't," said Bud the mothman. "I believe he already understands."

"I remember seeing an image of Bud when I was a young girl," Sheila said. "I was at church, people were singing a hymn. I closed my eyes. I saw him. He was making love to me."

"An unusual image to have in the throes of praise to Jesus," Bud said.

"The rip in reality is closing," I said, sounding like Katie.

"Yes," the mothman said, "it has."

"Don't you need to go back where you belong?"

"No."

"You intend to stay here?"

"Yes," he said, "with Sheila."

She went into his arms. His wings moved in around her.

"You don't want her," Bud the mothman said, "and I do."

"You have Katie," Sheila said. "I was mad at you about that.

I'm not anymore. Things have a way of working out."

I said, "He can't possibly exist in this reality."

"Of course I can," Bud said.

"How?"

"How does *any* creature exist in this reality?" he said.

"You make a good point." I stood up.

The mothman added, "There have been others like me, not like me, over the centuries, who have. It's called love."

I gathered up a few necessities into a suitcase and left.

I drove back to the desert, to Katie.

—October, 1998
San Diego

HARDBOILED ZOMBIE DETECTIVE

I. "WHO KILLED ME?"

...and then I woke up. I couldn't breathe. It was, in retrospect, the most godawful feeling I ever had and God had nothing to do with it. I didn't know where the hell I was. Mud, thick and wet like greasy shit, filled my mouth and it didn't taste like anything really; it was slimy and going down my throat—*I couldn't scream, I could not fucking scream and that was the one thing I wanted to do most of all.*

I was under the earth.

I reached out and broke free—my fist felt air and the storm. It was raining hard. The rain was making the dirt above me into mud.

I pulled myself up, I climbed out.

The grave I was in was shallow, dug in haste.

I had no idea how I got there.

I wasn't even sure who I was—my name, my profession, the year, what city I was in.

I was in a dark and desolate place. Thunder rolled across the sky like a giant bowling alley, and the rain came down harder. I spit out the mud from my mouth, blew it out of my nose, opened my mouth to the dark and stormy sky and drank the rain.

I was so goddamn thirsty.

I wore a gray and rumpled suit, torn here and there; my shirt was untucked and my thin black tie loosened. I didn't have any shoes on. I thought: they bury the dead barefoot.

But I wasn't dead.

Whoever put me in the grave fucked up.

And I was going to *fuck them up.*

I'm a Scorpio, I like revenge.

Funny: that's all I knew about myself: my zodiac sign and that I was, or had been, the unforgiving sort.

I touched my chest and felt the bullet holes. I'd been shot twice, and I kind of remembered *that*. Yes, I'd been shot in the chest, in the heart, but I didn't know who did it, or why.

I stuck my finger into the bullet holes. No blood.

Any other time, that'd be funny.

I began to walk.

The ones question in my mind, the only thing that was driving me to move through this storm and the night, was: who killed me?

Who the fuck killed me, and how the heck did I come back to life?

* * * * * * *

I found the road and the road looked familiar. I knew I had to walk west, that would get me somewhere. I walked with my bare feet and stared at the ground. The rainstorm subsided and became a manageable drizzle. It was cold but I didn't feel cold. I didn't feel much. I noticed light. I looked up. Two high beams. A car was approaching. The light hurt my eyes as the car got closer. I moved, slowly (my back somewhat at a hunch, my feet dragging) to the other side of the road and put my thumb out.

I could only imagine how I looked. *How I smelled.* Nobody in his or her right mind would give a horrid, ungainly fellow like me a lift.

But it was worth a try.

So I put my thumb out.

The car was a nice big Buick with tail fins. It stopped. The window rolled down. The man driving was in his fifties, wore a Hawaiian shirt and polyester pants. He took one glance at me and said: "Holy shit."

"I know," I said, "listen—"

He shook his head with apparent disgust, was about to gun it. Something took me over—something vile and ancient, something revolting and, in a grand and unspeakable way, *pure*. I took hold of the door handle and pulled. The door was locked; I had incredible strength and *knew* I had this powerful thing inside me—or the burning call for what I did next; it gave me the superhuman capacity to break the lock and literally yank the door off and toss the door aside, into the air, like it was cardboard.

So this is what happened: I grabbed the man by the collar of his Hawaiian shirt—complimented him on the fabric—then snapped his neck like a straw, bashed his skull in half a dozen times onto the hood of his Buick until his head was split open and his brains were exposed; then I clamped my mouth down onto his brains and had myself a feast.

Oh, it was sick and vile and somewhere in the back of my own brain (if I even had one now) I was telling myself to stop— *but I could not stop*. I relished the taste of the blood and skull meat…and the more I ate, the better I felt.

It was the only thing that mattered in the universe, in that very crucial moment: that I eat a human brain and shudder in the ecstasy and tasty delight of it all.

There was something wrong with me, sure, but I didn't give a fuck.

II. "THE GIDEON PRIVATE INVESTIGATION AGENCY"

I drove the Buick downtown. Signs told me that I was in Miami, Florida, Dade County. Oh yes, that rang a bell all right. There was a wallet in my jacket pocket; at a stop sign, I looked in it. $33 in wrinkled, wet tens and ones and a Florida Driver's

License. Arthur Laurence Gideon. DOB: 11-15-33. I also had a private investigator's license, with a business address. I knew where that place was, where my office was. *My office.* I knew who I was now; I just didn't know who the fuck killed me.

I knew that it was October in 1966. I was thirty-three years old and would be thirty-four next month. I'd been married ten years ago, when I lived in San Diego; my young wife had died of cancer.

I lived alone, I was alone, and I was a gumshoe in Miami....

That's all I could recall....

I parked the Buick in front of the building where I had my office. It was starting to rain hard again.

I had keys in my pants pocket. The light was on in my office, which was located at the back end of the third floor.

I went inside.

A woman's voice—a yelp, a small scream, one gasp—

"Arty?!?"

"Who goes there?" I said.

"Who do you *think?*"

She was a curvy, voluptuous brunette with short-cropped hair and large, pointed breasts in a very, *very* tight white blouse and a *very*, very tight black skirt cut two inches above the knee, in black stockings and black, three-inch pumps. She wore black-rimmed glasses and bright red lipstick. It took me a few seconds, but I remembered who she was.

"Miss Melfile," I said with a sigh.

Her name was Lissa Melfile and she was my secretary, had been for the past eighteen months.

"Arty," she said. "I mean, Mr. Gideon. Oh gosh."

"What?"

"Nothing."

"Tell me."

"I—I wasn't expecting you."

"Why are you looking at me like that?" I asked.

"I—"

"Tell me."

"You look *awful*."

I said, "I feel awful."

"I wasn't…," she started to say, and began to cry.

I glanced at the wall clock. "It's three in the morning. What are you doing here at this hour?"

"Waiting for you, of course," she said. "I've been worried."

"How long have I been gone?"

She looked at me with watery eyes like she figured I was nuts.

"How long?" I said.

"Three days," she replied softly.

"I don't remember the last three days," I said, "or even the last three weeks, or three months. My memory…has some… gaps."

I hoped I looked as confused as I felt.

"Maybe you're missing some of your, uh, memory," and she was looking at my head when she told me this, and cried more.

I said: "What is it? Why are you—?"

"Go look in the mirror, Mr. Gideon."

I went into the bathroom and turned on the light. Let's just say that I was not prepared for what I saw in the mirror above the basin.…

I almost screamed but did not. A man does not scream like a little girl when he's in his office and his secretary is near.

Not only was I pasty pale with dark circles under my yellow eyes, not only did I have two bullet holes in my chest and blood and mud and who-knows-what-else all over my suit and skin, but I was missing half the left side of my head and my brain matter was exposed.

Not only that, my left eye was dangling out of the socket. I popped it back in.

"Aw, shit," I whispered.

Plus, I was barefoot!

* * * * * *

I told my secretary to please stop crying please, and she nodded. I told her to sit down and she sat in the chair in front of my big expensive oak desk. I remembered paying a lot of money for this desk—I always wanted such a desk and the day I could afford it, I went and got it. Well, at least I remembered *something*. Little things were coming back, like torn parts of blurry photographs. I felt like drinking booze, for some goddamn reason, and I knew I had the stuff—right in the big desk. I opened a drawer and found a half-full bottle of Maker's Mark and a few little paper cups.

"Join me?" I said.

"Always," Lissa Melfile said.

She sat and crossed her long legs; I looked at her legs and knew I should be feeling something—a distant stir that had to be desire, sex.

And I felt nothing.

Miss Melfile sipped at her cup and coughed like she wasn't used to the burn of alcohol. "That always hits the spot," she said, and I remembered suddenly that she seldom drank.

I drank and again I felt nothing—not the singe, not the warmth, not the buzz in the head that makes people want to drink more and more.

"What happened to you, Mr. Gideon?" she asked.

"Do you call me by my first name, or 'Mr. Gideon'?"

She blushed. "Depends. Both."

"Depends on what?"

"Oh," she said and looked away.

"Are we sleeping together?"

"I could be insulted by a remark like that. I *should* be."

"I'm sorry."

"I understand—it's a memory thing."

"Well?"

"We were, for a short while...."

"But?"

"But it wasn't feeling like the right thing to do," she said. "I mean, I work for you. We have that employer-employee relationship. You said—"

"How goddamn typical for a private eye to be slipping the sausage to his secretary."

"Yes! That's what you said! And—"

I sat back in my chair and said: "I hate being a cliché."

"*Yes*, that's what you—you remember now?"

"No. But I figure that's what I'd say. It's what I'm thinking… right now."

"It was both of us," she said. "I didn't…well, Arty, if I can call you that, Mr. Gideon…I often wonder about your heart."

I looked at the holes in my chest.

She said: "Most of the time it's like you don't have any feelings in you. Like you don't have any emotions. I know you gotta be tough in this business, but when you're with a lady in the bedroom, a man has to drop the hardboiled act…unless it's not an act."

I nodded.

"You know what I mean?"

"No," I said, "but I'm beginning to hark back to a night or two that we fucked."

"Sometimes you can be a real *bastard*, Mr. Gideon!"

"I know."

"But that's okay," she said. "Most people are bastards."

"I still don't recollect a whole lot."

"So you don't know how—you got like you are?"

"No."

"Maybe it'll come back."

"Do you know what I was doing? What case I was on?"

"I should hope so," she said with a smile, "or else I'd be a very bad secretary. You were on a missing persons case—some runaway girl, came from a rich family. But don't they all?"

"I was about to say that."

"Of course you were."

We smiled at each other. I wondered how gory my smile looked; hers was very pretty.

Pretty. Yes. She was. I was feeling something down there,

that thing I called my prick.

"Was I making any progress?" I asked.

"You never really tell me the details of your cases. I write your reports when you give them to me, handle your correspondence and invoices...."

I nodded.

"Arty?"

"Yes."

"You look like you're dead."

"Yeah," I said, "I do."

"I mean, the wounds on you...."

"Ain't pretty, is it," I said.

"You *should* be dead."

"I think I am."

"I was afraid something like that happened, like your check got cashed."

But she was looking at my face with too much interest for me to believe she had any fear.

I said: "What's the girl's name? The one I'm looking for?"

"Jenna Rush. Her father is Samuel Rush."

"He's rich? A bigwig?"

"*Senator* Rush," she said. "The Rushes go back to the plantation days. Old money."

"A Senator?"

"Our very own Republican."

"Hmmm," I hmmmed. "Do I usually take cases for government officials?"

"Mr. Gideon," she said, "you take *any* case, as long as the money is green and it isn't counterfeit."

III. "WEIRD SEX WITH A SECRET NECROPHILE"

Obviously what I had to do was backtrack; I'd need to call on the Senator, find out just what, exactly, he sent me on. Miss

Melfile said I didn't have any other cases pending, so somewhere along in my sleuthing to find the missing girl I died and came back to life and had a desire to eat human brains.

It was a good thing I gobbled down the brains of that guy in the Buick and I was satiated on the matter, for now; or else I may have cracked open my secretary's skull and feasted on her mind. Instead, I kept looking at her pointy breasts and legs and feeling some other kind of want.

"What I really need to do is call Senator Rush," I said out loud, and reached for the phone.

"At *this* uncivilized hour?" Miss Melfile said.

I put the phone down. "Of course. It can wait till later."

She yawned.

"Maybe I should get some rest," I said, "go to bed."

"That would be a good idea."

"I have an apartment? A home? Or do I sleep here on the couch?"

"You have a bungalow by the beach. It's very nice."

"Do you have a car? I need a ride...home."

"Yes. What happened to your vehicle?"

"I don't know. I came here in a stolen Buick."

"Stolen?"

"Borrowed," I said.

"Oh Arty," she said.

"What," I said, "do I do this often?"

She sighed and said: "Let's go, I'll drive you home."

* * * * * * *

She had a VW Bug. I felt cramped inside but couldn't complain, she was concerned for me and that was an alien feeling. I kept looking at Miss Melfile's pleasing-to-the-eye (even if I had one that kept popping out) legs. She drove a few miles toward the beach, to a stretch of beach bungalows that looked pricey and cozy. Parked in front of one and said: "This is your bachelor pad, Mr. Gideon."

"Shit." I felt through my pockets. "I don't have any keys."

"I know where you keep your spare."

She walked and I followed and the way she moved her curvaceous hips and amble rump, things *were* going on inside me. At least there was some sensation returning to the body—but that could work against me: I might feel the pain that should be accompanying my wounds.

We stood at the front entrance of the bungalow.

She bent down and *that* did it for me—I had to fuck her. She turned and looked at me and her eyes said she wanted to be fucked. This was not wishful thinking, I knew that look if I knew only one thing in the world. "Here is your spare," she said, reaching under a flowerpot and producing a silver key.

"Yes," I said, "of course," but my thoughts were on her ass.

She straightened and opened the door and we went inside. She turned on the light and asked: "Does it look familiar?"

"I'm sure it will."

"Well, this is home sweet home."

"And where do you live?"

"Not too far away," she said, glancing at me with that *look* again.

"Miss Melfile," I said, pulling at my tie, "I thank you for the ride and your assistance; I'm going to have to apologize in advance for what I'm about to do."

"Oh," she said, touching her chest, "are you going to turn me into a zombie?"

"A *what?*"

"A *zombie*. That's what you are."

"I don't know what I am," I said, "but only vampires and werewolves can turn people into—"

"I think zombies can too," she said.

"Well, that's not what I had in...."

"What were you...?"

I was looking at her knockers and feeling a whole lot of lust. She said: "Oh."

"I know I'm an miserly sight—I stink of death and violence

and who-knows-what, so I'm telling you now that I'm sorry for what I'm about to do."

"Please," she told me, "just get it over with." She softly smiled. "Just do what you have to do," she said.

I lunged like a Bengal tiger on its prey and she did not fight me. She kissed me back. She pulled at my clothes. She let me take off her blouse and bra and play with those wonderful tits in my big decaying hands.

"I want your ass," I said.

"Oh, Mr. Gideon, you can have *every* part of my body!"

* * * * * * *

"You don't mind?" I asked.

"Not at all," she said.

"I thought I was going to have to ravish and rape you," I said.

"Ravish me all you want, Arty," she said, "rape me any way you wish. I just want you to take me and…and…."

* * * * * * *

In bed, she asked: "Does your penis work in this state? I mean, you're dead, but is your cock dead? Can it get hard?"

"Miss Melfile," I said, "I happen to be a stiff with a stiff."

"Oh my! I see that this is true!"

"And it seems to be bigger than it was before."

"I can attest to that."

"I don't know how, but should I complain?"

"I want to suck on it before you fuck me," she said, "*can* I suck on it, Arty?"

"I ain't stopping you," I said.

* * * * * * *

I came in her mouth and she made a face but she swallowed it like a good secretary.

"How does it taste?" I asked.

"Sour. Like—death."

"Oh."

"But I *like* the taste of death!"

"Really?"

"Oh, indeed. Oh, I see it's still hard."

"It's hard and ready for more."

"I want you to fuck me now," she said, and I did.

* * * * * * *

We fucked and my eye kept popping out and small pieces of me flung off when we got especially vigorous. You'd think I'd be embarrassed but if she didn't care, why the hell should I? Like the song says: we were having a grand old time.

* * * * * * *

"I have a confession to make," she said.

"I'm listening."

"I like dead people."

"I know that."

"I don't mean just now," she said, "always."

"Oh?"

"Before I worked for you, I had a job at a mortuary. I was fired."

"Why?"

"I was caught fucking a dead body."

"I bet he wasn't as responsive as me."

"I can't say that he was," she winked, "but I'll never be able to get a job at another mortuary or morgue again."

"So you've always been this way?" I asked.

"My secret desire," she said, "I'm what you call a necrophile."

"Yesterday I would have found that perverse," I said, "but now...I find it very nice."

"The sex was *nice*."

"Nice? It was fucking *great*."

"I love fucking a man who is dead; you don't know how satisfied I feel right now, Arty."

"I'm feeling pretty good myself, girl."

"Maybe this is the start of something…special."

Maybe.

Who knows.

I lived day-to-day like any other goddamn gumshoe, I could do the same as a zombie.

"Tell me," I said, "how long have you been into screwing the dead?"

"It all began when my high school sweetheart died," she said, looking sad in the bedroom with me as the sun started to rise outside. "I was fifteen and he was sixteen and oh we were in love so much. We never went all the way but he would put his fingers inside me and I would suck on his penis and I couldn't wait for the day until we were married and we could have sex like a man and a wife. I came from a good Catholic family, you understand, and while I did certain things, I wasn't about to have pre-martial intercourse.

"Anyway, one day we were walking home from school, holding hands, and then he was trying to be—he wanted—I don't know *what* he was doing, he was playing around, but he let go of my hand and he said, 'Watch how fast I can run!' He was on the track team, you understand. Anyway, he ran into the street and the garbage truck was coming down the way really fast and the truck hit my sweetheart and killed him right there on the spot. His twisted, broken body was on the street—neck, legs and arms completely broken…and he had this silly grin on his face, like he was smiling at me. I went to him,

"I went to his dead body, I held him in my arms, I was prepared to cry and scream like any girl who has just lost her love would, like Juliet, but I didn't. What I felt was…excitement. My body was on fire with strange pleasure and my crotch was so very wet and I kept having orgasm after orgasm until the ambulance arrived and they had to pry me away from his body.

But it was not grief that made me want to be with his body—it was delight.

"Did I think this odd, you ask? Yes. Yes, it was quite odd and—wicked. But every time I thought of him—that way: dead—my vagina started to spasm. Oh, you should have *seen* me at the funeral, I had to pretend I was crying and horrified, but I was secretly having many orgasms, just looking at his pale and still form in the casket. Then I would masturbate in bed, late at night in the dark, thinking about him. I still do."

Silence.

"Arty?"

Her breathing was hard, her breath rancid from having the taste of my cock on her tongue.

"Mr. Gideon," she said, "what do you make of my life story?"

"That," I said, "is a weird tale, Miss Melfile."

"Oh, Arty," she said, kissing me, "shut up and let's make love one more time and then we can sleep in each other's arms."

* * * * * * *

She slept, but I could not. I wasn't tired in the least. I had no idea if the dead were capable of sleeping—do they need it? She lightly snored as she snuggled against me and this was all right, this was nice.

I closed my eyes and tried to rest or sleep—

But like a car slamming into me, it all came back—

A flood of images—

The dead—so many of them—

The dead like me—

And naked young people fucking—

They were all laughing—

At me—

Laughing and hurting—

—me.

Me.

I screamed.

I sat up and screamed.

"Arty," Lissa Melfile said, her hand on my back, "Arty, what is it?"

I was shaking.

"I remember everything now," I said.

IV. "NOW I KNOW WHAT HAPPENED TO ME"

It went like this:

A tall leggy blonde in an expensive pale blue woman's suit and matching pill box hat waltzed into my office one day and asked if I was available for hire.

Don't these things always start with such a leggy blonde?

Nevertheless, I said: "What's the job?"

"Someone's missing."

"Isn't somebody always missing?"

"Do you want the job or not?" she asked with a huff.

"Sure," I said, "tell me about it."

"You need to come with me then."

"Why can't you tell me about it here?"

"I'm not the one who has anything to tell," she said, "it's my employer."

"Who is?"

"Sam Rush."

"As in—?"

"Senator Rush."

"Ah, *that* Senator Rush."

"So you know him."

"I know *of* him. Who doesn't around here? Hasn't he done enough to fuck up the south Florida economy?"

"His daughter is missing."

"I'm sorry to hear that."

"He'll tell you more, if you take the job."

"I'm willing to listen to what he has to say," I said, my feelings going out for a worried father but not for a rich politician, "and I'm willing to help if I can."

"Good. Let's go."

There was a car and driver waiting outside.

"Nice," I said.

"Yes, isn't it."

I scrutinized her legs and ass as she got into the car.

I said: "Nice."

She gave me a look.

"Help yourself to the wet bar," she said with a sigh.

I did.

"You?" I said.

"I don't drink during working hours," she said.

As we drove, I asked her name. We were sitting across from each other.

"Jill," she said. "Listen, Mr. Gideon, let me give you three points of advice before you meet the Senator: (1) don't have a smart mouth with him, (2) don't say anything about the economy to him, and (3) don't ogle my body parts in front of him—it'll piss him off and he's a man you do *not* want to piss off."

"Why, Jill? You his girlfriend?"

"I'm one of his top aides."

"One?"

"The," she said.

"But you're screwing the man," I said.

"That's none of your business."

"And what does his wife do? She heads the local chapter of the Red Cross, right?"

"Mr. Gideon," she said, "in this matter, I expect you to be a civilized, discreet professional."

I said: "My sincere hope, Jill, is that I do not disappoint you."

"Believe me," she said, "if it was my decision and choice, you wouldn't be riding with me anywhere."

The car went to the land of the wealthy, to the one hundred and fifty acre Rush Estate and its twenty-room mansion.

I whistled.

"Nice, yes?" Jill said.

"I'll never know, baby."

* * * * * * *

The Senator was waiting for me in his study. He looked like he hadn't slept for a few days. He appeared worried and I felt for the weight the man must have been carrying.

He was staring out one of the big windows, holding a stiff drink in his hand.

"Please, sir, sit down," he said.

I sat.

"Would you like some gin? Bourbon? Whiskey? Vodka?"

"I had two drinks on the ride here. My limit is two during working hours," I lied.

He smiled, but it was a sad smile.

"Mr. Rush," I said, "I understand you have a problem and maybe I can help."

"I hope you can help. I asked around: who's the best P.I. to hire? Your name came up several times."

"Is that good or bad?"

"You tell me."

"Let's say it's good."

"Good," he said, and sat down at his desk. "My daughter is missing."

"So I was told."

"Were you told anything else?"

"That's all Jill said."

"Jill is a good woman."

"So I gather."

"You 'gather'?"

"She seems good," I said, "a top aide."

"*The* top aide."

"So she said."

"And *great* in the sack." He grinned.

"I imagine."

"You don't have to imagine. I can arrange a meeting, in a hotel room. Would you like to fuck her? She's a good fuck."

"Well," I said, not knowing what to say to that.

"I tell you what," said the Senator, "you find my little girl, Jill's pussy will be a bonus."

"Tell me about your daughter."

"Her name is Jenna—Jennifer, but she goes by Jenna. Named after her sacred grandmother, my saintly mother. Jenna is thirteen and she has run away from home."

"How long has she—?"

"Two and a half weeks now."

"You call the cops?"

"Informally," he said. "I don't want this to leak to the press. It wouldn't be good."

"It might help find her."

"It would only look bad. Jenna was hanging out—with a bad crowd. You know this stuff with the kids now—all this *hippie* nonsense."

"I've heard about it," I said. "I've been seeing the hippies around."

"Drugs and free love and radical politics," he said with distaste. "Long hair and unwashed bodies and—*free love.*"

"Free love."

"Do you know what that is?"

"Not really."

"Indiscriminate sex," he said. "And sex with children. Jenna is only thirteen."

"Didn't you tell her to stay away from that riffraff?" I asked him.

"I tried, oh I tried. I lectured, I grounded her. This is what drove her to run away. The classic western culture parent-child situation of misunderstanding: she leaves home. Leaves a note: 'It's time for me to split, Daddy-o.' Can you believe that? What does 'split' mean? Where does she come off referring to me as 'Daddy-o'?"

"Kids these days," and I rolled my eyes for effect.

"Tell me about it," he said. "So you can understand my delicate problem, sir. Not only am I a member of the sacred body of the American Senate, there is the family name that goes back many generations in these parts."

"Yes."

"And if this were to get into the press—Rush Family daughter running around with unwashed hippies and taking that LSD stuff and engaging in 'free love'...."

"I understand."

"I believe you do." He opened the drawer in front of his desk and brought out some Polaroid pictures. "This is Jenna."

I looked at them.

"Pretty girl," I said.

I wanted to say *sexy*, for a thirteen-year-old, but that's not the sort of comment a grown man makes in front of a teenage girl's father.

"Will you find her for me?" asked the Senator. "Will you take the case?"

"I'll do my best," I said. "But where do I start?"

"That's your job, sir, not mine."

* * * * * * *

Rush gave me a handsome retainer, five times what I normally charge. I was feeling happy and wanted to celebrate. Miss Melfile was at the office when I was taken back in the car (without Jill, and I had two more drinks). I reached behind my secretary and squeezed her big tits and whispered into her ears: "I got some good dough, baby, and I think we should go out and have a night."

"Arty," she said, pushing me away, "don't."

"What is it?"

"You know...."

"Know what?"

"Like I said last night, we can't do this anymore. *I* can't. It's just not in me, and it's not right."

"Right," I said with a heavy, overdramatic sigh, moving away from her, giving her space. "Well, guess who I'm looking for?"

"Who?"

"A lost little rich girl."

"Another one?"

"She's very young."

"They keep getting younger. I don't even *remember* being a young girl." At first I thought Miss Melfile was being facetious, but I noticed how sad her face looked.

"She ran off with hippies," I said.

"Hippies?"

"Yeah."

"She *is* lost."

* * * * * * *

...and so I went to South Beach and did the footwork: showing the Rush girl's photo around to every hippie-looking person I spotted and could uncover, either alone or in groups, high and sober, coherent or, as they said, "spaced-out."

Most of them said they'd never seen her, but I knew they were lying; they just didn't trust me.

"You a cop, man?"

I said: "No."

"You look like a cop, man."

"I'm a private eye, man."

"Far out, man."

"So you haven't seen this girl?"

"No, man, never seen her."

Right.

"You a cop, man?" a girl who was fifteen and half-naked on the beach asked me, shading the sun from her eyes with a little hand.

"No," I said.

"You look square."

"I'm not."

"You *look* it."

"Well, I'm *not*."

"You wanna drop acid with us, man?"

"Are you sure you haven't seen this girl?" I said.

"I don't know, man, you see a lot of people but it's hard to really remember the faces, you know what I mean?"

But there was also this:

"Yeah, she used to hang around here, but haven't seen her in weeks."

"Oh yeah, she went by the name of, uh, Bright Sunshine, I think, I only met her once."

"No, she said her name was Wallflower."

"No, it was Daisy."

"Oh yeah, I fucked that little girl. Man, she was high that night. Man, that pussy was some *tight* pussy."

"She sucked my dick *twice* for beer and weed."

"I think she has a pimp, man."

"She goes to school with my little sister. Is that weird or *what*?"

"I haven't seen her in a month."

"I haven't seen her in *days*."

"I don't know where she crashes, man."

* * * * * * *

...and I was going to my car when a skinny, smelly hippie fellow with B.O. and dirty long blond hair came up to me and said: "Hey, man, $10 and I'll tell you where you can find her. Wallflower."

"How do I know your information is good?"

He shrugged. "Take it or leave it."

I got out my wallet and gave him two fives.

He gave me an address and an apartment number.

"That's where she's staying?" I asked.

"*No*, man," he said, "that's where a wild party is happenin' tonight."

"Wild?"

"Party. You know, lots of drugs and sex. We call them 'love-ins.'"

"Yeah?"

"Yeah, and she'll be there."

"How do you know?"

"She goes to *every* orgy in town, man."

"You know she's thirteen?"

"Yeah that's why she's popular. I seen twelve-year-old chicks at some of these orgies, man. Wild, huh?"

"Wild," I said.

* * * * * *

...and I went, that night, to the address and the apartment number. It was in a shitty part of town. There was loud music and a lot of moaning inside. I knocked and knocked on the door and was about ready to break it down or climb through the window when it opened. A naked woman in her twenties stood there; she was rail thin with frizzy red hair, glassy eyes, and a thick bush of dark pubic hair.

"Look at you," she said.

"Hello," I said.

"Trippy," she said, "look at you in the suit, man!"

Two more naked girls joined her and they glared at me up and down with silly grins on their pusses—uh, faces.

"Wild," one said.

"Who are you?" the other said.

"I'm looking for a girl," I said.

One said, "Well you came to the right place," and all three of them grabbed me and pulled me inside.

The room was thick with marijuana smoke and empty beers bottles lined the walls. What can I say about the floor? It was a sea of human flesh; it was, for all intents and purposes, a Mongolian Clusterfuck. I guess I *was* square, I'd never been to anything like this—I'd heard about such things but didn't believe they were true. But here it all was, before me: dozens of naked men and women of all ages fucking and sucking and moaning and groaning and coming and pissing. I don't have to describe what it all smelled like, even the pot smoke didn't cover that smell, a smell that I admit turned me on, along with the sight of so many nude women with their holes being filled with cock.

The three girls who pulled me inside were pulling off my clothes; they were saying, "C'mon, baby, let's get it on," and kissing me and grabbing me. I was waving Jenna Rush's photo about when I saw the girl, right in the middle of the orgy; all she wore were a pair of white panties and moccasin boots, her hair done in braids. She was marvelously tanned from head to toe and she had one man's cock in her ass and another in her mouth. Both men were in their forties and had long, thick beards and smiling at one another as they did the Senator's daughter.

I called out her name.

The music was too loud.

"What is this noise?"

"It's the Airplane!" one of the girls said.

I screamed, "JENNA! JENNA RUSH! YOUR DADDY IS LOOKING FOR YOU!"

All the fucking stopped and there were many eyes on me.

The music played on—

When the truth is gone....

"JENNA RUSH!" I yelled.

"Oh shit!" the girl shrieked, pushing the two men and their hard penises away.

"JENNA! COME HERE!"

"Fuck you, pig!" she said, grabbing a flower print dress from the floor and running past me.

I went after her.

"Hey!" said the naked women. *"Come back! You don't want her, she's a little girl. We're women. We know how to fuck!"*

As much as I wanted to stay, I had a job to do.

Jenna slipped on her flower print dress as she ran.

"Come back!"

"TELL MY DADDY TO GO TO FUCKING HELL, MAN!"

We were running down the street, toward the beach.

That's when some guys in leather jackets grabbed me.

One of them hit me in the back of the head.

They also grabbed Jenna.

"Is this her?"

"It's her."

"What the…," I said.

These guys, something was wrong with them—they had no faces. Well, their faces were skulls with rotting drooping flesh and eyeballs dangling from the sockets; plus they were slouched and moved about in a funny manner, like their bodies were stiff.

"What the fuck," I said.

I was hit on the head again and, as the story often goes, everything went black.…

* * * * * * *

…and I came to, back inside the apartment where the orgy was going on, but now it was no longer a "love in" with all the many sounds of pleasure, it was a slaughter house of madness and there were many screams of pain, fear, and death. The guys in leather jackets, these guys with skulls for faces, five of them in all, were killing naked men and women left and right, smashing their heads open and feasting on their brains, smearing blood all over their rotting flesh and laughing. A sixth one, who seemed to be the leader and was the tallest, held Jenna Rush by both of her arms; he watched and took glee in this sickness. Jenna tried to get free, but she was too small and weak. She looked at me with terror, and then I blacked out again.…

* * * * * * *

…and came to out in the middle of nowhere. A storm had rolled in and it was beginning to rain, thunder in the sky. Two of the skull faces were digging a hole in the ground. Jenna Rush was sitting on the ground, her arms tied behind her by rope. The leader was pointing a revolver at me.

"You were in the wrong place at the wrong time," he said.

"Who are you?" I coughed, rubbing the back of my head and feeling the two large bumps there.

"People call me The Power," he said. "My Momma calls me Stevie."

"Let her go," I said. "Let us both go, and you won't have any trouble."

"Trouble?" he laughed, and his five cohorts laughed with him. "We *are* trouble, my man. I should change my name from The Power to The Trouble from Hell."

"Let the girl go."

"Can't do that."

"Do you know who she *is?* Who her goddamn *father* is?"

The Power seemed to grin, if a skull can do that. "Yes," he informed me, "I do."

Then he shot me: two bullets in the chest.

I looked at the bullet holes, and the blood coming out.

"Oh shit," I said.

"You'll be dead soon, don't worry. Would you like one in the head? Then we'll bury you nice and comfy."

"Hey, Power, let's make him one of us," said one of his crew.

"Yeah," said another, "I bet his brains taste reeeeeeeaaaallll goooooooood."

"What?" said The Power. "You zombies didn't get enough at the party?"

"There can never be enough," all five said.

"True," said The Power. "Well," he said to me, "you'll come in handy, I think. When you rise from your grave, you'll deliver a message to Senator Rush. A very important message. You'll tell him The Power Platoon has come home to roost."

The other five converged on me as I lay dying from the gunshot wounds. They smashed my face in, broke my head open and began to greedily eat....

The last thing I remembered hearing was The Power saying: "Take off his shoes and socks. We bury the dead barefoot, remember?"

V. "…"

…and then I woke up. I couldn't breathe—

VI. "THE TRUTH ABOUT THE ZOMBIES"

"I can't breathe," I said, coughing.

"It's okay," Miss Melfile was saying, touching my back, "you're just having a flashback."

I'd told her everything as it came back to me—

I stood up.

"This is ridiculous," I said, "if I'm dead, how can I be breathing? *Do* the dead breathe?"

"You're dead, but you're not *really*.…"

"I don't like being like this. Is there a cure?"

"I don't know," Ms. Melfile said. "But I like you this way. You know? I really do."

"Obviously what I have to do is find The Power and rescue the Senator's daughter."

"How will you do that?"

"I'll go back to where this all started, where that party was."

"Some party!"

"Wait," I said, scratching my skull, the hair and dead flesh falling off, "can I even go outside in the sun? Will the light destroy me?"

"That only happens to vampires," my secretary (who was naked) said.

"Then I'll be okay?" I asked her.

"I don't see why not," she said.

"I'll have to use your car."

"The keys are on the kitchen table," she said. "Before you go, will you give me a sloppy kiss?"

"But of course," and I gave her a long one.

* * * * * * *

The sunlight didn't put an end to my being one of the undead, but I can't say it was all that pleasant. The heat and brightness were extremely annoying; and it was a sunny day with no clouds to boot. I couldn't believe that it was this very sun that made me move to southern Florida in the first place.

I drove to South Beach and turned on the radio. The local news was reporting on "riots and madness" on the streets of Miami.

"It is uncertain if this could be college students protesting the war," the news announcer said, "or some other form of civil unrest and disobedience."

"Hippies," I muttered, "goddamn hippies."

I heard a lot of police and ambulance sirens, but didn't see any signs of rioting or madness.

`The apartment complex where the orgy had taken place four nights ago was covered in yellow police tape.

There was one lone cop guarding it. He was young and in uniform and looked nervous. When he saw me, he drew his service revolver, pointed it at me and said, "Stop right there, you freak!"

"Freak?" I said incredulously, and then I remembered what I looked like.

"It's okay," I said. "Really."

"The hell it is. You just turn around and go back to what rock you crawled out from."

"Or what?"

"Or I'll shoot."

"Why don't you shoot, rookie," I told him, "because I don't think it'll do a goddamn thing to me."

Seemed like good a time as any to test this. The rookie shot me once, in the chest. I felt the impact but there was no pain.

There was a hole, but there was no blood.

"Holy crap," said the rookie.

All I could do was laugh, and the laughter brought out the apparent monster inside of me. I moved fast, slapping the gun out of the rookie's hand. "No, please," he said and this made me laugh more—like a maniac—and just as it overtook me last night, there was the sudden urge and need; so I bashed the rookie's head on the ground, opening his skull, and feasted on his squishy, yummy brains, savoring each bite. I could feel the brain matter and various fluids going down my throat and settling into my stomach. This felt good. But do the dead eat? I couldn't be completely dead then. Those people at the orgy, I saw them all die, rather violently, their brains being devoured by The Power and his buddies.

What the fuck. I got a hold of myself. With my jacket sleeve, I wiped mind goo away from my mouth.

I stepped under the police tape and into the apartment. Empty, as expected, with the walls and floors covered in dried, putrid blood. Lots of chalked outlines of bodies, many bodies.

...and then a voice.

Arthur Gideon.

"What?"

Gideon, why didn't you do as I told you?

"Tell me what? Where are you?"

Why didn't you do as I told you?

It was The Power. His voice was in my head.

"Get out of my skull, you motherfucker."

You are one of us now.

Distant laughter.

Go home, Arthur Gideon.

"Fuck you."

Go home, we're waiting.

* * * * * * *

On the radio, the news guy was saying, "...strange and

unconfirmed reports that dozens of bodies are missing from the police morgue. These bodies are from a mass murder that happened several nights ago...."

Ah, but it was true. Now I knew what was going on because I saw them all over town: naked and ugly zombies wandering around with that special zombie walk and causing all kinds of dastardly trouble, like killing hapless ordinary citizens on the streets.

* * * * * * *

The Power held Miss Melfile with one arm and had a gun to her head, the same pistol he used on me. His buddies were there, too, as well as Jenna Rush. Jenna was not the tanned pretty hippie girl anymore; she was like me, like The Power, like all her friends who were now terrorizing Miami.

"Gideon! We *just* missed each other," said The Power. "We got here and you'd *just* taken off. And *look* what you left for us, one hot bitch." He kissed Ms. Melfile on the cheek; she was struggling but didn't seem to mind. I don't think The Power realized she was into dead men.

Still, I said, for effect: "Let her go."

"That's what you blabbered last time."

"And now *look at me*," Jenna Rush said with a giggle.

"Before you were killed," said The Power, "I told you when you came back, you were to go to see the Senator and tell him about his daughter. You didn't do this. Tsk tsk tsk."

"Yeah," said one of his crew, "tsk."

The others went, "Tsk tsk tsk."

"Don't you know I'm the leader of you all?" said The Power. "I'm the fucken wellspring, pal!"

"We all do what he says," Jenna Rush giggled.

"The problem here," I said, "is that I've always had a problem with authority."

"You'd make a great hippie, Gideon. I had a feeling you'd be difficult. This is a-okay. So: here we are. And this is what I want you to do, Mr. Private Eyeball: you're going to call the Senator, you're going to say you have his little girl, and you're going to set up a meet with him. Say she's being stubborn, she doesn't want to go home, so you want them to have a father-daughter heart-to-heart on neutral ground. The meeting place will be where we killed and buried you. Nice and remote."

"And if I don't?"

"Your hot bitch here gets a bullet in the noggin."

"Let him shoot me, Arty," Miss Melfile said. "Don't give in to ultimatums from assholes."

"Ahh, honey, you don't mean that," said The Power, kissing her cheek again.

"Arty," my secretary said, looking right at me, "you must realize now what I truly want."

"Yes," I said.

"Just let him do it."

"I can't. This has to play out to an end."

She nodded.

"Do I kill her or not?" The Power asked.

I wanted to get to the bottom of this shit. I went to the phone and called the Senator's private line.

"Goddammit," he said, "I've been trying to reach you the past forty-eight hours!"

"I have her."

"You found her?"

"She's here."

"Good job, sir. And not a moment too soon; this city is going to hell right now."

"Literally."

"Bring her home."

"She won't go."

"What?"

I held the phone toward Jenna.

She yelled, "FUCK YOU DADDY, I WON'T GO HOME!"

I proposed the meet.

"I'll be there in thirty minutes," he said.

"Half an hour," I said to The Power, hanging up the phone.

"Works for me," he said with a shrug.

"Now let my secretary go."

"I'm a zombie of my word," he said, and released Miss Melfile from his grip.

She straightened her hair and smoothed down her skirt. She didn't look at me. Miss Melfile appeared disappointed.

* * * * * * *

That remote area just outside the city limits didn't seem so desolate and lonely in the daytime. Senator Rush showed up in his car with Jill and two bodyguards donning dark suits—I had no idea if they were federal or private; they were your typical thugs: well-dressed and -armed and willing to kill on command. Jenna Rush and I stood by Miss Melfile's car and waited. (I still had no idea where my car was, probably stolen or vandalized.) Jenna kept giggling, saying, "Man oh man, is Daddy having the surprise of his lifetime coming."

"Quiet," I said. "You like being this way?"

"What about you? We're the same, we're part of The Power now. He's going to rule the world in a month."

"Don't get caught up in that fellow's delusions of grandeur," I said.

"You know it's true. You can feel it. *I know you can feel it.* All us zombies, we're connected, man."

"Hush. Your father is here."

"You just don't know," Jenna said, "it's Daddy's fault we're like this now!"

"Jenna!" the Senator cried out. He stopped when he got a good look at his daughter and me: walking corpses on a sunny day and not smelling anything like a bed of roses. "Sweet baby Jesus," he said, stumbling. Jill and one of his bodyguards caught him. "Dear Lord," he moaned, "you've been turned into one of those monsters."

"And you're the monster-maker, Senator," said The Power.

I have no idea where his voice came from; it boomed like there were hidden loudspeakers. The Power and his men emerged from the ground, where they had buried themselves. They moved fast, overtaking Rush's two men before they could react, breaking their arms and legs and necks with an admirable swiftness.

Then they took care of Jill. She screamed, she tried to fight them. She died in a great deal of pain, and The Powers men took delight in her agony and blood. I have to admit I felt a tinge of glee myself, after the snotty way the woman had treated me during our last encounter. Then I recalled what Rush had told me: find his daughter, I could have Jill in bed. I wondered if Jill was like Miss Melfile and preferred dead men over live flesh.

There were four of us standing in a face-off: Jenna and her father, The Power and yours truly.

"What on earth are you?" asked the Senator as The Power took a step in his direction. "You're one of those things from the flying saucers, aren't you? I read the Roswell report."

"Don't you recognize me, Mr. Rush?" said The Power. "I used to be human, until you and your rich compadres sent me and my buddies to Vietnam."

"Excuse me?"

"Don't lie, Daddy," Jenna said.

"What have you done to my daughter, you sick bastard?!?"

"Exactly what you did to me," said The Power.

"What you did to all of us," said The Power's crew in unison.

"Listen, whatever in blazes you are," Rush said, "I have no idea what you're talking about."

"My name is Lieutenant Steven Carl Fitzsimmons," said The Power. He took a soldier's stance of attention and saluted. *"Sir!"*

The other five also saluted and yelled, "Sir, yes, sir!"

The Senator's jaw dropped and his face turned…gray.

"Ahhhh," said The Power, "recognition."

"This isn't possible. You and your platoon…are dead."

"Yes, *yes* we are. And we happen to be here for some payback. You see, Mr. Gideon," and The Power turned his rotting skull my way, "Senator Rush is on what you would call a Black Project Committee, a little unknown wing of the Intelligence Arm of the Senate. And our people's representative here championed a nifty little project to create an unstoppable, unkillable Marine. Well, the Marine could die in combat, but he'd come back. Usually takes two or three days for the stuff they injected into us to take effect. And what did they put in our blood? Activated only when the heart stops beating? Something cooked up in a secret buried lab? No. An ancient recipe he got from a voodoo priestess from Haiti. She gives him the recipe, she and her family get to come to Florida and prosper as bona fide United States citizens. Was that the deal, Senator?"

"You keep your mouth *shut*," said Rush. "You're discussing top secret information. You signed an oath of—"

"Yeah? And what will you do to me? Have me executed for treason?"

The Power and his men laughed.

Jenna Rush laughed.

I started to laugh.

The Power continued: "Well, my platoon was selected as lab rats. They injected us, told us it was in case we got bit by bad insects in the jungle. Fucking liars, but what do you expect from the government? To cut to the nitty-gritty, Senator, the recipe worked. Me and my men were killed in an ambush. A few days later we rose from the dead and we hunted down those gooks who killed us and them a bunch of zombies too."

"You went MIA," said Rush.

"We came home, for payback."

"You need to report back to your unit, your base. Immediately, Lieutenant! I can have you tossed in Leavenworth for this!"

The zombies laughed more.

"When I heard your daughter was a runaway," said The Power, "well, I came up with a *grand* idea for revenge."

"It's horrible what you did to these cool guys, Daddy," Jenna said. "But in the end, it all works out. I like being a zombie. It's the most far-out thing ever."

"Oh my God," said Rush. "Oh no...."

"And now you're going to join us," said The Power.

"No."

"Yes."

"No."

"Yes."

The Power's men held the Senator down.

"My sweet dear little one," The Power said to Jenna, "would you do the honors?"

"I'd love to." Jenna picked up a large rock and approached her father. "It'll hurt, Daddy, but in a couple of days everything will be all right and you'll thank me."

The Senator screamed and his daughter cracked opened his head and began to eat.

I turned and started to get into Miss Melfile's car.

The Power joined me, sitting in the passenger's seat.

"Ahhh, brains," he said. "It's like candy to a girl. What do brains taste like to you, private eye guy?"

"Steak."

"Pork to me. I'm a bacon man."

"Can I drive you anywhere?"

"Nah. So you're not pissed off?"

"What can I do now?"

"It's all his fault," and he gestured to the body of Rush.

"War mongers," I said.

"You understand what's happening," said The Power.

"All of Miami will be zombies within the week."

"And the state, and the country, and the world."

"With you as leader?"

He shrugged. "Who knows."

"I'm not a follower."

"I see that now. Join me anyway."

"I have my own life to live," I said, "as a zombie."

"Well," he said, "you know where to find me."

VII. "ZOMBIE LOVERS"

There were zombies everywhere in the city and it wasn't so bad; I was one of them and getting used to their presence.

I drove home. Lissa Melfile wasn't there.

I picked up the phone but the phone line was dead (no pun intended here).

I drove to my office.

My secretary was there, and she was naked.

"This is a sight," I said.

"I wanted you to see me like this," she said.

"I like what I see."

"I don't. Arty, I don't. You know what I want, what I need. Right?"

I nodded. "I've been thinking about it."

"It's some sort of form of evolution," she said. "And I've been waiting for this all my life."

* * * * * * *

Two and a half days later, she woke up in bed. Her flesh was no longer white and pink. Her brains, I must admit, were delicious, the best I've ever had.

"Oh, Arty!" she said, holding out her arms.

I went to her and we made love the way zombies do it, and let me tell you: it's the best I've ever had.

Later, I asked her, "What happens when the whole world becomes a race a zombies? What do we do then?"

"We grow," she said, and she was right.

—September, 2003-September, 2007
San Diego, Borrego Springs, Los Angeles, Seattle

THE ARRANGEMENT
WITH MR. GREEN

I.

Mr. Green pops into the back of the town car with me; he does that sort of thing, just zips in and out of reality with a chime from his old wood flute, being a supernatural creature; I don't think I will ever get used to it; it's a good thing the partition between me and the driver is up; I imagine a car crash if the driver looks into the rearview and sees this seven-foot tall humanoid with a leafy green head and smooth green skin wearing a tuxedo.

Yeah, he's wearing a tux, like I am. He thinks that's funny: Mr. Night on the Town, ha, ha.

"Off to the big banquet to get your award, eh, lad?" he says.

"Where have you been?" I ask.

"Here and there, doin' this and that. I enjoy New York."

"I thought you weren't 'keen' on big cities."

"They're growin' on me like a lean moss," he says, and laughs in that high-pitch chuckle I have come to adore.

"Are you going to accept the award with me?" I am hopeful.

"Now that would be *quite* the sight, eh, lad?" I see he has his mug a lager in his right hand, as always, the old wooden flute in the left. He's consistent if anything.

I want him to do it, to come with me and show the world the truth. I want to disclose it all, no matter what it would do to my life. I am tired of living this lie that is now my career and existence; I can't tell anyone what is going on because that one time I did, when I told someone I loved, she looked at me like I was completely nuts and left me because she knew I was serious.

Mr. Green holds up his mug. "Just wanted to congrats you, lad. You deserve it!"

"You mean *you* do."

"I'm the mouth, you're the writer. Your name on the covers."

Am I really a writer? When was the last time I used my imagination?

"We still have much more work to do," he says, "and many more awards and attention to grab. But you won't have to feel like such a fake no longer, because I am handin' the reigns over to your brain." He places the wood flute to his mouth and plays the three notes I have come to know all too well these past years.

II.

I arrive to the awards banquet of the International Fantasy Society. Hundreds of people look at me: there he *is*, Danny Boyd, best-selling author of *The Green Man Chronicles*. I accept the Best Novel Award with a smile, and nodding when the audience asks if there is a next book coming out soon. There are eight more in the cycle, correct? A new book every nine months? I clutch the award—a silver angelic being holding a mighty sword—close to my chest and nod and say, yes, yes, there are many more adventures of the Green Man coming....

I feel like a fraud, because I am.

III.

I was twenty-eight and washed up. I had "promise," publishing my first science-fiction story at sixteen and pumping out a hundred until I was twenty-two, when I switched to fantasy. My book publisher was not happy at first, but pleased as plump pumpkins when the first fantasy novel sold better than my science fiction.

A couple of trilogies later and at age twenty-eight, I hit a wall of emptiness. I had writer's block, really bad writer's block; I once could sit down and whip out two chapters before lunch, a short story before dinner; but when the block came, I simply stared at the blank screen for hours, days, weeks, and then months; I tried it the old fashion way: purchasing a 1970s Olympia manual like one of my influences, Harlan Ellison, used, but the end result was my staring at a blank sheet of twenty-two-weight white paper for hours, days, weeks, months.

The first year was true hell, and I had to accept the fact that this was the end; I had milked the creative cow dry. Sure, with some smart investments, I could take my royalties and live frugally for the rest of my life, never having to worry about getting a job; that was a different kind of hell I did not want.

A fellow writer friend suggested I go to Hollywood and take script jobs: revising or fixing dialogue, something that did not require too much brainpower, and perhaps it would jump start the flicker to a flame. I tried that: rented an apartment in Santa Monica, my New York agent talked to his sub-agent in LaLa Land; all my books had been optioned, right, so *that* was something (although there was no word on further development); I took some meetings, got a few jobs, but I couldn't do it.

Another writer friend suggested composing erotic romance under a female pen name: take on a persona, the genre was flourishing. Tried it, but I was too mentally impotent to create scenes of romance and soft porn.

Two years, then three; I was thirty-one. My agent sent me a tearsheet from one of the trades, headline: *What Happened to the Promise of Daniel T. Boyd?* "Yeah," my agent scrawled over the text, "what's going on?" I had to tell him; he suggested drugs, sex, booze, anything. No, no, and no. Then he suggested getting out of the United States, travel, go to Europe. "I know the perfect place you can borrow for the season," he said, "a wonderful cottage in the Scottish countryside that I am sure will bring you back. It's owned by your British publisher...."

IV.

The cottage was located on the outskirts of the town Crinan in the Argyll and Bute coastal region of Scotland. There was this marine layer warmness from the gulf breeze that I found immediately appealing, after too much time spent in large American cities. I felt as if I had been transported back in time, surrounded by giant, gaunt trees hundreds of years old, ancient fortresses that must have dated back to Arthurian times, antediluvian castles atop distant hills, a variety of small islands off the fogy coast. I expected Tolkein's Hobbits to come running out of the shires and forests, leading me to some wild adventure that would be my next book.

And that sort of happened.

The first week there I went exploring, walking deep into the Crinan Woods and the Argyll Forest Park, even considering climbing the Arrochar Alps and Loch Goil Mountains (if I'd had the equipment and physical stamina), exploring the outermost land of Castle Stalker and Castle Sween, Fincham Castle and Carrick Castle, imagining the old stone structures filled with kings and princesses, knights and maidens, evil wizards and ghastly dragons; I took a ferry to Isle of Bute and walked long trails from one end of the isle to the next; I tried to summon the ghost of the handless piper that was said to haunt the Duntrune Castle north across Crinan Loch; pictured the line of kings who were crowned over time at the hill fort of Dundadd, each with the heavy burden of monarchs awaiting them—oh, their stories I could tell!

The townsfolk of Crinan paid me no mind; it seems Yanks often came here at the behest of the London publisher who often opened the place up to writers who needed to get away from it all and refresh their batteries.

The third week, I felt I was ready. I would write a novel about brave knights and nasty, multi-dimensional beings, a tale of honor and courage; but when I sat down at the laptop, nothing came forward except the first line: *The roar of the Corrievrekam whirlpool was as fierce as the unearthly cries of the marching army of zombie elves.*

I got drunk on the twelve-pack of Guinness I had purchased in the local store, which was better than running to the nearest coastal cliff and plunging myself deep into the Scottish sea.

V.

The sound of three notes from a flute woke me up; my head was pounding hard from the alcohol and I wanted to vomit. In the main room of the cottage I could make out the familiar pat-pat-pat of the laptop keyboard, and what seemed to be a high-pitched giggle. An intruder, I thought, looking around the bedroom for something I could use as a weapon.

Empty-handed, I walked out of the bedroom and saw, in the dim light from the fireplace (I had not ignited it), sitting at the card table, was a large shadowy figure slumped over my laptop and typing. I noticed there was what appeared to be an old, wood flute on the table, and a large, warped drinking mug that was also made of wood.

"Who the hell are *you*?" I asked, my voice hoarse.

"*There* you are," this person said in a squeaky Scottish or Irish voice. "Tied one over, eh, lad? Well, no worries, we'll get your career back on track."

At first I thought it might be my British publisher who owned this cottage, come to check on me, wearing an odd hooded jacket, but when this person turned and the light of the burning embers showed me a better view, I could only stare in a dumb-founded, hung over state, my mouth agape like a cartoon character, at this person who was *not a human being.*

He—it, whatever—was green from head to toe, with regular human features of eyes, nose, and mouth, but instead of hair there was a growth of foliage, branches, and leaves from its head; instead of skin on the body was a fuzzy green moss; and instead of feet were giant leaves. It wore a loose tunic and loincloth that appeared soiled and ancient, with a bentwood dagger tucked in a vine rope belt around the torso.

"Don't scream, lad," he, it, said.

"I won't," I heard myself say.

"I will explain more tomorrow evening. Meanwhile, take a look at what I have put down on this mechanical contraption. Keen, I say, but nothing can beat a quill and parchment to tell a *real* story. Ah, I yield to progress, lad, if this is what it is called! I planted that first sentence in your head, the way a farmer plants a seed, when you were taking a stroll through the woodlands, hoping it would give you inspiration to make something up. You cannot create lies out of the truth, yes? So I will help you. Yes, there *was* a war between the undead elves and the peoples of the forests long, long ago. You can read about it...."

He stood up, I backed off.

"Tomorrow," he said, picking up the flute and placing the instrument to his mouth; out came the three notes that had woken me up, and the leafy green man vanished in front of my eyes.

He left the drinking mug.

I made myself some tea (green tea, nonetheless!) and it took me an hour to gather the courage and gumption to sit behind the laptop and peer at what was on the screen, sloppily typed on the word processing program, a narrative after the sentence I had left.

There was about three thousand words of explanation of a ghastly war fought among dead elves resurrected by a dark lord of mystic origins and the fisherfolk of the Isle of Jura, who joined forces with the simple townsfolk of Sell and Mull, who opposed this travesty; they were aided by the fairyfolk of Crinan Woods in this struggle, yet despite their valor and pureness of heart, they were no match for zombie elves who, when struck down, merely rose again, for the dead cannot die twice.

Only a being of similar enchanted proportions could defeat such foul creatures; so the good folk with the aid of ferries made a request to The Great Tree of Gaia, found in the center of the woods, for an army that could take care of the job. Their prayers were answered, but they did not get an army; from the ether of neverwhere came a tall and mighty man who was part tree, part flora and fauna, and part blood and bone, who single-handedly defeated the zombified elves and killed the dark lord who created them. This entity was named Gweydelthoth Mywar, who then resided in the woods and forests, and let it be known that whenever he was needed to defeat evil, he would come.

It was quite a story; I wanted to know more. I fixed the grammar and spelling, broke the narrative into paragraphs, and started to believe in the possibilities....

VI.

As promised, the green man returned that evening. I was opening a bottle of white wine when I heard the three notes from the flute; I quickly turned around and there he was again, sitting at the desk and looking at the laptop.

"So what do you think?" he asked.

"I was wondering if you were real," I said, "or if I wrote all that in a drunken sleepy stupor."

"Of course."

Of course what?

"Are you Gweydelthoth Mywar?" I asked.

"That's one of my names, but you can call me Mr. Green. Can I have some of that wine?"

He picked up the wooden mug and tossed it my way. I almost didn't catch it, my hands were shaking. I poured some wine in the cup, approached and sat down across from him. His eyes and lips were green and he had a rich forest aroma about him.

"You like the story so far," he said, slugging the wine back.

"Yes, very much. Is there more?"

"There is a *lot* more, lad."

"Will you write it down?"

He pushed the laptop my way. "I will tell you, and you write it down as you see fit. I can speak a good saga, but I don't have the gift of story structure and dramatic turns."

VII.

And so Mr. Green told me how after that battle, there were many more to be fought and won around the world: cultures and tribes on this very continent prayed and beseeched the earth mother and the ground that was her essence for a variety of needs, and from the plants and dirt and roots he arose. He was not alone, for soon his brothers and sisters were required; they resided in every corner of the earth.

"Our image has been drawn in caves and on rocks," he told me. "One can view our likeness on the doors of churches where, while the worship is of Christ, the old ways of the woodlands is not completely forgotten."

He came to visit every night for a week, staying until an hour before sunrise when he would use his flute to disappear. I asked him how that worked and he shrugged and said, "Does it matter how? It simply does. The problem with you modern men of this world of science and gadgets is you want to take the magic apart and find an answer that is *not* magic."

VIII.

His stories began to form into a book, and after one month of visits and long tales of vast wonder, I had 110,000 words that did not take long to break down into chapters and three main sections. I titled it *Rise of the Green Man.*

My British publisher was delighted with it, as was my U.S. publisher. Half a dozen translation rights were sold before the book came out. It was rushed into production and on the shelves in hardcover nine months after completion. While not a bestseller, it did well in the genre market and my publishers contracted me for two sequels.

I returned to the cottage the next year to work on the second book. I went into the woods and called for him and that night, he showed up as he did the year before, and once again we sat together and he told me the adventures of his life, which went back six thousand years or more, he was not quite sure. "Maybe seven or eight," he said with a sigh.

The second book was titled *Path of the Green Man*, and the third *Interview with the Green Man*.

When the third book was nearly done, he told me I did not have to keep coming back to Scotland, he could find me anywhere on the earth, all I had to do was ask. "I am not keen on the big cities," he said, "but I can do it."

From then on, he showed up at my New York condo on Park Avenue; the fourth book, *Wars of the Green Man*, had hit the bestseller lists, the first had been made into a Hollywood film, there were TV shows and comic books in the works; I was doing quite well.

We had a nice arrangement: I kept his story alive in the imaginations of mankind and he kept me alive with material for consumer consumption.

IX.

Romancing the Green Man was a breakthrough title, attracting the lucrative paranormal romance audience and developed into a three-season series by the BBC, which was adapted for a five-season series by Showtime. There was a primal drive in the notion of sexual encounters between human women and leafy men. *The Green Man vs. the Martians* caused some friction with fans, who did not care for the science-fiction element of devious space invaders wanting to strip the earth of its resources and being stopped by the Green Man Family. *Kingdoms of the*

Green Man, the first in a ten-book cycle I called *The Greenman Chronicles*, won my fans back, and the International Fantasy Society gave the Best Novel Award to the second title, *Nights of the Green Man*.

X.

Returning home from the awards banquet, Mr. Green appears in the back of the towncar again, still wearing that ridiculous tux.

"How you feelin' now, lad?"

"As always, the fraud," I confess.

"You have money, fame, happiness, what more could you ask for?"

Happiness? Really? Every time I tried to have a relationship with a woman, they were either fans who thought I was something I was not or gold-diggers who wanted me to help them get their own fantasy and romance novels published, so they could get rich and famous. And there was that one who left me, claiming I was insane, when I told her the truth....

"You won't have to feel like a fraud any longer," Mr. Green says. "'Tis time for you to get creative, lad. I have no more stories for you. I've told you all. You're on your own. I know you can do it."

The blood leaves my face. "What do you *mean*, you have no more stories?"

"I've given you all I got, sir," he says with spread hands, sounding like Scotty on *Star Trek*.

"But...but...I'm contracted for eight more titles in this series! Ten million advance, one million per book!"

"I have faith in you," he says.

"That's good, because *I* don't. Look, Mr. Green, please," I say helplessly, "for nine years now I have not had to use my imagination. I'm simply an editor shaping your words into commercialized product. I don't have a creative, original bone in my body. I'm worse than a hack."

For the first time since I have known him, Mr. Green appears troubled. "I see this is true, Danny boy."

"Don't leave me out to dry," I say.

"I need to ponder this new quagmire," he says, lifting the flute to his mouth.

"Wait!" I try to grab the flute but he plays the three notes and he's gone, leaving that damn mug behind like he always does.

XI.

Mr. Green says he has faith in me; maybe I can prove him right. But for three nights I sit behind the computer and nothing comes out after typing *Book Three of the Green Man Chronicles.*

"I give up," I say aloud, and that is when I hear the wonderful, lovely notes of his flute…except this time there are six of them, not three.

He is not alone; next to him is a female of his kind, lovely green skin with longer braches and leaves on her head, thicker green lips and saucer-shaped green eyes.

"Allow me to introduce you to Mrs. Green," he says, "my wife of two thousand years."

"You never told me you were married," I say.

"You never asked. Say, lad, have any wine around here?"

The three of us sit down with two bottles of white wine. Mr. Green says he knows how to fix my problem. "I don't know why it didn't occur to me before," he says, "the noggin is getting' mossy with age. My wife will tell you her stories, how she came to me, the events we shared, good for *at least* three books. After that, her sisters and my brothers and our cousins will come to tell you their yarns. From all over the world! Lad, your grand-children will have to pick up where we leave off!"

"I need to work on getting some children first," I say.

"I know a few good human women I can introduce you to," says Mrs. Green.

I think I blush.

"So where do we begin?" she asks. "The battle with the winged giraffes of Mount Vosto or the invading horde of the uni-dolphins on the French coast?"

"Either is keen," says Mr. Green.

"I need to open a third bottle," I say.

"Make it four or five," says Mrs. Green.

"My wife can outdrink me any hour of day," says Mr. Green. "Been doin' it for fifteen hundred years at least."

"It was *you* who introduced me to the barley and hops," she says, kissing him on the cheek. To me: "I think we can begin with how my husband caused me to become an inebriated branch wench and we...well, we *made love*. It was a chase, and I was his catch."

Sex? I can see the reviews now...and the fan response...*and the new TV series....*

"Wine coming up," I say.

I have not felt this giddy in quite a while.

—November, 2012
Portland, Oregon

THE LAST
BUSHEL OF GRAPES

I.

When Armageddon came, and the people of the world suf-
fered greatly, trembling in fear, praying to various gods, I was
doing five-to-ten for bank robbery at Hawthorne State Prison
in California. My cellmate was doing twenty-five-to-life for
second-degree murder: he had beheaded his wife.

"The funny thing is," said my cellmate, Greg, "I have ended
the world at least three times, maybe four." Greg was a former
film and TV producer in Los Angeles.

I was a former con man and heel.

But we got along well.

"This sucks," he said about the end of the world.

The warden and guards had abandoned the prison—they all
went home to be with their families and they were either dead
or waiting to die, just as they had left the incarcerated to die.

But when you got several hundred hardcore criminals in racial
gangs, murderers, rapists, terrorists alike, facing end times,
you're not going to find very many frightened human beings;
in fact, most of the inmates at Hawthorne Prison welcomed this
change in history, because the end meant freedom.

First, they went after each other: the Aryans and the blacks,
the Hispanics and the Asians, the Christians and the Muslims—
pent-up hatreds, old scores and debts. You might think the last
days would be cause for harmony and peace, but you'd think

differently if you witnessed how these men butchered each other.

Greg and I hid in the shadows, not wanting to be a part of it. We were both Caucasian middle-aged men and we didn't run with any gangs or religious creed, but that didn't mean some crazed maniac wouldn't hesitate to take us out just for the hell of it. No one ever thought that when Armageddon came, a lot of dangerous and insane people would be released onto what was left of the world.

II.

When things settled down, we walked over the dead and mutilated bodies and left the prison grounds. It was so easy. No guards in the towers, no locked gates.

In the distance, the remnants of a mushroom cloud loomed like Goliath in a bad mood and made the sky purple and orange.

"What do you think they hit? San Francisco?" Greg asked.

"Or Sacramento," I said.

"There's the Alameda military base. My bet is on San Fran."

Los Angeles and San Diego had been taken out, this much we knew and was evident when looking at the skies south.

"How long you think before the fallout hits here?"

I didn't know, and I didn't want to know. We already knew we were dead, as did everyone else.

III.

The California prison system creates economic communities wherever a prison facility is located; outside the prison are small towns populated by the guards and other employees needed to maintain the stir, along with the families of these employees. Stores, gas stations, bars, and restaurants are needed to maintain American town life. The first store Greg and I found was completely empty, having been looted from the first bomb.

The only item we found was a lone bushel of grapes in the large storage refrigerator in the back of the store.

"Grapes," Greg said, amused. "If we could only make wine. You think they're radioactive?"

I ate one of the grapes. "Sure tastes good."

"One bushel and two of us."

"50/50?"

"All the way, buddy."

IV.

Greg wanted to head east and I wanted to go north. We shook hands. There were plenty of cars around to take. I passed on the ones with dead drivers in the seats. Some of them looked like they committed suicide instead of murdered. We both wound up with SUVs, his black, mine white. "It's fitting," Greg said, "all the irony left in the world: I'm the wife-killer and you're the bank robber, so who's evil and who's good?" We shook hands and with our grapes, we went our separate ways. There were many days when I hated sharing that small cell with the guy, and many times I wish he would go away forever, but I knew I would miss him: I had no one to talk to now.

V.

There were no radio stations broadcasting. No surprise there. The CDs left in the vehicle were all rap. I listened to lyrics about thug lives, homies, killing the enemy, rape, and urban mayhem.

The drive to Santa Barbara took three hours. The city was abandoned, or people were hiding and waiting for the end. Several people walked the streets in a daze and looked like zombies.

I went to the bank.

The bank I had robbed.

The robbery that had put me in Hawthorne for five-to-ten.

VI.

They say criminals always return to the scene of their crime and here I was: I wanted to get one last look at the place that symbolized my downfall. The doors were locked but the glass windows had been shattered. All the tills were emptied; twenty and fifty dollar bills lay scattered on the floor. Either the bank employees or citizens had taken the bombings as an opportunity to do what I had done—this made me smirk, because what value or good would money do now?

Still, money is nice to hold and look at. I picked up a few bills and smelled them; they were new. I even put them in my pocket like I would have use for them.

I went to the vault, thinking I should have emptied that during the robbery, instead of the $6,000 I acquired from the tellers; at least the conviction would have been worth it, if I had walked out with, say, $250,000. A quarter million or five bucks, I would've gotten the same sentence.

I could have had a lot of fun with a big take, maybe buying some invisibility, erasing my tracks, moving to Venezuela where there's no extradition treaty. It took the feds two months to find me and by that time the six grand was long spent; with $250,000 or more, I could've been a Vegas high roller or lived like royalty in a third world country.

A lot of what ifs went through my head: what if I had been more careful, what if I had left Santa Barbara, what if I had not robbed the bank at all?

I was desperate at the time. The sinking economy meant no jobs for a regular guy like me with only a high school education; I needed to eat and keep a roof over my head, and my sick mother needed some help too: that's where most that money went, and it was she who gave me up to the FBI.

She lived in San Diego and I figured she was dead, as the whole city was dead.

As I would be soon.

As for the vault, it was empty. Again I wondered what anyone would do with useless currency. The government was vaporized, and I'd bet the money I had in my pocket that Fort Knox was a crater.

A criminal will sometimes return to the scene of his crime, the moment that changed his life.

It was time to go.

VII.

A noise startled me, Behind me. A bang on one of the metal desks. Probably an animal, but I went to look anyway.

A young woman was squeezed under the desk. She wore jeans and a sweater and had short blonde hair.

"Don't hurt me," she said.

"I'm not going to hurt you."

"Don't rape me, please."

"I'm not going to do that either. Come out from under there."

Slowly, cautiously, she stood up, keeping her eye on me, looking at my hands to see if I had a weapon.

"A gentlemen, how nice," she said.

"What were you doing under there?"

"Hiding from you."

"I mean, what are you doing in here?" I asked.

She looked at me hard. "I know you," she said, "I remember you. You robbed us two years ago."

I didn't recognize her.

"My hair was longer then," she said, "and dyed black."

"You're a teller here?"

"I was," she said.

"So what are you doing here?"

"I could ask the same."

"You look hungry," I said.

"That's because I am."

"You like grapes?"

VIII.

Her name was Irene, "This job was all I had," she told me as we had a meal of grapes together. "I loved my job, I loved the people I worked with. They're all gone now, I don't know if they're dead or what. I was afraid you would kill one of them, or all of us, two years ago."

"There were no bullets in the gun," I told her.

"If you'd had bullets, would you have shot anyone?"

"All I wanted, needed, was some money."

"Funny thing is," she said, "I understand that. I would've done the same if I had no job."

IX.

The fallout was beginning, giant white pieces of debris, and a smell that's hard to describe.

"Nuclear winter will be here soon," I said.

"I must ask a favor of you," she said, "and a gentlemen would never say no."

"Anything."

There was a handgun in the desk she'd sat under. It had belonged to the bank guard.

"Do you know how to use this thing?"

I nodded.

X.

"It was nice meeting you," Irene said, and gave me a quick kiss.

"Do you have a boyfriend, a husband?" I asked.

"No."

"If things had been different...."

"Maybe," she said, looking out the window. The debris was getting thicker. "Get on with it, please."

I pointed the gun at her head.

XI.

I did as I promised, gave her that favor. The plan was that I would kill myself after and our bodies would lie next to each other, maybe hand in hand.

I couldn't do it.

I tried.

I put the gun to my temple.

I couldn't do it.

Let the radiation do it.

XII.

I drove fast, getting ahead of the fallout. I had three grapes left on a stem. I would save them for the last moment. I would at least have something delicious in my mouth when the time came.

—March, 2011
Los Angeles

TROUT FISHING ON THE OUTSKIRTS OF OBLIVION

I.

I spend most of the time trout fishing at Old Duncan's Lake because there is nothing else to do here. There might not be any people, but there are plenty of trout. I am wondering if the trout will over-populate and starve. Maybe that's why they bite so easily when I take the rowboat out to the center of the lake. I know I will eventually get sick of frying up trout for breakfast, lunch, and dinner.

I woke up one day—there is no morning noon or night— and I was alone. There wasn't a single person in town. Town is Mount Henderson, even though there is no mountain named Henderson anywhere near.

My parents were not in the house; both their cars were in the driveway and this was not like them. I called for them. I looked for them at several neighbors' homes and the neighbors were gone. There were no kids playing in the streets; their bikes, Frisbees, and toys lay scattered on driveways and lawns.

I was planning on leaving when I graduated high school in May, I would get up and go and never look back—New York, Los Angeles, Seattle, anywhere but here. I wouldn't tell my parents or buddies anything, not until I made something of myself; I would return home a success and people would say, "That Tommy Temple, he sure fooled us, we all thought he was a Big Nobody, and now look at him."

Now look at me: in an empty town where there is nothing but a dull gray void of sky.

I adjusted well and quickly to all this; the biggest blow was when I went to my girlfriend's home. Dee. Her folks were not there and she was not there, of course. I had to check. I took this opportunity to go upstairs to her bedroom and explore a world I had never been: Dee's private things. I looked in her closet, at the dresses and skirts and jeans; I looked at her collection of three-dozen shoes; I looked in her dresser drawer and pulled out a variety of bras and panties, smelling them. They smelled like her. I was surprised she had a black thong panty tucked away deep under her regular, typical underwear. When and for whom was she waiting to wear this? We had never gone all the way, and I was planning on breaking up with her one month before I headed off, so not to break her heart too much; Dee was a tall, pretty blonde, but she was not in my future, no matter what plans of marriage our parents had for us. I found her diary and read through it; mundane stuff like "went to the movies with Sammy" and "talked to Beth about Billy."

Then I came to this:

"I will break up with Sammy after graduation and before I go to Stanford. I have not told him I was accepted. It's for the best. There is no future with Sammy. He will stay here in Mt. Henderson and work at a garage or construction and never amount to anything."

That was the blow, but it was also a relief—and I would have had the last hurrah because I had intended to dump her first.

II.

I did the expected thing: I helped myself to food and property; I entered into homes and took what I wanted: jewelry, guitars, clothes, and money. I smashed windows into stores and raided cash registers. In three days I amassed $40,000 in

Federal Reserve notes and I felt rich…but, of course, where would I spend it? What use of it was to me?

I slept in different homes, different beds every "night," or when I was tired and needed sleep. I slept in the beds of friends and enemies, of that hot Ms. Allison who taught Senior English and all the guys wanted to date, of the coach and his young wife, of the mayor of Mt. Henderson. I went though their things, their folders, and their photos, and learned all their secrets, sweet and nasty.

After a while that became boring so I went fishing.

I love trout fishing.

At least the trout remained; sometimes I talked to them after I caught them, my own voice now a stranger.

III.

Boy Scout training on how to build a fire came in handy; there was no other way to cook the trout or any other food I found in the stores. The meat lockers contained rotting beef and chicken, so that was no good. All the milk was sour. I started to really crave a steak, eggs, a tall glass of milk, all the things I took for granted when life was normal. I yearned so much for the return of that life that I couldn't believe I had planned on leaving it. It is only when something is taken away from you that you begin to appreciate how valuable it is to your existence.

I missed my family: my mother and father and aunts and uncles and cousins. I especially missed my grandfather, as I had missed him since I was ten and he died.

IV.

Grandpa taught me how to fish for trout at Old Duncan's Lake like he did with my father; Grandpa's father had also taught him; it was a tradition among the men in our family; and of the women, the women would fry up the trout for a family dinner. My mother didn't seem particularly keen on cooking trout, but she would do it when my grandpa and I, from age seven to ten, would bring trout home. I was proud of my catches and my mother did not want to take that feeling away from me, despite her own impulses toward fishing and game hunting: she felt such activities were not necessary in this age when one could easily go to the store and buy food.

My father only went with us twice, as I recall; he had outgrown fishing and was too busy with the hardware store he owned and ran in town; he expected that I would one day take over the family business, something I did not intend to do—at fifteen, I had vowed to never wind up trapped in Mount Henderson, and now here I was: with nowhere else to go; Mt. Henderson was my universe.

V.

There was no way out, there was nothing beyond the gray walls and skies. Oh, I tried. I went to the end of the roads leaving the town; I went into the deepest parts of the woods and the county lines of Mt. Henderson; I met a wall of gray fog that, when I entered it, would take me straight back to my house. Of course I wondered how this was possible, and I continued to walk into the gray fog and I continued to wind up at my house, always the same place: my bedroom. I eventually accepted it; accepted that Mount Henderson was my personal lonely hell— and that's what I started to believe: I had died and gone south, paying for my sin of hubris, my desire to leave my family and life and seek fame and adventure elsewhere.

VI.

One time I jumped out of the row-boat and into the lake; I had the notion there was an exit point at the bottom of Old

Duncan's, but all I found was water teeming with trout of every possible size.

VII.

Things changed at my father's hardware store. I went there feeling nostalgic. I had worked there for three summer vacations, learning the trade and hating it; now I was wishing for it back, to see my father leering over paperwork, keeping an eye on employees; I wished for the stockroom, the register, the customers. Especially the women customers; hardware stores get few of those, but every now and then a woman from town, some pretty, married or single, would come in; some college age and my age—as a healthy teen lad, my eye was always on the lookout for all kinds of women.

And it was a woman I found in the store.

It could have been two days or two years or two hundred years I had been alone in Mount Henderson, I had no idea, and I had resolved that I would never see another human being again: yet there was one in my father's store, in the hammer and nails aisle. She was around five-foot-five with very long light brown hair, hair so long it went to her ankles; the longest hair I had ever seen on a girl—and girl she was, not yet a grown woman, a girl my age or younger, sixteen at least, small round face with big blue eyes and crooked teeth. She was as surprised to see me as I was to see her.

She ran.

I went after her.

"Hey!" I said, my voice a curious creature, not having heard it in quite a while.

She ran out of the store and I chased her.

"Hey, come back here!"

I was not going to let her go. She was fast but that long hair held her back the way a cape would on a super hero. I caught her, wrapped my arms around her; she tried hitting me, she kicked me and I lost my balance and we both tumbled to the ground. I was on top of her and she knew she was defeated.

"Please," she said, "don't hurt me."

"I'm not going to hurt you," I said, breathing. "Don't fight me, I promise, I'm not going to hurt you."

"Then let go of me."

I released her from my grip, expected her to jump up and take off again. No, she lay there on the ground and stared at me.

I sat up. "See?"

"Who are you?" she said.

"Was going to ask you the same."

"How did you get here?"

"I thought maybe you would have the answer to that," I said.

VIII.

Her name was Elaine. She was sixteen, as I figured, and she knew as much as I did: one day she woke up and she was in Mount Henderson and alone. Like me, she went to the two grocery stores for food. Why had we not crossed paths until now? She kept to herself at her grandmother's house; she needed to fix something, needed a hammer and nails, and went to the hardware store....

"I wish I knew you were here," I said.

"Ditto," she said.

"Do you think there are others?"

"I don't know. I don't think so."

"Maybe we should go house to house and look."

"They may not be friendly," she said. "They might be scared, they might have guns."

"They might have answers," I said.

"Is it so bad, just the two of us?"

IX.

I wondered why I didn't know her; I knew almost all the teen girls in town: we had only one high school. Elaine told me she and he mother had left Mount Henderson to live in Charleston, South Carolina when she was thirteen, to live with her new stepfather. "That didn't work out between them," she said, "so Mom and I came back here just a week ago—or a week before everyone vanished. I was about to register for the last semester," she went on, "even though I didn't want to. No one would have remembered me. You don't remember me, do you?"

"We met before?"

"Middle school, silly, and sixth grade," she said.

"No, I'm sorry, I don't."

"I remember you, Tommy."

"I'm sorry...."

"I looked different, I was younger and geeky, and my hair was really short. My grandmother always cut my hair short. She said long hair only got the women in our family in trouble."

"Oh yes, I remember you now."

She smiled, showing her white but crooked teeth. "No, you don't. You're just saying that."

"I don't mean to lie."

"Well, it's okay," she said.

X.

We spent a lot of time together. We were the only two people in the universe, so what else would we do? We stayed in the same houses but did not sleep in the same beds. One night she joined me and asked if this was okay. I said of course. "I don't feel like sleeping alone right now," she told me; I could tell in her voice that she was disturbed by something. I wasn't sure what to do; while I had had plenty of experience with sexual intimacy with girls, I had never actually spent a whole night with one; I wasn't sure what was appropriate in these moments. I put my arm around her and she reacted well, she moved toward me, we spooned as they call it. Her body was soft and warm. Her long hair was pulled into a massive pony tail; it was thick and amazing, like it was an entity all of its own. The tail found its ways around my torso, hugging me; the sensation was like the feathered wing of a bird protecting a hatchling. It was the best six hours of straight sleep I'd had since this all began and seemed to be the same for Elaine.

XI.

But something was still bothering her. When we had dinner later the next "day," a dinner of canned spaghetti I cooked up after making a campfire, and we ate outdoors like we were camping in the wilderness, she spoke up. "Do you miss her?" she asked.

"Who, my mom?" I said. "Yes, I miss her a lot."

"No, Dee."

I had not mentioned Dee. "You know about her?"

"The second day we came back, I saw you in town with her. I remember Dee going back to fourth grade. She always got the attention of boys."

"Yeah, she has—had a gift for that."

"She got your attention."

"She did," I admitted.

"You were steady for almost a year."

"How do you know?"

She shrugged. "I asked around. People said you two were an 'item.' Talks of marriage."

"I never talked about marriage." I told Elaine about my plans to break up with Dee and leave Mount Henderson; and how I read in Dee's diary that she also wanted to break things up with me.

Elaine seemed pleased with that information. "So it was

mutual, no one gets hurt."

"Yeah."

"Not like my mom and stepdad. He found another woman and just said, 'I want a divorce,' not even thinking about how much that would hurt her…and hurt me. Are all men like that?"

"I don't think so," I said. "Were you hurt? Was he like a real father?"

"My mom was hurt the most; she thought they would live happy until old age. Me…yeah…I wished he was a better father, like a real father, but it wasn't in his makeup."

"I guess some things never work out the way you hope," I said.

She asked again, "Do you miss Dee?"

"I miss the way everything was, this simple, small town life."

"But you wanted to leave."

"I thought there was a better world out there."

"Beyond the gray," she said. "Now there is no world out there anymore. All gone."

"We don't know that for sure, right? Millions, billions of people."

"All gone. I feel it."

"So there is just us, here," I said. "That doesn't make sense."

"Nothing ever really makes sense," she said.

We discussed the possibilities of what may have happened: from this was hell to aliens did it, we were in some kind of zoo and being observed; to it may have happened to towns all over the world, and for whatever reason, maybe DNA, only a handful of people were not affected; to an extended dream, mine of hers.

"Or we're both dreaming," she said, "sharing it."

She joined me in bed again and I held her close and her long wrap wrapped around my shoulders, moving on its own. She ground her rear, tenderly, into my crotch. I wondered if she knew about sex, if she was a virgin; I had not felt a reason to ask. I did not respond to her movement; sex with her was not on my mind, which was unusual, I was like any other seventeen-year-old who was often preoccupied with sex. There was nothing wrong with

Elaine that would make me not feel an attraction toward here; she was no Dee, she was petite and had crooked teeth, and had I met her at a beer party I would not turn away an opportunity to go down in the basement or park the car for a quick moment of satisfaction.

I just wasn't feeling it, and I knew she was expecting me to make a move. I wasn't feeling a need for anything beyond the cuddling.

"Maybe," she whispered, "we are in a virtual reality game."

XII.

We went fishing. She was quiet. She sat in the boat staring at me.

"You should cast your line," I said.

She held only the fishing pole and said nothing.

I was feeling uncomfortable. "What's wrong, Elaine?" I asked.

"This," she said.

"What?"

"This whole situation, here with you. It isn't going the way I had hoped. You don't love me."

"I don't understand," I said, but I did know.

She said, "You didn't make love to me last night. I was ready and willing and you do nothing. Am I ugly to you?"

"Look, Elaine," I started.

"This isn't working," she said, "because you still love Dee. Don't lie. It's the only explanation. You'd rather have her here with you than me."

Before I could respond, the world around us fell apart. The gray sky vanished, replaced by some kind of white wall with florescent lines. Old Duncan's Lake and all the trout disappeared, as did the boat and Elaine.

XIII.

Elaine was replaced by Dee sitting in a chair in what seemed to be a hospital room. She was holding a small baby in her arms.

A man in a white lab coat was removing something from my head and eyes, headgear with green-tinted glasses.

"You're back," Dee said. "You gave us a scare. Look," she said, "Daddy is back."

The baby, a girl, looked at me and smiled and went, "Daaaaaaaaa."

"Elaine was worried about you too," Dee said.

"Elaine?"

She rolled her eyes. "Our daughter, silly."

"He'll be disoriented for a while," the man in the lab coat said. "It may take two or three days before all his memories will return."

"Is there a chance he's lost some memories?" Dee asked him.

"There has never been a case of complete damage," the man said. I didn't know what they were talking about but I could tell he was not being truthful.

"I think it was a bad idea for your dad to give you a VR session for your 18th birthday," Dee said.

"If there are problems later this week, hallucinations or loss of memory, bring him back for a check-up," said the man in the lab coat before he quickly left.

I touched the headgear and glasses. "What happened?"

"You got trapped inside that virtual world and they couldn't bring you out. You were in la-la land for more than a day. They had to do some kind of special progress, inject you with a drug, for you to 'let go.' I hope you had fun in that fake world for all the trouble. Where did you go?"

"Home," I said.

"What?"

"I don't remember," I said.

"A waste of money," she said. "You dad could have given us

something we could use for the baby."

XIV.

Dee drove a beat-up little car and I sat beside her, holding Elaine, our seven-month-old child. Asking careful questions, I figured out that Dee had gotten pregnant at the beginning of senior year and we married after graduation. We lived in a small, one-bedroom apartment and I worked all day at the hardware store as an assistant manager; Dee stayed home taking care of little Elaine.

That night, in bed, Dee wanted to make love: she did all the right touching and kissed all the right places; I was ready, despite what sex had gotten us into. Dee mentioned wanting another baby, but not until we were twenty-three or so, when I started earning better money at the hardware store. "Someday you'll inherit the business and we can have a big family," she whispered.

Before the action of married life got under way, the baby woke up and cried in the crib next to the bed.

Elaine groaned and covered her face with a pillow. "Whose turn is it?"

"I don't know."

"I'll take care of it," she said, getting up, naked, and tending to the baby.

Dee changed a smelly diaper and I lay in bed, staring at the ceiling and trying to find my memories of how I wound up here. A teenage father, married, a full-time job, never enough money for luxuries, beat-up car. Everything I was afraid of and did not want to happen. I was stuck here in Mount Henderson and was wishing for that other realm, still stuck here but without responsibilities. Perhaps it would be best if I didn't regain my memories, I thought.

I knew the memories would reveal I was far more miserable and empty than I was feeling right now.

XV.

The next day, my father called and told me not to come to work, since I had not recovered from my virtual reality accident. "No good if you don't remember how to run the place or who your employees are," he said. "We'll come visit you for dinner tonight, okay?"

Sure, okay.

Dee was irritated about a couple of things: she felt my parents came around too much, my mother always informing her what she was doing wrong with the baby; that she had to show me how to clean the baby and put a fresh diaper on her.

I held little Elaine and felt nothing: no connection, no love.

I looked at Dee and felt nothing: no connection, no love.

I decided I was dead and this was hell and that empty town was purgatory, a place where I waited my ultimate fate: above or below.

I wanted to run.

Why didn't I leave like I had planned? Was it knocking up Dee? I should have left anyway; let me say I was a bad father and a man without honor. One day I would return home and make up for it all, and they would forgive me because I was a success and had a lot of money. Hell, I would buy the whole town.

XVI.

I knew this was not right when my parents came by at seven o'clock for their visit, and with them was my grandfather.

"Let's see that cute sweet little button of mine," Grandpa said, picking Elaine up and kissing her. "Papa loves you so much."

"You're dead," I said softly. I wanted to run to him and hug him but this wasn't right. "You died nine years ago," I said.

"What?" he said.

"Good grief," my mother said with a long sigh, "what did

that place do to you?" To my father: "I told you that VR stuff is nothing but dangerous."

"I thought it would be harmless," my father said.

"You're dead!" I yelled at my Grandpa. "I'm not falling for this—I must still be in the virtual place—you're not real! You died when I was ten."

I had to get out of here so I ran out the door. I would keep running until I found my way out of here, until—

Elaine, the girl with long hair, stood outside the apartment complex; she stood street, waiting for me.

"Tommy," she said, "I'm sorry."

XVII.

The world of the gray sky, the Mount Henderson in a void, returned. People disappeared—no more Grandpa, no more Dee and the baby, just Elaine and me.

I felt better about that, but I wanted answers.

We returned to my parents' empty house and sat on the stairs. She told me, "I created this reality. For us."

"You? How?"

"It's something women of every other generation in my family can do," she said. "That's why my grandmother always cut my hair. The magic is in the hair, like Samson from the Bible: the power is in the length and thickness of the hair. This power skips between generations, my mother didn't have this power, and my grandmother knew I would learn about it sooner or later. She was afraid I would misuse it as a child. I'm still a child. Look what I have done."

"Why did you do it?"

"I had to know, Tommy. I had to know if you still loved Dee, if marriage and family was what you really wanted. You said no, but your heart might tell another story. I see now that life is not what you wanted, or want now, and that's a relief."

"Not that," I said, "why did you do it in the first place?"

"Oh. Well, because I have been in love with you since I was twelve," she said. "You don't remember me from middle school, but I could never forget you. My true love. A love you had no idea about. You were kind to me in seventh grade. When we had P.E. and forced to play basketball, no one wanted to pick me to be on his or her team. I was small and geeky and had messed up teeth and pimples. The ugly duckling, and shy, too shy. But that one day when you were team captain, you picked me and didn't even wait until I was the last choice like everyone else did. I felt like a princess with a knight coming to her rescue. And then a week later in biology, I did not have a lab partner. I sat across from you and you asked me to be your partner. You thought I was smart and would help or do your work for you, but I didn't care. I thought you picked me—both as a lab partner and to be on your team—because you secretly loved me. I knew better, but that's what I chose to imagine."

I remembered her now. "You."

"Short hair, crooked teeth," she said.

"How? How do you have this power?"

"I don't know how, it's been in my family for hundreds of years, I was told."

"How do you do it? How do you change everything?"

"It's like a wish. I wish for something and it happens. The energy comes out of my head, and my hair, and reality conforms to my wish. We moved back here and when I saw you in town holding hands with Dee, my heart was crushed. I thought, 'I wish it was only me and Tommy in the world,' and the world went away, and it came true. There was only you, and me right now. Forever."

"Can you change it back? Can you bring the world back? My parents…?"

"I suppose I could, but they would not be real. They would be constructs of imagination. I already tried, when I put you in the reality where you were married and a father; I brought it all back, but the people were like robots. I don't know how to use my power properly. My grandmother knew this. I should have kept my hair short."

I stood up. "You did this without my consent."

"I didn't mean to, Tommy. I made a hasty wish and it happened."

"This isn't what I wanted or want," I said. "I don't want to be stuck here with you for—what? Forever?"

"We could be like Adam and Eve," Elaine said. "We'll have babies and they'll have babies and we'll repopulate this reality."

"No," I told her. "I won't have that with you. I would rather be alone again. How could I ever trust you not to keep changing reality? I just want to go back home, the way it was."

She began to cry. "I'm sorry, Tommy. I wanted this so much…I didn't consider your feelings…I'm sorry…I wish, I wish I never had this power and none of this ever happened." She looked up. "Oh crap," she said, and vanished.

XVIII.

I spend most of the time trout fishing at Old Duncan's Lake because there is nothing else to do. I am alone and have accepted that; there are worse lives to live than forever trout fishing at the outskirts of oblivion.

—July, 2012
San Diego

THE SMALL BRIGHT
WHITE LIGHT AT THE
CENTER OF THE EYE

I.

When we ephemerals found the wrecked vessel, we were excited about meeting a new race and disappointed when we discovered all but one of the crew of five had expired. The fifth, a male named Gregory Ellis, was nearly dead from many wounds. We slipped into the manufactured bodies we had been using to interact with other beings on this dimensional plane in order to engage in medical procedures to save the creature's life.

We had not begun in a timely manner, and we were not familiar with the body, although it was based on general body formations found in this realm. The moment Gregory Ellis "died" and the conscious essence left the body and went back to where it came, one of us—you—departed from your manufactured body and gained easy entrance into the Ellis body; this act kept it breathing and the heart beating, allowing us to finish repairs.

The creature was no longer Gregory Ellis and you were now known as the Guest.

What is the body like? we asked.

Very strange, you responded, and: It has many aches and pains, despite the repairs—a curious sensation indeed. Not very well put together, not like the bodies we make.

II.

It was decided that you would remain in the Ellis body and return to the home world of these creatures. You would observe and report on the planet, how these beings formed society and culture, and whether or not they were worth further interaction. You would also experience and report on being human.

The vessel was not so damaged that it could not make it back to the home world. There was on onboard computer that had the coordinates programmed for a return trip. It was not difficult to handle the machines; you accessed the Ellis memories and knew what to do.

We hope this mission will not be too taxing, we said before you, the Guest, left for Ellis' home world.

I look forward to the experience, you said.

III

While you were able to access Gregory Ellis' memories, you could only experience it piecemeal; along with the human memories on the home planet were the emotions. Human emotions were difficult to grasp and comprehend. You had plenty of time to do this—six months was the estimated trip back to the home planet. It took seven. You did not use the sleep chambers that slowed the Ellis body's metabolism; this is how the other four had died: asleep. By the time the vessel reached the home planet, you had accessed 75% of the Ellis memories and knowledge of human life. You felt prepared to take on the role of Gregory Ellis, to resume the man's life—at least, enough to obtain the information you required for the mission.

IV.

The vessel had been missing for ten years, you soon found out. When the vessel entered the home world's orbit, three armed warships that demanded to know why you were invading sovereign territory immediately met it. When it was deduced that the vessel was a missing scout ship from ten years back, the human beings became excited with wonder and awe, not unlike how we were when first finding the wrecked ship.

V.

What happened? the human authorities asked.

We collided with an unexpected asteroid, you said, and: It wasn't on the charts.

So the flight recorder indicates, they said.

The others were killed in the power surge, you said.

But you were not?

I was lucky, I suppose.

And now you're going to be famous, they said.

Famous? you said, not understanding the concept.

Your face is all over the medias, they said, and: Everyone wants to interview you. You're the hero of space adventure, the prodigal son returned to earth, Lazarus risen from the dead!

Oh, you replied.

There's just one complication, they said.

Yes?

Your...wife, they said.

Fiona, you said, seeing the image of the woman inside Ellis' imagination. You had experienced all memories of this wife, and felt the emotions: love, loneliness, loss, longing, fear. None of these emotions made you feel comfortable.

What about Fiona? you asked.

Well, they said, and they explained the facts....

You showed no emotions, which the other humans seemed

perplexed by. You knew that a human man would register shock and dismay about losing one's mate, one's "wife," but you did not know how to properly convey that with Ellis' face or body language.

VI.

You talked to men and woman who were called "reporters" and took down every word you said, either by recorders or writing on notepads.

Next, you appeared as a guest on a "news talk show." You engaged in a conversation with a human man with silver hair and deeply tanned skin.

So, this man said, ten years....

It did not seem like ten, you said.

Not when you're in cyro-sleep most of the time.

No.

Never done it. Do you dream when frozen?

You didn't know the answer. You simply said: No.

You're the only fellow to have been in space that long, you've made the history books. How does it feel?

I'm not sure, you said, and asked: How is it supposed to feel?

It should feel fricken awesome, the man said, and: I mean, *I'm* famous and I love it. Now *you're* famous.

It is awesome then, you said.

I knew it! And the babes?

The what?

The women, the groupies, *the spaceman strumpets*, the man said.

Oh.

Awesome, right?

Yes.

I bet your wife is regretting it.

I don't know.

Who needs wives, right?

Right.

We have to cut to a commercial, the man said.

VII.

Several days later, you were escorted to a place called San Francisco where, you were told, Fiona Aaronson lived with her husband and two children. She was no longer Fiona Ellis.

She lived in a big house on a hill. It was a rainy day. You sat with her on the porch and drank a liquid called coffee. You enjoyed the drink.

Fiona had short blonde hair and green eyes. She was thirty-five years old. In Ellis' memory, she was younger and had longer hair and less body fat. You experienced Ellis' emotions: love, loss, a certain pain.

I waited three years, Greg, she said, and: Three years was long enough, Your tour was only supposed to be a year. They said it was hopeless. They said all contact was lost. They said there was not enough food on your ship to last three years, not for five men. They said you were as good as dead.

I almost was, you said.

I had to get on with my life, I had to let you go, she said.

I understand, you said.

Do you? Do you really?

Yes, you said, feeling Ellis' sadness.

She cocked her head to the side, looking at you, and said: You're different, Greg.

I am?

Yes.

How am I different?

I'm not sure how to express it in words, she said, and: It's more like a feeling.

Been away for a decade, you said.

She was looking at you in the eyes, and you felt she was seeing you, the Guest, and not her former husband.

It's your eyes, she said.

My eyes?

They're different, they're not like I remember, but it has been ten years and that's a long time.

I believe there is a problem, you said.

What is it?

Our marriage, you said, accessing memories to determine what Ellis would say in this situation.

Our marriage, Fiona said with a heavy sigh.

Since I'm not dead, we're still technically married, you said.

I know, I've talked to the lawyers about it.

That makes your current marriage invalid, you said.

I'm not sure about that, she said.

Where is your husband, by the way?

He didn't think it would be a good idea if he was here for your visit, Fiona said, and: And he's talking to the lawyers right now. You were declared dead and I was...do we need to really talk about this, Greg?

Do we?

I don't want to. I know we have to at some point. But I don't want to right now.

Where are you children? you asked.

Inside, taking a nap, it's nap time, she said.

May I see them?

What?

I would like to see these children, you said.

All right, she said.

She took you inside the house on the hill; the government escorts waited outside by the government car with the black tinted windows. Fiona led you upstairs and to a bedroom, a children's room, where two little human males, ages three and four, slept in separate beds.

They look...peaceful, you said.

They are my angels, she said.

Do you remember when we talked of having children? you said, accessing those Ellis memories and feeling sad.

Please, don't, Fiona said.

Something odd took you over: the incredible Ellis emotions, and the Ellis memories, the recall of Fiona's body next to the Ellis body. It was as if Ellis was back in his body and taking over: you reached out for Fiona and kissed her on the lips.

Gently, she pushed you away.

Please, don't, she said.

Fiona, you said.

I still love you, she said softly, but I have these children, and I have a husband who loves me, he's alive and he loves me.

One of the small boys woke up and looked at them.

Mommy, said the boy, pointing at you, who is that?

A very old friend, Fiona said.

A new emotion from Ellis' memories filled your body: anger, and jealousy, and more anger.

I must leave, you said, shaking.

That might be best, she said.

May I come back?

Yes, she said, and: We do have things to talk about, eventually.

VIII.

From San Francisco, you were flown by government transport down to Los Angeles. That evening, you were on another news talk show, but you did not want to be there.

That night, you were in a hotel room in Beverly Hills, provided by the talk show producers. You could not get the Ellis body to rest; the body—and yourself—were still feeling the variety of emotions associated with Fiona.

There was a knock on the door. You opened the door and a woman with long black hair and many gold necklaces walked in. In her hand, she held a small animal, what was called a "toy box terrier." This woman wore high heels and a short silver dress and sunglasses, even though it was night, indoors, and the room was semi-dark.

Wow, you *are* real, she said.

May I help you?

You sure can. Let's get to bed, baby!

She dropped the small dog to the floor and grabbed you, kissed you.

Gently, you pushed her away, the same way Fiona did to you.

Don't you *know* who *I* am? she said.

No, you said.

Oh yeah, you been gone and ten years ago I was nine and not so famous.

Who are you?

I'm Wendy Talman, man, she said, and: Duhh, my daddy is Miles Talman, the third richest movie producer in town.

I'm sorry, you said.

Look, I paid a fortune to bribe your handlers and get in here. Why?

Why? she said, and laughed, and said: What woman *doesn't* want to fuck the spaceman hero? *Duhhh!*

More memories and feelings: sex. You accessed Ellis' sexual experiences, the dozen women he'd gone to bed with, including Fiona. Desire filled your inner core. Again, it was as if Ellis had reclaimed his body and you were not in control: you grabbed this woman, kissed her, removed her dress, pushed her onto the hotel bed....

IX.

Wendy Talman slept soundly, after two hours of sexual intercourse. You paced about the room. The small dog followed you, barking at you. You picked the dog up. The creature was so fragile. You touched its body. So fragile. You grabbed its neck and twisted. The bones broke so easily; the animal's body went limp.

Ellis' voice in your mind: *How could she? Doesn't she still love me? How could she marry another man and have children with him? The whore!*

You and Ellis knew what to do.

X.

You woke up the government escorts, who were in the next room, and told them that you had to return to San Francisco immediately. They were not pleased about this, at one in the morning, and said San Francisco was not on the schedule, you were due to be in New York the next day. Ellis knew what to do: from your mouth came threatening words, that you would inform their superiors that they took bribe money from Wendy Talman to gain access to his room. This motivated the two men.

Within an hour, you were aboard the transport and in the sky. It only took an hour to get to San Francisco. The escorts drove you to Fiona's house, and even though it was four in the morning, and the sun was not in the sky yet, the escorts did not question your actions.

By this time, Ellis' emotions and memories were in complete control, moved by feelings of betrayal, jealousy, and hate.

XI.

Ellis was well-trained in hand-to-hand combat from his previous job in the military, before he joined the space program; accessing this quality, combined with the Ellis body strength and the emotions, you overtook both the escorts once you had arrived to the big house on the hill in San Francisco.

The two male humans were not expecting such a thing from you, and they were exhausted from lack of sleep. You easily knocked them both out with strategic blows to the back of their necks. You then removed the weapons each had: hand guns that shot twelve bullets.

You knocked on the door and activated the "buzzer," knowing

that Fiona and her husband would be asleep at this hour in the morning. It had been raining all night, so the world was wet and cold. These elements enhanced the feelings of anger from Ellis' deepest pit of emotional turmoil.

How unpleasant it is to be human, you mused.

After several minutes of repeated knocking and buzzing, Fiona's husband—a man called Steve Aaronson—opened the door, wearing a robe. His hair was shaggy and curly.

What the hell is the meaning of this? he said.

You raised the handgun and fired. The first projectile went into the other man's chest; you fired two more into his face. Half of his face was destroyed. Blood, bone, and cranial matter splattered everywhere, including onto you.

You tasted his blood in your mouth.

How unpleasant, you mused again.

Fiona came down the stairs, screaming.

She stopped. Tears emerged from her eyes and rolled down her face.

What have you done? she said.

These words came out of your mouth, not yours and belonging to Ellis: How could you, Fiona? How could you leave me for dead? How could you marry another man? I'm your goddamn husband, you bitch.

She looked at the bloody carnage that was her second husband and said again: What have you done, Greg?

Remember what I said? What I told you?

This was the memory: once, after a marital fight, Gregory Ellis said to Fiona Ellis, quite seriously: If you ever cheat on me, if you ever leave me or sleep with another man, I will kill you both. I will kill him first and make you watch, and then I will kill you, and then I will kill myself.

Oh my God, Fiona said, and: I *knew* there was something wrong, I knew you'd changed. It's in your eyes. *Those are not your eyes.* What happened to you in space? Why have you done this? *Do you know what you've done to our lives?*

You raised the gun.

Please let my children live, she said.

You injected her with five projectiles, until her face and chest were nothing but meaty pulp and slippery blood.

You walked up the stairs.

The door of the children's room was closed. You heard them crying inside.

You opened the door.

The two children were huddled in a corner, holding each other. They were afraid.

Ellis: They must die too.

You: They are innocents.

Ellis: No one is innocent.

You raised both weapons.

You were on the floor before you could fire. The weapons were taken out of your hands. You were hit in the face by human fists. The two escorts—they were conscious, and with their bodies they held you down.

You gave no resistance. You could have prevented them from doing this. The experience was so unpleasant that you could no longer sustain Ellis' memories and emotions. You slipped out of the Ellis body and returned home, the realm of the ethereal.

If anyone had watched closely, they would have seen you leave the body, via the eyes: that small bright white light at the center of the pupil that was the essence of the Guest. The light dimmed, and all there was left was darkness.

XII.

The Ellis body lived without the Guest. It was an automaton now, moving by instinct. It could not speak or reason. It did as it was told, an empty husk going through the motions of life.

There was a publicized trial. Millions watched it on their screens. The jury found Ellis guilty of first-degree murder and Ellis was sentenced to death. After the trial, several jurors told the news media that when they looked at Ellis, it was like looking at "pure evil."

I look at him and there's no life in his eyes, said one juror.

Something horrible must have happened to him in space, another said.

—July, 2009
Los Angeles

TRANQUILITY

I.

The end of the five-year sentence is soon to come to a close and you are anxious for the government to return what they removed from you: your other half, of who you are, that criminal who has been denied a right to life in society, detained in some mainframe hell where all the five-to-tens go. Two more weeks: in two weeks you will be whole in real time, and you will know what heinous act of malfeasance you committed.

Your wife, Anna, knows, but by law she cannot tell you; no one in your family, at work, friends or foes are permitted to say what it was that you did, otherwise the final phase of the punishment would be moot: that real time moment when your missing half is downloaded back.

You have been going about your life the past four years, eleven months and two weeks as half a person, and it was not easy. Sometimes the curiosity and torment of not knowing can get to a person, make a person go mad; sometimes when reunification happens, and the horrible crime is realized, a person wants to die and self-terminate. This is why some decide not to go whole again. You had that option.

But you had to know.

Anna disagreed. "I think we'll both be better off if you didn't," she said several times in those last days.

Of course, you wanted to ask her why why why; what did you do, why would it be bad to remember?

"Things might not be nice anymore," she said.

Home life was generally tranquil and you liked that. So did Anna. Tranquility was the best avenue for all families, especially one like yours: man and wife, late twenties, and one small child, age three.

Tranquility, as the government liked to remind everyone on the billboards and screens, *keeps society productive.*

And: *Love makes for a happy home.*

And: *A happy home makes for a tranquil world.*

"We have a happy home," Anna said; "would you want it any other way?"

II.

In the second year of the incarceration, you went underground, and paid considerable money to find a mind-cracker to fish around your skull for residual remnants. The cracker was a teenage speed addict, but you were told he was the best. You met him in an abandoned building, an apartment where people once lived and loved, and he sat you down and connected various contact wires to your skull, which connected to a small, no-brand-name tablet in his hand.

"When they erase part of you, they can never *really* erase it all," the cracker said. "A shadow is there, hiding in the murky gray matter, bits and pieces and sometimes even a whole. They shove it all back in redundant packs into the medulla oblongata."

"Lovely," you said.

"Now, before we do this, I am not responsible for any ugliness you might find out—you know, whoever you were when you were whole."

"I'm paying you."

"I find nothing, no refund."

You don't know what happened. He gave you something in liquid form to relax and go into REM-sleep mode, then next thing: your body shaking violently and blood flowing out of your nose.

"Goddamn it all to shiznet," the cracker grumbled, pulling the contacts and nodes off.

Weakly, you: "What did you *do?*"

"Nothing. It's what *they* did: put a block on all residual. Whatever you did, it must have been pretty bad, dude."

"Try again."

"No way."

"Try again!"

The cracker was stubborn. "You'll die, and I'm not going down for that, half-head!"

"I want a refund then."

"I said—"

"You found *some*thing, not nothing, and you say it'll kill me...that's not what I paid for."

The cracker threw up his hands. "I'll give you 25% back, just 'cause I feel sorry for you, half-head."

You didn't argue with him.

You knew you had been a bad person; that was enough.

III.

After the first year, it was easy to spot those in your shoes: the criminals who were walking around as "half-heads." The hollowness of the eyes, the confusion of *what did I do wrong* on their faces...even the way they walked, because they walked like you: slowly and carefully, and something told you that there was a time you strolled through society with a lighter step.

You watched debates, read sociological reports, and listened to the speeches of pundits who were against this sort of punishment.

"Does removing the criminal from the mind of the body also remove the spirit of the criminal from the body?"

"This is cruel and unusual. The removed memories and personality are tortured in some cyber prison, a data dump kept secret, and when reunified with the body, the results are unpredictable."

"We have tens of thousands of people suffering and they don't know why they are suffering. How can we, in a country that promotes tranquility and love, call that fair and just?"

IV.

The day before reunification, Anna cries and cries; weeping like a widow at a funeral.

"What's wrong?" you ask. "Tomorrow I'll be the man you knew, always knew...."

She just cries.

V.

They come: the two government agents come in their gray smocks and their machines (a small metal box with blinking lights that you know your other half is stored in), hooking up the contacts and electrodes and putting the helmet and visors over you. They do this right in your home, sitting you down in the living room. They are quick and efficient and seem genuinely concerned for your well-being.

"It might hurt a bit," one says.

"I'm ready."

"We mean after," says the other.

VI.

...and when it is done, when I am a whole, when I am with you and you are with me and there are no more secrets: *then comes the pain.*

The pain of five years inside the mainframe.

Five years of digital anguish.

Five years without a body, and reliving certain memories

over and over in virtual hell.

Memories of my alleged crime.

"No," I say, pulling the helmet and wires off my head. "For *that?* Just for that, I was made to *suffer?"*

"Law is the law, pal," one of the agents says.

"Fives years," I say, "because of *that?"* I say this to Anna, my wife, my darling loving wife. She is standing behind me. I turn to her. She is crying again.

"Anna," I ask, "you condemned me for *that?* Because I didn't want to stay, I didn't want a child, I didn't want to be a married man and tied down to this life?" I say to her.

I rise.

She backs away....

One of the agents grabs my arm. "Easy, buddy."

"You *filed* a criminal complaint because I didn't love you," I say to her, resigned now to the pain, the exile, the truth.

"You were going to leave me, alone and childless!" she whimpers, her back against the wall.

"It was a choice I made," with great emptiness. "A *choice."*

"Free will doesn't make a tranquil society," one agent says, "you know that."

"Happy home, happy family," says the other. "It works."

"We lived in peace and bliss," says my wife. "For five years...."

"There was never any love because I didn't love you," I tell her. "Maybe I acted that way, when I wasn't whole, because I knew no other way. But that means it was all a lie. Don't you see? I was half a person, I was...."

"They said you'd be *better!"* Anna cries. "You were supposed to have learned!"

"Ma'am," one agent says to Anna, "you can file an extension on your complaint. Looks like five years in censorship wasn't long enough for him to get it."

"It's okay," I say, hands up. "No, all is fine. I've learned." I smile as best as I can, hoping there is a twinkle in my eye.

"Do you want to be downloaded back, buddy?" says an agent,

gesturing to the metal case with the memory cell. "Return to a half-head life?"

"No," I say softly. "No."

"You going to be happy?"

Nod. Smile. "Happy as a clam in the ocean."

"Then go hug your wife."

I move to Anna. I hold out my arms. I smile.

"Tell her all is fine."

"Anna...I didn't know what I was saying. I was...I...."

"The shock of re-unification does that sometimes," says an agent.

"I'm okay now," I say. "Anna, I know what I did was wrong. I've paid my debt. I'm ready to move on...with our life...."

I think I sound convincing.

"Where's our child, Anna? I want to hug and kiss her."

Anna smiles. She comes to me, into my arms, and the agents clap their hands and congratulate me.

VII.

I sit with Anna and my child for a family portrait at the shopping mall photo studio. The three of us smile. We are happy and tranquil. I can play the role, for a while, until I figure how to break out of this prison.

—October, 2012
San Diego, California

WELCOME TO
THE MEMOIRS

I.

Ah, the Lieutenant; let us consider the Lieutenant: I had every bit of admiration for the poor bastard, even though I knew he was insane. But: who could blame him? The unbearable conditions have to be taken into consideration: the war. The war was getting inside the shells of the best of us, and caused us all to be perverted.

II.

Gentleman:

Once again I request that I be released from this confinement, that I be let out of the enclosure and given (if not all) some of the freedoms I once enjoyed. We are a free people, are we not? Even in this time of war, and as a loyal soldier of our fine democratic government, I have certain guaranteed rights as set forth by our founding fathers four hundred and twenty years ago.

I have written my report and verified its veracity. My report is the truth and nothing but the truth. I have answered all your questions and endured hours of interrogation. I have taken the fabulation-detector tests and allowed wires and gewgaws to be hooked up to my head and my limbs.

This just won't do. I need to at least get out and exercise. Perhaps you can arrange for a pretty female to be brought into my enclosure and satisfy my needs? I know this is not beyond the scope of your abilities. I, like anyone else, have basic requirements.

III.

In medias res, folks, here I come: back from the battlefield and onto the homeland, where I determined it was my duty to pay a personal visit to the Lieutenant's wife and explain to her how her husband died; that he was, in fact, a hero, and his death was for the defense and our survival as a civilized people. I had seen photos of the Lieutenant's wife: he had shown everyone in the platoon the three pictures he always kept with him, and she looked pretty, but I must say she was far more attractive in person. She was a striking bitch with a shapely form and large, dark eyes. I think she already knew the truth; she looked like she'd been having a good cry. "Excuse me," I said, "but I served with your husband; he was my commanding officer and the most staggering, patriotic, and intelligent individual I've ever had the pleasure of crossing paths with." She reached out to me with her long thin arms and wrapped those appendages around me and we held each other and she cried. She cried so hard that I almost broke down myself, but I could not: it is not something an honorable soldier does. She held me tightly and the next thing I knew: we were kissing, we were passionately "making out," and then we were in the bedroom on the bed and we started to make love. I inserted myself inside her and she hissed and I said, "That's it, take it, take it," I said, "I bet the Lieutenant never fucked you this good, you whore," and then I told her the truth: I told her that the Lieutenant was a pathetic sorry case for a leader and that he was crazy and as well as disgusting; that he had done something so vile, so weird, he *deserved* to die. "How do like *that news*, bitch?" I said, and her mouth opened wide and she *came*, she came hard, and then I came and fell down on top of her. "I hate you," I whispered, "I hate you."

IV.

The Lieutenant often kept morale up by telling us how evil the enemy was. "They have to die, for all their crimes," he said late at night, before morning arrived and the killing would resume. "Take into consideration how they live," he said; "the color of their skin and the way their eyes are situated in their skull. *And how they smell!* And how they fight—with their sad guns and bullets and grenades. For all their weapons technology, we are *winning* this war using tried-and-true swords and arrows. For that, don't they *deserve* to die? Eh?!"

V.

This will never work.

Gentlemen, look: the Lieutenant was not the officer you think he was, and there is nothing I can do nor say, other than outright lying, to change that. I believe he was born that way: he was a deviant. He could not help himself.

VI.

"My wife is not enough for me," the Lieutenant confessed to me one evening after he had too much bug juice to drink. "Oh, sure, she's a sexy creature," he said, bringing out the photographs, holding them like small treasures, "but I have an insatiable appetite, I am a monster when it comes to sex. I am a pleasure machine, and it doesn't matter where I get it, as long as I make the conquest"; and while I like to tell myself the Lieutenant was merely inebriated, I understand now that a true self was emerging from his shell. He reached out for me and touched me tenderly. "I think you're the same way, soldier," he said.

I pushed him away. I was disgusted. "You have me wrong, sir," I said, "what makes you think I'm 'like that'?"

"Don't be so *backwards*, soldier," he said. "These are progressive times."

"I'm old-fashioned, sir."

"I could order you."

"And I could *kill* you," I said; "it would be justifiable because there are laws about such things."

"This is *war*: the old laws do not apply on the battlefield."

"I am going to walk away, sir," and I did.

"This is just between you and me, soldier!" he yelled. "Just you and me and the breeze of the night!"

VII.

"Get out," his wife said after I spent myself inside her a third time, after hours of fucking; "you disgusting bastard, get out, I hate you, *you're just like him*, get out of my house!"

VIII.

From my report:

We were doing a mop up in one of the enemy's cities. Estimation is that 95% of the enemy had been removed like the revolting infestation they were; now it was a matter of seeking out and removing the stragglers who managed to slip away. It was a tedious operations that grunts such as ourselves were sent out to do: we went from structure to monolith, from domicile to dwelling, finding the vile vermin of our odium and terminating them with mercy and pity. It was best for the platoons to separate and become solo when entering the large facilities, those monuments of metal and glass erected in worship of whatever false god the enemy worshipped. This is when I heard the familiar cries, in the language and tone of a female enemy, inside a room. So in the room I went, and what I observed, I was not prepared for. I know the Lieutenant was an insane and disgusting excuse for one us, but not to this extent: I witnessed him holding down a female of the enemy and violating her. The Lieutenant had torn off her fabrics and was inserting his sex organ, by sheer brute force, into this female's sex organ. My gorge nearly became buoyant upon seeing this blasphemous act of carnage and I yelled: "Lieutenant, stop what are doing now!" He laughed, oh yes: he laughed. He said, "Do not judge me, soldier, it is not as bad as you think, she is quite nice and you should take a turn when I am done!" Yes, indeed, yes, the Lieutenant had completely lost his mind, and per military mandate, I performed my duty, I did as the manuals instructed: upon such sexual deviation on the battlefield, I became judge and executioner. I unsheathed my sword, approached the Lieutenant, asked him to forgive me (for I was willing to forgive him) and inserted my blade with academic precision into his back, penetrating his heart, exiting the other end and killing the female enemy as well. I wept when I did this, even if I knew there was no hope for a obstinate member of our society: I closed my eyes and wept and said a prayer for his soul. ...

IX.

Dear Sirs:

Enclosed, please find the manuscript to my memoirs as a soldier in the last campaign, entitled *Beyond the Enclosure*. My accounts, while horrific and explicit, are nevertheless true and I strongly feel it is important that the truth be told. Therefore, it is my sincere hope that your esteemed company will publish these humble pages.

There is much debate in the press lately about whether or not the war was justified. Many of our citizens died. I, too, wished we had never left the confines of our underground dwellings and invaded the surface lands. But we must face the facts: the human beings were destroying this planet with their vehicles and their industry and their need for too much of the planet's resources. We needed the same resources, and we needed this planet to be well in order to survive.

So, yes, I am of the camp that concurs that while it was indeed genocide, it was quite necessary for our survival. And yet, the war is now over, and very few humans are left. I support the idea of the reservation on Madagascar where no more than 200 of the vile creatures' infants will be maintained in a sterile environment, ignorant of their true lineage and history. And so, once again, the insects are the Stewarts of Earth, and we will do what is right to keep this round rock clean for democracy.

It is my hope that you will find this manuscript suitable for publication.

I look forward to your response.

—May, 2008
Borrego Springs, California

THE DREAMER

I.

The third week I was there, the Dreamer—deep in the core of Ganymede—made contact. The Dreamer said to me: I know what you need. I replied: No one knows what I need because I don't know what I need. The Dreamer said: I know what is destroying your soul and I can fix that—please let me help, it is what I do, it is why I was made.

I had no idea what the Dreamer was: alien, machine, spirit, god.

I had shipped out to the Ganymede Station to conduct sociological research on men and women in confined cramped quarters and limited personal space while in space. I applied for the grant and won. This is was what I needed at the time: to get far away from my old life. Off-planet seemed the best route for a woman in pain. My previous published books and papers made me a fine candidate for the study.

Then I had the dreams: dreams of the Dreamer, and with the Dreamer was my dead son. I did not know how this was possible but I did not care; I held my dead son in my arms and I whispered: I love you. My dead son said: Love you back, mom.

His name was to be David. David Kelly Greene. If he had lived.

The Dreamer says: He does live.

I said: Only here.

The Dreamer said: That can change, with a simple thought, a

request, a desire, and he will be yours.

And I cried.

II.

Sally first said what we all wanted to say. During breakfast, the morning shift—half a dozen men and women—ate quietly, deep in thought, and I knew what was going on. I felt the same, I felt the energy in the air: fear and confusion.

Sally said: You know, I've been having the strangest dreams all week about this gigantic alien creature with hundreds of tentacles....

Everyone stopped eating.

Everyone turned at stared at her.

Sally said: What?

Someone asked: What color is this thing?

She said: Gray.

Someone else asked: Where is it from?

Sally said: Down on the moon, I think.

Everything looked at each other. We didn't have to say it; we had all been having the same dream.

Sally said: It speaks to me, it says it's name is—

The Dreamer, I said.

Yes, she said.

The Dreamer, everyone else said.

The senior officer, Captain Nathan Lee, spoke what we were all thinking: Okay, what the fuck is going on here?

III.

The Dreamer: ten thousand feel tall. That is not an exact measurement, it is a guess. It towers into the skies deep below the surface of Ganymede, surrounded by the ancient machinery that keeps it alive, in stasis, keeping the enormous body functioning as the entity sleeps and dreams. Its forty eyes, each the size of a Mac Truck, closed. Tens of thousands of tentacles stretch out of its body like filaments of brain tissue, connecting to machinery and rock and a mist that permeates the interior space where the Dreamer rests.

IV.

Captain Lee gathered both crew shifts—twelve in all—and said: Obviously we are dealing with an intelligent something, a source, a being, and it's made contact. What I want everyone to do is wrote down every detail—what was in your dreams, what was said, what you saw, what happened. Then we will compare everything and maybe we can figure what the hell is going on and what this Dreamer wants from us.
Sally said: What if it doesn't want anything?
Every living thing wants something, said the Captain.
I said: Or needs.
Indeed, said the Captain.

V.

The Dreamer: *Since before your species crawled out of waters and knew the difference between the soul and the body, I have been here, asleep. I have been a prisoner of my own free-will, exiled for my philosophy by my own kind, left behind on this dead moon, alone, so terribly alone. I have been reaching out to you and for thousands of years you have not listened. I would give you anything. I touched the spark that made you crawl from the sea. I sent you love, and still you would not listen. Now you are here, Erin, and you say that you will listen.*

VI.

I will listen, I said, I will listen and I will dream with you.
A bell rings. Come in, I say. The door to my quarters opens.

Sally walks in, wearing only shorts. Her breasts are small and white. She does not ask first, she crawls into my bed and holds me. She knows I need the contact, and I know she needs it too.

I'm scared, Erin.

Don't be.

What does it all mean?

I'm not sure yet.

She kisses me and I kiss her back,

She says: Do you know what I wanted to be when I was a teenager, when I was nine, when I was fourteen? I wanted to be a movie star. Is that funny?

No, I say, and ask: That was your dream?

It was, yes, it was, and when I was seventeen I started to go out to auditions, I tried to find an agent, I got headshots done, I did some modeling but the only modeling I could find was taking my clothes off. Your tits are too small, they told me. I refused to get plastic. I wanted to be real, nothing fake. But no one would cast me, no agent would take me on. You don't have what it takes, they said. You don't seem to reliable, they said. An agent said: You need training, you need school. The agent said: Go see this scout from Rutgers University. So I went to see this scout, this man, this older man, and I auditioned for him and he said I could get a scholarship to Rutgers, if I agreed live with him as his lover for six months. After six months, he said, I would have my foot into the mix and he would find another girl to replace. He wanted me to be his whore, Erin, and I said no, I said I would never sell my body to be an actress and he said: How the hell do you think any woman becomes famous in this business? He said: Everyone is a whore in Hollywood and if you're afraid to be a whore, you're afraid of success. I fell apart. I cried for weeks. Then I enrolled in the space program. My test scores were amazing. I was told: You can go places with these numbers, girl—you could go to space. I traded the stars for a different set of stars.

I held her close, feeling and knowing her pain.

She continued: But the Dreamer says that can all be different, that I can have my first true dream back, that if I forgive myself for all my mistakes, I can be the big actress I wanted to be ever since I was nine. Do you think this is true?

I don't know, I said.

How could it be possible? To erase all my life and have a different life than this one? Would it be real?

I don't know, I said.

When I was a teenager, I only made love to girls, Sally said, and when I went into the program, I only made love to men. I have been wanting to be next to a woman for so long.

I had a girlfriend in college, I tell Sally, but I disappointed her, I didn't know what the hell I was doing and she tried to teach me, but I was too dumb to be a dyke.

We both laughed.

He said: I know what you're thinking, Erin.

What?

You want to go down there.

I looked down at her belly, and beyond....

I mean Ganymede, she said, laughing.

You're a mind-reader now, I said.

She said: I will go with you.

It's a risk.

Of course.

We could get in trouble.

Of course.

If we live, I said.

If, she said.

VII.

We're in the shuttle pod, Sally and I, departing the station and descending toward Ganymede's surface. Captain Lee comes online: What the hell do you two think you're doing?

I said: You know the answer, Captain.

Come back, now, that's an order.

I'm not military. I'm here to observe.

Exactly! You're not even trained to fly that pod.

I'm flying it, sir, Sally said.

We have not been cleared for a surface jaunt, the Captain said helplessly. The Captain knows this is futile: we will not abort.

Captain, Sally said, you know we have to do this. We're being called.

Silence.

I wish I was there with you, the Captain said.

XIII.

The Dreamer: *For those who ask what does it all mean, the answer is simple: it means everything. Your dreams are my dreams and together we experience them together. But first, you must forgive: forgive yourself and forgive others and float on the cloud of your desires, and then you will have everything you always thought was only possible in another life not lived.*

IX.

I held my newborn son in my arms, and placed my overflowing breast to his mouth so he could feed and I could give him life. I sit down with my child and watch a movie starring Sally Evans.

—June, 2009-September, 2010
Borrego Springs, Los Angeles, Tijuana

THE CHRONOTOPE

I.

And here I am getting the inoculations for two jaunts: one half a million years into the past and one half a million years into the future.

A good number of timers had died so that I, and my contemporaries, will not. Every new method of travel—by sea, by land, by space, and by time—is paved with gravestones from the folly of trial and error. In the first jaunts, into the distant past or future, the notion of deceased or new microbes, bacteria and viruses alike had not been considered by the great minds that were too busy dealing with equations, physics, and the nature of time as the fourth dimension.

This is what the doctor tells me as he gives me the shots that will keep me alive.

We must thank them in our prayers, says the doctor.

I thank them before each jaunt, I say.

They sacrificed for the future, says the doctor.

Which future? I ask.

All possible times, says the doctor, and all possible worlds.

II.

And so I do not get stricken with any illness when I jaunt back half a million years to collect the data from the machine left by a timer who returned with an extinct virus that spread throughout the lab and killed many. That lab, in Denver, had to be nuked.

I pray for those who died, and I thank their souls for the sacrifice they made so that I can jaunt and carry out my job safely.

III.

And so I do not fall ill when I go half a million years into the future to an earth where no human beings live, only insects and small animals. I like it here in this time: no crowds no stink of overpopulation, but the bugs and rats...and these giant land lobsters who seem to be the dominant intelligent species.

IV.

And still, when I return, I am subject to three days of quarantine to make sure my body is not host to something new, what we call the hee-bee-jee-bees. It's an uncomfortable feeling, to think that, unknown to me, hee-bee-jee-bees are swimming like happy fish through my bloodstream. Not all hee-bee-jee-bees attack the body right away; they could swim around for days, weeks, months, maybe even years, and then one day decide to destroy their home, not unlike we humans do, and make a mess of things.

V.

And my jaunt point is the old military base on Coronado Island, part of San Diego, California. My jobs are tasked to southern California. I have worked out of points in London, Miami, and New York before. I like San Diego, the weather is nice in any era.

VI.

And I find myself in the city of Tijuana, Mexico, near the border by San Diego, in the year 1987. The city is a mixture of poverty and wealth; the haves and have-nots; third world and modern world. A hungry child begs me for money as I see a limousine drive down the street.

My job sends me to the red light district of Tijuana, an area the locals call Zona Norte. Here the streets are lined with prostitutes dressed provocatively to entice men to pay them money for sex. Inside the clubs and bars, naked women dance for the delight of men's eyes. On street corners stand musicians with accordions and guitars, singing of better times and better days. Many American men walk up and down the streets, enter the clubs, looking for women to pay to have sex with.

This is a delightfully decadent city. I have read much about it. I like the atmosphere, which is festive despite the poverty; I like the smell of street vendors selling hot dogs and corn. It is too bad that in 2037, the city will topple in a large earthquake; for now, in 1987, is thrives on various human needs for connection.

I walk into the restaurant of the Hotel Nelson and have a meal of tacos and small beer. The food is magnificent. Men and women come to my table to sell me things: bracelets, wallets, hats. Children try to sell my gum and candy.

It is from the vantage of the restaurant window that I see my job, just as I was told: a group of five off-duty sailors walking down to where the prostitutes are. I take the knife I had been given for my task and place the knife in my pocket. I get up and follow them: into the Hong Kong Club, where they sit down and drink beers and watch local women dance on the stage. They give these women one-dollar bills, and for that they get to feel the women's body parts.

I am patient.

I am a man, too, and I enjoy watching the display of flesh.

One of the sailors gets up and goes into the men's restroom.

He's happy drunk. He is my job.

I follow him.

We are alone in the restroom.

He is at the urinal, relieving himself.

I take out the knife.

I quickly reach around and slit his throat.

He turns and I jab the knife into his chest.

Leave the restroom, walk back into the streets of Tijuana, waiting to jaunt back to my time now that the job is done.

VII.

And I'm told I did a good job, and reminded why the young sailor had to die in 1987. He would have gone on to be a career man in the Navy, reaching the rank of admiral where, in the throes of madness, he would order several submarines to launch a nuclear attack on Beijing, instigating a war that I once remembered but has now been erased from the timeline of my memory.

One life to take, to save the lives of millions.

It would give you an incredible headache to ponder on how future history was changed, from 1987, by that one death.

VIII.

And it's never that easy. I am tasked to remain years in a certain era before my job becomes clear. I have spent five years in the fifteenth century, before the colonists came to the area that would be Southern California, where I killed a simple crewmember of a Spanish ship. I have waited three years in the eighteenth century, where I killed a writer whose philosophical works would have become the basis for a tyranny far greater than Hitler's. I waited one week when I went five hundred years into the future and I have waited one minute when I was ten thousand years in the future. I stayed one year as far back as two hundred thousand years from my time, to kill a simple hunter-gatherer and his tribe before they evolved into what I was told was dangerous. I had no idea how or why such sincere folk could become dangerous. I do as I am told; I do my job, and I jaunt back—

IX.

And I wait for my next assignment, which could come within days, weeks, months. I have waited two years. I do not know who in the government or military decides that someone from the past or future must die. I am not sure what the criterion is, beyond the good for mankind's timelines.

I am a soldier.

I am a time assassin.

And I am lonely.

X.

And I go to San Diego back in 1938 and am met with a surprise. There is a parade and the parade is for me. I am downtown San Diego, on Broadway, and there is a large banner that reads:

WELCOME TIME TRAVELER!

Hundreds of people cheer as I make my arrival, as I appear out of thin air in the middle of the street. A portly man in jacket and tie, the style of the times, approaches me, and in his hand he holds a large gold key. He tells me he's the mayor and this is the key of the city, presented to me. He explains that many timers get the key to the city, and there is always a parade whenever "one of you people from the future" shows up.

Something is wrong; something is not quite right. This is 1938, nobody here should know of timers, or of time travel, let alone throwing parades.

Another man emerges from the crowd. I know who he is. He tells me his name is Jack Jennings and he's ready to meet his doom, to ensure that the future will be a better place without his influence. He's a young scientist right now, but twenty years later he will develop a weapon used in the Korean War that is so devastating that it stops Vietnam from happening, and President John F. Kennedy doesn't get assassinated, and Richard Nixon doesn't take office, and Ronald Reagan never becomes President which means both George Bushes, father and son, do not become President, and 9/11 never occurs, yet Al Gore does become President in 2012....

That, of course, has to be set straight.

And so Jack Jennings must die.

Jack Jennings waits for his demise.

I point the weapon at him.

The major smiles.

The crowd cheers me on.

Fight the future! they yell.

I kill Jack Jennings and the crowd goes wild, fireworks are shot into the air, confetti rains down, a young man in uniform grabs a woman in a nurse's outfit and kisses her right next to me, the perfect photo op.

XI.

And back at base, I am told that a paradox has occurred and I say no shit a paradox has transpired, 1938 is all wrong. The whole future is wrong, they inform me, and things need to be done to make sure we don't all suddenly vanish without a trace in history.

Here is what happened:

There is a rogue faction of timers who have broken away from the program and have been acting on their own, stopping certain assassinations or taking out people who were not on the hit lists, at least not from the time point they launched from. It has been difficult to find them because their whereabouts in time is unknown. They have absconded with technology and hidden it somewhere in the past.

When I ask who they are, I am told they are not fellow timers I am acquainted with; they are a group from three hundred years in the future, when there is no more United States and a different form of the time program exists.

Things are a mess in the past and the future.

XII.

And I remain five years in San Diego from 1906-1911, the longest stretch of time before I find my target. Something must have gone wrong with chronotope settings, or the wrong data were input. I await a pull-back but it never comes. I am marooned in this era, and I must survive. I take off jobs, and wind up working the grape fields in an area known as Temecula.

In 1908 I meet a woman named Catherine who also works the field. She is a simple woman, a widow at age twenty-eight with a child. I fall in love with her after she falls in love with me.

Against all better judgment, I marry her and we have two children a year apart. We live modestly but we are happy.

In 1910, a man passing as a migrant worker calling himself Miguel tells me he knows who I am, he knows what time I come from. He says he comes from 2314, and he is part of resistance group called the Anti-Chronotope Brigade, who have been changing the past and the future in ways they believe are more beneficial to humankind than what computers and politicians and military men in power believe.

Join us, he tells me.

I say I cannot, I am loyal.

What will your loyalty get you? he asks me. Once you complete your mission, you will be taken out of this time and you will leave your wife and children behind. Join us, fight with us, and we can return you to this year whenever you please. You will no longer be a slave to time.

I ask him: doesn't he see himself and his cronies as time slaves themselves, slaves to their cause, pawns in altered histories.

Clearly, we cannot help you, he says.

I didn't ask for help, I say.

You are doomed, he says.

Eventually, we all are, I say.

XIII.

And so I wait another year for my target. He is a field worker with charisma. By 1915 he will be a leader of labor revolt. We will usher in the rights for the downtrodden worker earlier than it is supposed to happen, resulting in an economic collapse in the United Sates prior to the Great Depression, which will result in the Great Depression never happening, which will result in the United States never joining the Allied Forces in Germany, and the consequence is Hitler's rule of much of the world until 1953, when Berlin is nuked by the Russian Resistance.

All because of one man working in the grape fields of Temecula, California.

And I find myself unable to kill him.

Why is this? I have been here for five years and I have changed. I have a wife and two wonderful children that I love. For them, I am willing to risk it all: time, history, and my rank.

So I let him live, to do what he must.

For a year, nothing happens. Catherine gets pregnant again, my target moves on elsewhere.

Then word gets to me that he was murdered, and I know that they sent someone else to take care of my failed task.

XIV.

And perhaps I should have known better, because I am jaunted back to base while I lay in bed next to my sleeping, seven-month-pregnant wife. I am taken from that life.

XV.

And when I return, I have only been gone five minutes, not five years, despite the gray now in my hair and beard.

I am forced to shave and get a haircut.

I sit in an isolation room and wait for my interrogator, a woman who looks a lot like my daughter will when she becomes a woman, I think.

She demands to know why I failed. I demand to know why I wasn't sent to 1911 when I could have gotten the job done swiftly, why was I marooned for five years where I had to blend in, where I had to fall in love and marry.

There was sabotage by the Anti-Chronotopes, she informs me, and you are not the only soldier who was displaced.

I tell her about my visit, how they attempted to recruit me.

For my loyalty, I will not be prosecuted and demoted.

To redeem myself, they have a special mission in mind, one where I will prove my ultimate loyalty to the cause.

Send me back to 1911, I suggest. I will take care of the job, and then I want to retire. Leave me there. I have a wife and three children.

Your marriage and progeny have altered the future, I'm told.

How? We are no one. We are simple people.

I am told that my great-grandson will become an important man in world politics, and that was never meant to be; he was never meant to exist.

How do you know? I argue. How do you know that isn't the correct future, the one that is truly meant to be?

I receive no answer.

XVI.

And you never want to ponder too long on the concept of paradox; it will only give you a headache. They tell you this first day of training. Leave the paradox in hands and minds of scientists and philosophers. I am a soldier. A pawn. A piece of metal in the large machine.

And yet, how can I resist? They could send someone to pull me from 1906, resend me to 1911. Seems to be an easy solution.…

XVII.

And so they send me back to 1899 to murder Catherine as a child, thus ensuring she will never give birth to children where a great-grandson one day might exist and cause detriment to the preferred timeline.

I wait for her outside the small schoolhouse sitting in the middle of a dirt mound. There are fifteen students. I see her and my heart melts. She's a child, but she's still the woman I love. She is a smaller version of my wife. I want to run to her and take her in my arms and kiss her.

I cannot do it.

I am not that loyal.

Walking away, I hear behind me a voice: They'll just send someone else to take over the job.

I turn. It's Juan, the man who tried to recruit me.

The world is full of murders happy to kill, he says.

I say, I want to join.

It's too late, he says.

Then why are you here?

Look, he says, pointing,

I notice in the distance a number of men and women dressed for the wrong era.

Time tourists, says Juan, here to observe the death of a

paradox.

Catherine. No.

I see her approached by a tall man with blonde hair. He smiles at her.

I yell her name.

It is too late. The man stabs her with a knife, and he laughs. He laughs.

She falls to the ground and laughs.

What kind of man laughs at the murder of a little girl?

You see, says Juan.

I'm doomed, I say.

We all are, he says.

XVIII.

And I find myself back in 1938, downtown San Diego, and the parade that awaits. But it doesn't seem to be for me. The banner reads:

WELCOME TIME ASSASSIN!

And in the crowd I spot dozens of time tourists who did not even bother to dress in period clothes. No one notices. They are waiting for the show. The Mayor of San Diego approaches me, but he doesn't hold the key to the city. A man next to him holds the key, a tall blond man whom I recognize immediately: the assassin who killed Catherine.

We are honored, the Mayor says to me, to witness the protection of the future.

And the blond man smiles at me.

You laughed when you killed her, I say to him.

I find it all so amusing and ironic, don't you? he says.

This isn't fair, I say.

Don't dwell on it, he says, it'll only give you a headache.

And then he raises his arm and points a pistol at my heart.

And the crowd cheers for my death.

And I see Juan in the crowd, observing, and finally I understand his cause.

—August-September, 2010
Tijuana, México

ACKNOWLEDGMENTS

"Brothers" first appeared online at *New Dead Families*, edited by Zack Wentz (2009). Copyright © 2009, 2013 by Michael Hemmingson.

"Of Proms, Time, and Aliens" first appeared, under the title "Solid Memories Have the Lifespan of Tulips and Sunflowers," in the anthology, *Prom Night*, edited by Nancy Springer (DAW Books, 1999). It also appears in the author's collection of literary fiction, *Pictures of Houses with Water Damage* (Black Lawrence Press, 2010). Copyright © 1999, 2010, 2013 by Michael Hemmingson.

"Something Weird Happened on the Way Back from Borrego Springs" first appeared at *Galaxy Online* (1999). Copyright © 1999, 2013 by Michael Hemmingson.

"Hardboiled Zombie Detective" first appeared, under the title "Hardboiled Stiff," in the anthology *Badass Horror*, edited by Gerald Brennan and Gary Kilworth (Dybbuk Press, 2006). Copyright © 2006, 2013 by Michael Hemmingson.

"Tranquility" originally appeared in *Fiction International* (2013). Copyright © 2013 by Michael Hemmingson.

"Consequences of Steam," "More Allisons Than I Know What to Do With," "Six Days Apart," "Trailer Park Trash," "The Arrangement with Mr. Green," "The Last Bushel of Grapes," "Trout Fishing on the Edge of Oblivion," "The Small Bright White Light at the Center of the Eye," "Welcome to the Memoirs," "The Dreamer," and "The Chronotope" are published here for the first time. Copyright © 2013 by Michael

Hemmingson.

ABOUT THE AUTHOR

Michael Hemmingson lives in Southern California and Baja California, traveling back and forth like a crazy Ping-Pong ball on chai tea lattes. His first independent film, *The Watermelon*, was released in 2009. He is working on other films, other books, other tales. He is a cultural anthropologist and sociologist, publishing papers on the subject, such as *Zona Norte: An Autoethnography*. He won the the 2009 Norman Z. Denzin Qualitative Research Award from the Carl Couch Center and University of Illinois at Urbana. He is a two-time Everett Helm Fellow at the Lilly Library of Indiana University, where he conducted research into the papers of Gordon Lish/Raymond Carver, and the art books of William Vollmann. He serves as a radio host with a Wednesday show, *The Art of Dreaming*, at Revolution Radio (freedomslips.com), where he focuses on the lunatic fringe and exopolitics. This is his first book of speculative fiction, after publishing many books of crime noir, erotica, and literary fiction, from *The Rose of Heaven* (Prime Books) to *Wild Turkey* (Forge Books) to *Hard Cold Whisper* (Black Mask Books). There will be more SF coming soon.

POISON FROM A DEAD SUN

Since childhood, Nolan Bender has had a psychic connection to the nuclear fish monster known as Goldgotha. He could summon Goldgotha by thought, and Goldgotha defeated many nefarious aliens and their monsters. As an adult, working as a reporter, Nolan has not summoned his kaiju in many years, until a group of devious aliens known as The Consortium invades earth with the intent of enslaving mankind. Nolan once again calls on his trusty radiated goldfish to save the day…but is he being deceived about the truth, and has reality been usurped?

Borgo Press Books by MICHAEL HEMMINGSON

The Rose of Heaven
In the Background Is a Walled City
How to Have an Affair and Other Instructions: Erotic Tales
The Dirty Realism Duo: Charles Bukowski and Raymond Carver
Auto/Ethnographies: Sex, Death, and Independent Filmmaking
Sexy Strumpets and Troublesome Trollops
The Stripper
The Yacht People
Star Trek: A Post-Structural Critique
Judas Payne: A Weird Western
The Chronotope and Other Speculative Fictions
Poison from a Dead Sun: A Science Fiction Tale
Zona Norte
Vivacious Vixens & Blackmail Babes: Tales of Erotic Noir

POISON FROM A DEAD SUN

A SCIENCE FICTION TALE

MICHAEL HEMMINGSON

THE BORGO PRESS
MMXIII

POISON FROM A DEAD SUN

DEDICATION

For Rominna Michelle Hemmingson

CONTENTS

—cross the wounded galaxies we intersect, poison of
a dead sun in your brain slowly fading—

—William S. Burroughs, *The Soft Machine*

PROLOGUE

I woke up.

Everything was quiet. Kelly was beside me, deeply asleep, and she was pregnant. She told me she was pregnant.

Outside in the world, in the city I lived in, the explosions started. The invasion had begun. I knew I would call on Goldgotha....

I just didn't know what timeline I was in.

* * * * * * *

I was in a large gray metallic room. I was not alone. A man I knew, but could not place his name, sat holding his head in his hands. He was bald and had dark Haitian skin....

He looked up. "They fooled us all, Nolan," he said.

CHAPTER ONE
GOLDGOTHA V.
ARMADILGEDDON; OR, THE
ETHNOGRAPHY OF MONSTERS

I left my homeland in Okinawa and went to college in California. I'd received enough negative response from my family (both my American father and my Japanese mother, divorced) and friends when I expressed a desire to do graduate work under the tutelage of Dr. Ethan Lory. I started to have doubts: was I really doing the right thing? Was this my true path? Should I stay in Japan and become a scientist like my father?

When I arrived at the University of California, San Diego, and went straight to Dr. Lory's office, I knew this was the correct path for me.

There could be no other.

UCSD was a beautiful facility composed of five colleges on a cliff in La Jolla, overlooking the ocean, in the heart of San Diego's wealth and prosperity; many movie stars who lived in Malibu and Beverly Hills had second homes in La Jolla—Dr. Seuss and Raymond Chandler had once called the place home.

Ethan Lory was speaking to a very tall blonde female

graduate student about her M.A. thesis on H. G. Wells. She wore a very small and short skirt and revealed a lot of tanned, long leg, and I thought she should be posing for *Playboy* and not writing about the works of a dead author. She looked at me and got up, flustered, told Lory she would see him later, and departed quickly.

"Nolan Bender," I said.

"*Ah*, you're here, finally," Lory said. He motioned for me to sit down. He was in his mid-fifties, wore a Hawaiian shirt (which he did every day) and khaki slacks and tennis shoes.

"Yes, sir, I am."

"*Sir.*" He laughed. "Say, let's go get a drink."

* * * * * * *

"*Why* monsters?" he said and sighed. We were sharing a pitcher of beer and tequila shots at Porter's Pub on the UCSD campus. "I tell you," he said, "I come from a more innocent time. A time when things were black and white, when you knew what and who was evil and who and what was good. There were the bad monsters that wanted to do nothing but wreck cities and cause general havoc and mayhem; and there were the good monsters who helped mankind fight off all kinds of nasties, like the bad monsters and invaders from other dimensions and time travelers with ill intentions. *Now*, you don't know *who is who* and *what is what*. A monster can be both good and bad; it will save your life and then turn around and stomp on you. You just can't tell anymore."

"For me, it all has to do with Goldgotha," I said, trying to hide how buzzed I was getting. I wasn't much of a drinker, not like Lory, who could put them away and still maintain his composure.

I hiccupped.

He smiled. "*Ah*, yes, your claim to fame."

Goldgotha was attached to me—like a cancer, is the way I felt at the time; the famous monster had been with me ever since I was a child.

History—my father was a nuclear physicist, working on Okinawa. He accidentally left some radioactive samples in test tubes at home where I could see them one nosy night when I was seven years old. I intentionally poured the liquid nuclear matter in my goldfish's bowl, to see what kind of effect it would have on my poor, unsuspecting goldfish. One could academically argue, in the Lacanian or Freudian mode, that deep down in my child psyche, I wanted (desired) to create a monster...and created one I did.

My goldfish grew slowly overnight, after I had gone to sleep, and by morning it had escaped its water bowl. It was the size of a cat. It smashed a window and went out into the world. Within a week, it was the size of a Goodyear Blimp, and growing bigger by the hour. It could move on land and swim in water and fly whenever it needed to; it also could emit a laser beam from its fishy eyes, for protection and destruction. At first it was considered a bad monster, until, one curious day, three mutated spiders merged into gigantic twenty-four-legged beast and attacked Seattle. Goldgotha (that

was the name the media had given my fish) fought this big arachnid and won. Now Goldgotha was considered a good monster. It (he) retreated back to the sea, waiting for another day of kaiju glory.

My father wasn't very happy about what I'd done. "There are enough damn monsters in the world, real and imagined," he said, "and what do you do? *You bring another one in it.*"

Lory burped. "So," he said, "there hasn't been much activity from Goldgotha lately. Certainly not for the last seven years. Is it true you can just call upon him and he'll show up?"

"I only did that once," I said; "I was ten."

"Hmm. What *is* it with kids and monsters?"

"This was when that mad scientist's diseased lung detached itself from his body and wanted to wipe out all of mankind."

"Ah, *yes*, Lungilla! I remember that beast well. Breathed out carcinogens onto people, killing them instantly. Indeed, the disease inside the lung was from a parallel universe. Then Goldgotha, the giant laser-breathing goldfish, emerged from the sea and did battle with Lungilla."

I said, with pride, "Goldgotha *squished* Lungilla *flat.*"

"That's what I have been talking about when I talk about monsters," said Lory. "In those days, good *always* triumphed over evil! Nowadays, you see the bad monsters winning and going off to stomp Tokyo."

"Why is it always Tokyo?" I asked. "Doesn't Tokyo

get tired of rebuilding only to have everything smashed down again months later?"

"Economics, kid. The developers and construction companies love it. A steady stream of labor. Frankly, I always had a theory that the yakuza was controlling those monsters—what a great way to wipe out your enemies, blame it on the kaiju, get rebuilding contracts funded by sympathetic world governments. It's all a political game, always was. And," he said, "I think Tokyo takes some kind of sick pride in always being wounded. Look at the worldwide attention it gets. But the monsters—well, the monsters have *always* been merely an extension of our avantpop, post-post-modern, post-kaiju selves. They are connected to the oldest fears and desires of humankind. That's the meat of our academic field."

* * * * * * *

I, too, was quite fascinated with the cross-disci-plinary, interpersonal, and post-ethical historical and contemporary interactions between humans and monsters. After all, my take was beyond academic—I had an interpersonal, historical, and empirical connec-tion with Goldgotha. I think the other graduate students in the Monsters Studies Department resented me for this; none of them had ever had a close encounter with the object of their theories; everything about this field, for them, was distant and suppositional—their infor-mation came from books, the TV, and interviews with those who had had contact. While their research was

quantitative, mine was qualitative and participant-observer in nature when it came to the ethnography of monsters. I ignored their sneers behind my back and their false smiles and praise when speaking to my face. This sort of attitude was common in all departments in the halls of academia; why should my vocation be any different?

Over the past ten years, critics and scholars alike have speculated that Goldgotha was dead; no one had seen neither gill nor fin of him. "Goldfish, as it is, do not live for long," one person wrote, "so perhaps, even as a kaiju, Goldgotha had a limited lifespan."[1] I have never believed this. I could *feel* Goldgotha out there, somewhere in the sea, waiting to emerge when mankind, and the world, would need his help the most. I also knew I could call on him, like I did when I was a kid—if I really wanted it, he would appear for me.

There were some people who also realized this. Well, maybe not "people." They were aliens from the seventh dimensional realm of Jupiter, inhabitants of the city Startopia, and they wanted Goldgotha for their pernicious plans.

* * * * * * *

This is how it happened....

During my second quarter at UCSD, I acquired quite a taste for beer and tequila, no thanks to Ethan Lory. I

---

1. Reamy, Thomas. "Unexpected Lives—On the Mortality Rate of Monsters in a Post-Structural Society." *The Journal for the Academic Study of Contemporary Kaiju.* Vol. 5, Issue 3.

was spending more and more evenings at the campus pub. This is where I met Sachiko. She was everything you'd think a sexy, savvy, twenty-first-century Japanese girl should be, wearing skin-tight back jeans that had a few styling tears in the fabric, one right below her left ass cheek, showing an enticing smidgen of sultry flesh. She was wearing a yellow halter and no bra, the dark nipples of her small breasts hard and obvious and calling to any man's eyes. Her lips were bright red with lipstick and she wore a classy beret on her head. I was looking at her and she was looking at me; she was alone and sipping a pint of Chinese beer. She got up and approached me. She sat down with me. We talked. She said she was a grad student in quantum dimensional theory, but monsters had always fascinated her. I said the study of other dimensions always got my synapses fired up, and this was no lie.

You know the story—we have some drinks, we're drunk, we're connecting well, she says she has on-campus housing, would I walk her home? She smelled like...well, she smelled like sex. Like she *wanted* me to screw her.

And so I did.

I have to say, it was great.

We fell asleep in each other's arms.

I woke up, naked, strapped to a cold metal table inside some kind of spaceship.

Sachiko was there; she was wearing a tight silver spacesuit. So were several other women. They were all looked exactly like her—clones, I thought.

* * * * * * *

"This is the human shape we took, for this dimension," Sachiko informed me. "Our true form, in our own dimension—which happens to be the seventh—is a gaseous matter. We are from the planet you call Jupiter, soldiers for the Municipality of Startopia."

Gee, I thought. The greatest lay of my life turns out to be an alien that's a chemical cloud.

"We want Goldgotha," she said.

"What?" I said. I played dumb.

A jolt of pain went up and down my body.

"Don't act ignorant," one of the Sachikos said. "We can inflict grave discomfort for many hours. We know all about you. We know about Goldgotha."

"What do you want with that fish?"

"Simple. We wish to control the monster and use it. We know you can call it from its hideaway place."

"I don't know if...."

"We know you can."

"We know," they all said at the same time.

I said, "I won't do it."

They said, "We shall inflict horrible pain."

Oh, they caused me a lot of agony all right, and I almost broke, I almost gave in, but I was strong, I was determined, I wasn't going to participate in whatever foul, ill deeds these aliens had in mind.

I passed out from the torture, sweating and bleeding.

* * * * * * *

I came to.

They had Dr. Ethan Lory captive. One of the Sachikos pointed a large, black, oval weapon at his head.

"Don't cooperate with these bitches, kid," Lory said.

"We will kill him," a Sachiko said.

"They're serious," I told Lory, "they will."

"Let them!" Lory said, and laughed. "I know all about these trans-dimensional Jupiter aliens! Their entire agenda is to conquer all planets in the third and fifth dimensions of the solar system! They need monsters to do it. You can't let them have Goldgotha!"

I asked, "Even if you have to die?"

"Even if I die." He winked. "Death is so three-dimensional anyway. They won't really kill me. They need me."

One of the Sachikos said to me, "Will you cooperate?"

I said, "No."

The one with the weapon fired the weapon. Lory's head vaporized. His headless body slumped to the floor. It was a clean vaporization, no blood.

"Oh shit," I said.

"Proceed to Plan C!" one of the Sachikos said.

I'm sure Lory would have taken pop culture delight in knowing that his capture and death was Plan B from outer space.

* * * * * * *

Plan C was to release one of their monsters onto the Earth. They decided to pick their kaiju from the desert

of New Mexico. A Sachiko told me, "In the 1940s of your planet and nation, one of our ships crashed in New Mexico. Its crew was subject to torture by the American government. So, by right of justice, we have chosen to mutate a creature from that region. Behold," and she laughed manically, "the awesome death power of Armadilgeddon!"

The monster was a giant armadillo with an impenetrable shell, and a tail that shot out lightning bolts. First, it destroyed Albuquerque, which was no great loss, and then it made its way west. It obliterated Phoenix, Arizona, and started for the port town of San Diego, California—where I now lived.

Oh, the military tried to kill it, like militaries always try and fail. They sent jets, tanks, and missiles, but Armadilgeddon really *did* have an invincible shell.

"Our monster will not die!" one of the Sachiko aliens said to me. "Do you believe Goldgotha can stop Armadilgeddon?"

"Oh yeah," I said.

"If so…," she grinned, "call for it."

* * * * * * *

I had no choice. After all, human lives were in jeopardy. That spaceship I was in—a big saucer-shaped thing—was hovering over Mission Bay as Armadilgeddon made its way through San Diego, smashing buildings and slaughtering people by the will of its Startopian masters. I didn't put any blame on the kaiju. It had once been a mere simple armadillo in the

American southwest; its only worries being coyotes that wanted to eat it, or speeding cars going down the highway, wanting to run over it.

I concentrated. I closed my eyes and imagined Goldgotha in my mind, as best as I could recollect. In my head, I said, *Goldgotha, help us again!*

I sounded like a child inside my mind.

In many ways, I was.

I had to touch upon my inner child, my memories, to make a connection with my former goldfish.

I opened my eyes and screamed, "GOLDGOTHA! WHERE ARE YOU?!?"

And from the nether regions of the sea and my subconscious, the kaiju heard my plea…and came forth like a hidden nightmare, a forgotten romance with fantasy. Like a trumpet from an angel of wrath, Goldgotha sprang from the deepest parts of the Pacific Ocean and leapt onto the beaches of San Diego, standing on his fins, screeching—beseeching Armadilgeddon for BATTLE.

"Finally!" all the Sachiko aliens said. "Goldgotha will be ours!"

I said, "Don't be so sure of that, ladies."

"Once Armadilgeddon defeats Goldgotha," one Sachiko told me with a snicker, "we will place our mind-controlling devices into the monster, and with it we shall smash the cities of the Earth, and we will rule this planet like we were destined to!"

I started to have my doubts about Goldgotha's power to win…but I should have known better. I thought about

how long it had been since Goldgotha had done battle, at least any battle that I knew about…but Goldgotha had never let me, or the world, down, and he wasn't about to start.

With the Sachiko aliens, I watched the war of the monsters from a view screen in the spaceship. It was quite a fight. Both monsters did considerable damage to each other with lasers and lightning bolts, not to mention the physical blows to each of their massive bodies. It wasn't looking good for Goldgotha—he'd lost part of his dorsal fin, he was bleeding green blood, so he retreated into Coronado Bay. The Sachikos were cheering for their creature. I felt doomed. I wanted to tell Goldgotha I was sorry. But Goldgotha attached himself to a nuclear aircraft carrier that was docked at the North Island Naval Base, sucking away at all the nuclear power; this made Goldgotha twice as big, and with renewed strength, he was back in action and quickly stomped on Armadilgeddon, ripping out his foe's intestines.

He whopped that big armadillo's mutated ass three ways to Jupiter.

The Sachiko aliens were scared now. With Armadilgeddon dead, Goldgotha turned its fishy attention to the spaceship. Before the Sachikos could get the craft started to fly away, Goldgotha hit the ship with his laser breath. The ship crashed into the water. The Sachikos turned into their gaseous form and escaped out the air vents. Goldgotha sucked them into his gills and feasted on them.

I was able to get myself free—I always could, but I didn't want the Sachikos to zap my head off.

Goldgotha ripped open the spaceship with his giant teeth. He peered in.

We were face-to-face, in a matter of speaking.

"Goldgotha," I said, very softly.

He made a sound...*a sound of compassion.*

I could feel him.

He was happy to see me again.

We still had our connection. We always would.

* * * * * * *

Goldgotha returned to the sea and I was a hero. My personal kaiju—my friend—saved the earth from the evil aliens from Jupiter's seventh dimension.

Hero. This was fine by me. I didn't mind the unwarranted attention. I only wished Dr. Lory could have been there to witness it, share it.

I blamed myself for his decapitation and death.

I returned to school to finish my graduate work, but my heart was no longer in the academic study of monsters.

I switched to communications, with an emphasis on print journalism.

And ten years later, I was a professional reporter... leaving the ethnography of the kaiju far behind me, but not too far when it came to invaders and the fate of the earth.

CHAPTER TWO
CYRANO KINSMAN

It had been decided to cut a story I was working on—money laundering among the urban developers in downtown San Diego.

"We can't run it," said my editor, Vern O'Reilly.

I knew why, but I asked: "Why?"

He said, "This comes from up top."

Up "top" was Duane McMasters, the newspaper's publisher, or his wife, Ellen.

"Look, Nolan, you know the drill. These developers buy a lot of ad space. You know Duane's motto: 'The advertisers put the food on the table.' 'The advertisers—'"

"'Are the boss,'" I said. "So these crooks just get away with their scams?"

"*Some*one will eventually get them," Vern said. "They always do—a naïve new city councilman or an ingenuous young D.A.—"

I smiled. "They'll be bought off."

"Always so cynical, Bender. Look, I have another story for ya—tonight, at the Marriott ballroom. I think you'll like it." He handed me a two-page press release.

"A shindig for a company that has moved out here from New York. Go there, write it up, have the story to me first thing in the morning."

I scanned the release.

"This is fluff," I said. "'Reach Your Highest and True Excellence'?"

"Hey, it's hot material these days."

"It's just *another* scam."

"Bender," he said, "you *like* scams, and this organization doesn't have an ad account with us."

I said, "Yet."

He nodded. "So go get 'em before they do."

* * * * * * *

I drove to Kelly's apartment. She'd called in sick. She was a researcher at the paper, seven years younger than me. I usually didn't date co-workers, I'd learned better from experience. Kelly was an exception. Yes, I loved her; it felt like I'd always loved her. I had my own key to her apartment; Kelly had given it to me last month.

She was lying on her couch, wrapped in a blanket, watching TV with the sound off. Cable news. I could never sit through more than five minutes of political disinfo and infotainment for the masses.

"How you feeling, babe?" I said, leaning down.

"Better," she said, kissing me on the cheek. "Must've ate something bad last night."

"You didn't have dinner."

"Lunch," she said.

"They cut my money fraud story," I said, sitting next to her.

"You *knew* they would."

I looked at the TV. The news. I was surrounded by the news.

"Well," Kelly said, "maybe we can order a pizza and drink a six pack and call it a night."

"I have a story to do this evening." I handed her the folded press release. "And," I said, "you're in no shape to eat pizza and drink beer."

"I said I feel fine." She read the press release and frowned. "The Excellence Group. Never heard of them."

"They're from New York, just moved their ops here. Throwing a *soirée* to announce their arrival."

She sat up. "Wait, *this guy*, their leader. Cyrano Kinsman. I've *heard* of him. I think. Yeah, I know who this guy is."

"Yeah?"

"Late night TV and insomnia," Kelly said, and laughed. "*Nolan*, do you know what he *is?*"

"God?"

"I bet he thinks so. He's a *motivational speaker.*"

"Why am I not surprised."

"I've seen his late night infomercials. Finding your inner power, the marriage of spirituality and money, living your life to the fullest," and here she read from the press release, "'reaching your pinnacle of excellence.'"

"Sounds like fun."

She gave me a look.

"Maybe my problem," I said, "is that I haven't found my inner power."

"You're going to hate it," she said, "your bullshit meter will go haywire."

"I'll go and come right back. That is, if you want me to come back...."

"Don't be silly," Kelly said, giving me a kiss on the lips.

Going to my apartment would feel strange, anyway; I seemed to be spending most of my nights here.

* * * * * * *

I had the downtown beat so, yes, this *was* my kind of story. I put on the suit and tie for the event, assuming the atmosphere would be business formal. I was right. There were many men and women in suits, business attire, briefcases, shiny black shoes, the works. The air was filled with stylish and costly colognes and perfumes. I hoped I applied sufficient underarm deodorant. There were three hundred people, give or take, crowded into the Marina Marriott ballroom, where rows of seats had been placed before a stage. On stage: a large red plush chair—the kind you'd think a king or prime minister might sit in—and a piano. I noticed a few faces from other media outlets; they nodded at me and I nodded back.

I wondered where the rest of these people came from; listening to conversations, I figured some of them were regulars the way they talked about other seminars, what

Cyrano Kinsman was wearing at certain events, what he'd said, what foods were consumed. Other people were professionals in various realms of the business world, as I heard them talk about what happened on Wall Street today, what the dollar was faring against this and that foreign currency, what war for oil was on the verge, brimming scandals at the White House, and the high cost of printing books against the diminishing market of readers and the demise of independent bookstores.

I sat in the back of the ballroom; this was always the best place to relax and observe. I crossed my legs. The chair to my left was vacant, and to my right sat a guy in his early twenties, blond hair slicked back; he was wearing a white shirt and a red tie, and looked lost.

A short man with thick glasses and wispy hair sat behind the piano and began to play something slow and beautiful. The chatter in the ballroom ceased and everyone listened. The man played for ten minutes. I could've listened to him all night. I wondered if he was a pro, a concert pianist. During this music, a tall, well-built black man in a pinstripe gray suit took to the stage and sat in the big chair. He sported dreadlocks and mirrorshades; his fingers formed a temple; he crossed his legs with the air of a monarch and turned to the short man at the piano. This had to be Cyrano Kinsman. There was plenty of applause when the short man was done; several dozen people stood up. He was given a wireless microphone and addressed the audience.

"Thank you, thank you very much, and welcome one and all," he said. "That was a beautiful prelude by Claude Debussy. I have always found that Debussy sets the right mood for select situations. And this is quite a situation, isn't it? Here we are—here we *are* in San Diego *at last*; it's been a long and necessary journey, and there is still much work to do. But we're here, you're here, and we should rejoice."

Applause.

"There are many familiar faces out there, and many new faces. For those of you who don't know me, allow me to introduce myself. My name is Paul Remnick, I'm the Chief Operations Officer for The Excellence Group."

Applause.

"Thank you. Let me tell you a little bit about myself, how I met Cyrano Kinsman, and how we started The Excellence Group. Eight years ago I was working as a psychoanalyst in New York City. A young man," he laughed and looked at Kinsman, "came to me, asking for my help. Little did I know that the tables would soon turn and it would be *me* asking for *his* help. A tragedy had happened to Cyrano Kinsman, a terrible loss that I will allow him to tell you about. Nevertheless, I did what I could to help Cyrano with his life, and he helped me. Together, we found the excellence in each of our souls, and we coached one another to achieve our maximum excellence. We knew there were others we could help, those who could help us in turn, and so we formed The Group, as we like to call it, and now

here we are in sunny San Diego, ready for the next chapter. Now I give you Mr. Cyrano Kinsman."

Applause. Kinsman stood, took the microphone. Remnick sat at the piano again. Kinsman's voice was deep, well-projected, and confidant—with only a slight trace of a Haitian accent. "Thank you, Paul. He makes it all sound so simple, doesn't he? We just formed The Group like *that*," and he snapped his fingers and some people laughed.

"But it wasn't so easy as one, two, and three," Kinsman said. "It took a great deal of time, pain, patience, and energy. *Any*thing that is worthwhile to yourself and to humanity in never easy, *al*ways a challenge to procure. There is considerable labor to do, and the darkness looms from above. We must endeavor to keep that iniquity contained. I will tell you about the darkness—some of you here have heard my story, so I apologize."

A woman in the audience shouted: "Tell us, Cyrano!"

He took in a breath. "My family came to this country when I was ten years old. Haitians right off the boat. I grew up in some…very bad neighborhoods in both Florida and New York; the education available to me was, it goes without saying, lacking. But I vowed at that early age that I would not allow my environment to dictate my future. I studied hard, scored high on the SATs (I will not reveal my numbers out of sheer modesty, of course)"—some laughter—"and I won myself a scholarship to Notre Dame. But do you know what kind of scholarship it was? A hint: sports. No, not

football or basketball. Golf. Golf put me through my undergrad years."

Lots of laughter, even from me.

Kinsman continued. "From Notre Dame I acquired a degree in literature and realized that was not practical for this world, so for graduate school I went to Columbia in New York. I earned my MBA from Columbia and I was ready for Wall Street. I was ambitious and focused. Let us say I believed in divine providence—and I still do, to some extent. I wanted to be *rich*, I *knew* I would be rich, and within five years I *was* rich. *I was very rich.* I was twenty-eight-years old and a multimillionaire. I had an apartment in the Upper West Side of Manhattan, I drove a BMW, I rented limousines and ate at the finest restaurants. Now all I needed was someone to share this with; I needed love.

"And so I found love. Her name was Irene McCaine. Yes, we turned a lot of heads because we were an interracial couple, but we were in love and it was right. I married her, and soon she became pregnant. We were going to start a family. I was the happiest man on earth.

"One night I came home late. I often worked late, it's the nature of Wall Street; Irene understood this. I came home to what is now my personal hell: there were intruders in my home. These intruders wished to do harm to both my wife and unborn child. I tried to stop them, I even injured one, but another hit me and knocked me out cold.

"When I came to, firemen were pulling me down the stairs. I was choking on smoke. My home was up

in flames, an evil deed done by the intruders. Yes, my wife and child perished."

Here, Kinsman turned my direction and seemed to be looking straight at me. I felt very uncomfortable.

He said, "I lost my family, just like that," snapping his fingers, staring me in the eyes.

There was a heavy silence in the ballroom.

"How could this be possible?" I wondered. I had millions of dollars, I was powerful, I was righteous, I had divine providence on my side. I couldn't comprehend my loss, and what happened that night. I stopped working. Why did I need to work? I had no family and enough money to last several lifetimes.

"For a year I hardly set foot outside. I didn't take phone calls, I didn't answer mail. I alienated many of my friends and colleagues. I knew I needed help. I opened the phone book and the first name I saw was Paul Remnick. Ph.D. I went to see him and…well." He broke his gaze. I was relieved. Was he really looking at me, or just in my direction?

* * * * * * *

After Kinsman's talk, some people left and others gathered in the adjoining ballroom for the open bar and a long table with a lot of delicious-looking finger foods. I wanted to get back to Kelly, but I also wanted a drink or two. A woman approached me as I got a second drink; she had long and curly reddish-brown hair that went down to her waist, and wore a flowing skirt with a southwestern feel—earthy, natural.

"You're from the press," she said.

I touched my press badge and said yes, and told her what paper I worked for.

"What did you think of Cyrano Kinsman?"

"Well," I said, "he's one of a kind."

"That's quite the understatement."

"I take it you know him."

"Oh yes. I am part of The Group."

"Moved here from New York?"

"Rhode Island," she said. "My name is Clarissa Gregory."

I shook her small hand and told her my name.

"Mr. Bender, if I may," she said, "I am drawn by your presence. You seem to be the kind of man who is often in-the-moment."

I was flattered. "I try."

"I imagine that has to do with your line of work. Tell me, how old do you think I am?"

"Well," I said, "I don't know."

"Oh, come on, Mr. Bender, you can guess."

"I would be afraid to."

"What would you say if I told you I'm sixty-five?"

I laughed.

"You don't believe me?"

I said, "No."

She said, "But I am. I can show you my ID if you'd like; it has my birthday on it."

"There's no need."

"I am sixty-five, Mr. Bender, but I look—what? Thirty? Thirty-five? Would you say?"

I nodded.

"You see," she said, "once I joined The Group, I learned the power of cellular regeneration. The fountain of youth, you can say! I reversed the process, and so have many others. For instance, Cyrano Kinsman will never look older than he is now. Why don't you touch my face? My arm? Feel how smooth and warm my new skin is."

"Clarissa," a voice cut her off, "are you harassing our guest?"

It was Paul Remnick. He joined us.

"Just getting to know him," she said.

"Yes, a reporter," he said, looking at my press badge pinned to my jacket. "There's been a request," he told me. "Cyrano Kinsman would like to talk to you privately."

"An honor," Clarissa said.

"With me?" I said.

"An honor you shouldn't pass up," Clarissa said.

I looked around. "Where is he?"

Remnick said, "Oh, Cyrano doesn't like these little after-lecture get-togethers. He's on his boat. Please. It won't take long."

I said, "Lead the way."

Clarissa said, "We'll speak again, Mr. Bender."

"I hope so."

"I *know* so."

"We love members of the press," Remnick told me.

I saw this as an opportunity to interview Kinsman; I didn't know he was going to interview me. Remnick

led me out of the Marriott and onto one of the docks on the Marina, where there were rows upon rows of yachts and pleasure boats of all sizes that rented docking space from the hotel. I'd interviewed a man on a yacht here before; although I knew the area, it was still an alien landscape to me.

The yacht I was taken to was a hundred-footer, tops; I figured it had three guest cabins and a main quarters. Five million dollars' worth of boat was my guess.

On the deck stood Cyrano Kinsman, wearing a long, dark coat. He gazed out at the bay, sipping from a glass of champagne.

"Mr. Bender," he said, "Mr. Nolan Bender."

"Mr. Kinsman," I said.

"Please, call me Cyrano."

"Call me Nolan, but not Ishmael."

He didn't register the reference.

"I'll leave you two alone," Remnick said.

"Thank you, Paul. Ishmael, some champagne?" He gestured to a silver bucket and the bottle sitting it in. "I *have* read *Moby-Dick*, by the way."

I smiled at that. I said, "No—but thanks. I had two drinks and I have to drive."

"I understand. Please, sit down."

We both sat on foldout chairs on the deck.

"I love San Diego," he said. "It is why I moved my organization here. This is the city of the future. Did you move here, Nolan, or are you a native?"

"Been here since I was a kid."

"Lucky man."

"I enjoyed your—speech," I said.

"Yes, I could tell."

"You could?"

"I noticed you. I'm sure you noticed me noticing you."

"I did, but—"

"But *how* could I, with all those people there? And you sitting comfortably anonymous in the back?"

"Yes," I said.

"You thought it was your imagination, that I was speaking directly to you?"

"Yes," I said.

"Over the years, I have learned—I have trained myself—to pick certain people out of crowds. People with, let us say, power. I don't mean money or position, but that—well, that something in French we call *je ne sais quoi*." He laughed and shook his head. "You have no idea what I'm talking about."

"No, I don't."

"You don't need to right now."

"I have to admit, I'm confused. Why am I here?"

"I'll get to the point," he said. "I want to make you an offer. I would like you to join The Excellence Group."

"I'm afraid I couldn't pay your corporate style fees. I saw the brochure. I don't make that—"

"Not as a student, as a member. We need you. And you need us. You don't understand this right now, but later you will. You do not have to give me an answer right now. Think about it. The answer will come to you."

"Why me?"

"You have something that can assist us with our mission," he said. "We have beneficial qualities that will aid you."

"I don't know what to say."

"Don't say anything."

"It's quite an offer."

"You think we're all crazy, don't you?"

"No."

He laughed.

"Be honest," he said.

"Look," I said, "I'm a skeptic."

"That's good! I like that!"

"For instance, I met an attractive woman who claims to be sixty-five—"

"Clarissa."

"She looks thirty-three."

"She is indeed sixty-five."

"Am I supposed to believe that?"

"Cellular regeneration and reversal. It takes a great deal of energy and resolve, but it is possible."

I rubbed my nose. "I have to admit, I'm not clear what you're all about. What's this mission?"

"I spoke of the darkness earlier tonight," he said. He looked up. "They'll come from the sky. They'll say they are friendly; that they want to help mankind; that they are here to liberate humanity and bring in a new world. The truth: they wish to enslave us. The truth: they wish to destroy us."

"Who are 'they'?"

"Think about my request, and I'll get back to you." He stood up.

"Thank you for your time," I said.

"No, thank *you*."

We shook hands. His grip was strong. We looked at each other for an extended moment. He released my hand, turned, and stared out at the ocean.

CHAPTER THREE
KELLY BELLINGHAM

My encounter with Kinsman left me—charged. I don't know what it was—his touch, his words; I felt the energy growing, flowing inside me—slowly and surely—as I departed the Marina docks and got into my car.

My head was buzzing as I drove. By the time I arrived to Kelly's apartment, I was in a state of aroused frenzy. It was a little past ten p.m. She was in bed. I gently woke her up. "Hey," she said.

"I want you," I said.

She mumbled, but she didn't turn me away; she was in the mood. She was wearing a short T-shirt and thin yellow panties. We kissed as I removed the panties and slipped a finger inside her. She was already wet. This pleased me. "I was having a strange dream," she said.

"Hush," I said, getting out of my pants.

"All these flying saucers were falling from the sky," Kelly whispered; "when they landed, they became cars."

I moved my body on top of hers and entered her. She made a surprised sound. "Falling stars that turn into

cars," she said into my ear, "what does that mean?"

I was delirious with the smell of her body, like an animal.

"I love you too, Nolan," she mumbled and when we were done, she was fully awake and said, "Wow."

I said, "Yeah."

"Where did all that late night energy come from?"

"I have no idea."

"I'm not complaining."

She went back to sleep. I lay in bed, looking at the wall and thinking about Kinsman. I drifted to sleep and Kinsman was in my dream. He wore a white outfit, like martial arts clothing—he stood on the deck of his yacht, the boat in the middle of the sea. It was a bright and sunny day, the sky was as blue as the water. "Look," Kinsman said, holding up his hands, "they are here." Dozens of spaceships appeared in the sky; they were oblong shape, and finely detailed with windows and weapons. The ships looked familiar. I'd seen them before.

* * * * * * *

Kelly Bellingham had started at the paper a year ago. I would be lying if I said I never took notice or interest. I was attracted to her from day one, but she was younger than I and a co-worker. I'd had some bad experiences dating women I worked with, especially in the newspaper business, and never had much luck with younger women. Seven years doesn't seem like a gap, but sometimes it can be.

She was originally from back East, the state of Maine, and I could tell she loved the southern California sun because she always had a deep tan. Her hair was brown, long and straight, with tints of natural bleaching from the UV rays. She often did research for me and when she would get physically close, I'd close my eyes and take in her perfume, tasting the scent on my tongue.

One morning, we had a late breakfast. She'd done some work for me and I said, "I'm hungry, are you?"

"A little."

"How about some bacon and eggs?"

"I could go for pancakes," she said.

She sat across from me at the breakfast nook; she was wearing a low-cut shirt and she caught me looking at her chest. I felt like an ass. She smiled and didn't say anything.

A month later, there was a company softball game. I usually avoid these functions, but Kelly talked me into it. Someone else told me to bring my video camera. The event turned into a drunken laugh-fest, with men and women from all departments at the paper flashing one another their private parts.

Kelly asked if I could drive her home, she was too drunk. "I mean, *can* you drive?"

"I think so," I said.

When we got to my car, I said, "You know, I don't think I can drive."

"We can sit here until we get sober," she said.

"That might take a while."

"You still have any tape left in that thing?"

My camera. "Yeah," I said, switching it on. I pointed the camera at her. "So, Ms. Bellingham, how many beers *did* you have?"

"So many that I flashed everyone I work with, and I'll be too embarrassed to go back to work."

"Hey, you didn't flash me," I said.

"I didn't?"

"I don't think so."

"Well," she said. She was wearing a pair of white shorts and a green tube top. She pulled her tube top down and said, "How's this? *Now* you've been flashed and you have it on film."

I lowered the camera. "We can always call a taxi cab," I said, and we started kissing, and one thing led to another.

* * * * * * *

I finished a 600-word story on The Excellence Group and their welcoming party. I didn't mention my brief one-on-one with Kinsman. I emailed the piece to my editor and felt good that I'd done an honest day's work.

I returned to the bedroom. Kelly was in the bathroom on the floor, and throwing up in the toilet.

"Maybe I should take you to the doctor," I said.

"No," she said, looking up at me. "I know what it is. I don't have the flu or food poisoning. I'm *pregnant.*"

"Pregnant."

"That's what I said."

"Are you sure?"

"Pretty sure. I know this feeling. I was once preg-

nant."

"I didn't know that."

"That's because I didn't tell you," she said, irritated. "I was a teenager, I made a mistake."

"Did you have an abortion?"

"I gave it up for adoption," she told me. "Him. I mean him, *my son*, I gave him up. I had to. I was too fucking young, okay?"

I didn't know how to respond to that.

"Nolan, look at me. *Listen*. Is this a good or bad thing?"

"I don't know."

"I want to keep this baby," she said.

CHAPTER FOUR
FAMILY

Took a couple of days to get over that typical initial shock, then I started to warm to the notion of becoming a father, starting a family, doing that thing what normal people in the world do.

We went to the doctor for a check-up and verification; Kelly was three months along. This didn't show on her belly, but we were assured there was a human being growing inside her. Doing the math, this happened early in our relationship; we'd only been together four months, minus a week or so.

Maybe, subconsciously, this is what I wanted all along.

* * * * * * *

Kinsman left a voice-mail message the day after the story ran: "Good piece, Nolan. I'm sure you've been giving what I talked about some thought. No need to answer me yet, but the answer should be sooner than you would think." I didn't try to figure out the cryptic-tone of his words. I had other things on my mind—other stories, and the child growing inside Kelly.

We didn't tell anyone, not yet; especially nobody at the paper. Very few of our co-workers knew we were romantically involved. Kelly and I always kept up the necessary professional appearance, once in a while sneaking in a kiss or an ass-grab in an empty hallway or down in the basement research room. It was harder now; I found myself constantly, obsessively, glancing at her belly and wondering if the truth was showing yet; I wanted to jump up on my desk and announce to the world that I was going to be a father and that, for the first time in my life, I was truly happy.

Happy—I was happy. Those words, that feeling, were foreign. I'd spent most of my thirty-two years pretending that things were cool, that I was on my chosen path, that I knew what I wanted and where I was going. This is probably the case for most of the people you meet. The *real* truth: all that was half-true, accompanied by a lingering loneliness and buried emptiness. With Kelly, the past four months I discovered the loneliness had gone away, and with idea of fatherhood began to fill the void.

My heart felt good.

Not that I was completely in the clouds. There were worries and obstacles—what to tell people when she did show, would she come live with me or would I move in with her or would we find a place, maybe a little house somewhere? How were we going to afford a child? Would we get married? Kelly and I hadn't discussed marriage, but having the child was a certain thing in our future. We didn't *need* to be married, and

I wasn't sure I wanted that.

* * * * * * *

Kinsman didn't phone me, yet he was in my life. I found myself, at odd times during the day, thinking about him. I'd see him in my head and I would hear his words, like he was standing next to me. And then there were the dreams.

He was in my dreams every night.

He was telling me about the coming darkness, how The Group was ready to fight for the future of humanity and so on and so forth.

Kelly interrupted one of these dreams; inside the dream, she showed up and she was naked. Kinsman looked her up and down and said, "A beautiful woman."

"Nolan," Kelly said, "something is happening."

"What's happening?"

"Nolan! *Nolan!*"

Kelly was shaking me awake. Her face was sweaty and she looked terrified.

"Wake up!"

"I'm awake. What's wrong?"

"There—there was something in here, in the bedroom. More than one."

"What?" I looked around.

"They went away. The whole bedroom was lit up, blue light. White light. Both. And they were standing… right there."

"Who?"

"It was a dream," she said very softly.

"Are you okay?"

"I was having a nightmare," she said. "Monsters. Can you believe it? I wake you up—*monsters*."

"What did these monsters look like?"

"I don't know. Tall, skinny, big eyes. They smelled like—oranges. Rotten oranges. I don't know."

She got out of bed and went to the bathroom.

Something was happening all right.

Kelly came back, her face washed and her hair pulled back into a tail.

"I just want to go back to sleep," she said. "No bad dreams this time."

"No bad dreams," I said, holding her to me.

* * * * * * *

The monsters returned two nights later and this time I saw them. I was awake—at least I thought I was awake. Kelly was asleep. I yelled at her but my voice sounded hollow, like it was going through a tunnel. I couldn't move my body. I was paralyzed on the bed.

There was a soft and bright blue light all around. The monsters were tall and thin; they wore white flowing robes and had large blue eyes. They didn't have big bald heads like you might think; they had thick and flowing dark hair and their heads were the same size as mine. They just happened to be nine feet tall.

There were five of them and they were very interested in Kelly. One of them had what looked like a metallic wand. The wand touched Kelly's stomach.

"Leave her alone!" I screamed.

"It's all right," one of them said. "Do you not remember us?

"The time is now," said another, "for the Sons of the Sun."

* * * * * * *

When I could move—when I seemed to be awake and I was no longer eight years old—the sun was just starting to rise and I heard a groan, a whimper. I sat up. Kelly was crouched in the corner of the bedroom. She was naked and her body covered in sweat. There was some blood on the floor by her.

"They took it," she whispered. "It's gone."

"They took what?"

"Our baby."

"Who?"

"The monsters."

"Kelly," I said.

"It's gone," she said, touching her abdomen.

* * * * * * *

Her doctor was baffled—the woman looked at Kelly's charts and shook her head, saying, "This makes no sense."

It had taken me all day to talk Kelly into seeing her doctor.

Kelly said, "What's the point?"

I said, "To make sure you're okay."

The doctor informed us that Kelly was no longer

pregnant, and there were no signs she ever was. There was no indication of a miscarriage, either.

"Your womb is normal and healthy," the doctor said to Kelly.

Kelly didn't say anything; she stared at the floor.

"I don't see how that can be," I said.

"Either can I," said the doctor.

"We were just in here last week—"

"I know, of course, I know," the doctor said. She was distraught, she didn't know how to deal with the strange and unknown. "The fact is, there's no fetus and no trace of a fetus."

"They took it," Kelly muttered.

"What did she say?" asked the doctor.

"Nothing," I said.

"I'd like to run some more tests," the doctor said.

Kelly looked at the other woman and said, *"No tests."*

"I think we should," her doctor said.

"You'll find nothing."

"I want to double-check—"

"It would be *pointless*," Kelly said. "The baby vanished—*poof!* Just like that. Bye-bye."

The doctor said to me, "I'd like to prescribe her something that will help her sleep. She's…under a lot of stress."

"Let's do it," Kelly said. "Let's medicate me up."

Driving back to her apartment, we didn't speak. Kelly stared out the window, hugging herself.

My cell rang.

"Nolan."

"Who is this?"

"Cyrano Kinsman."

"How did you get this number?"

"I didn't get where I am in life without being very resourceful," he said.

"*What* do you want?" I demanded.

"We need to talk," he said.

* * * * * * *

They were waiting for me on the yacht—Kinsman, Remnick, Clarissa Gregory, and two others: a tall, blonde woman in a black leather jacket, and a pink and plump fellow in a Brooks Brothers. They were all drinking champagne. The interior of the yacht was white and plush and very soothing-looking.

I was not soothed.

"A drink, Mr. Bender?" Remnick offered.

"No thanks."

"Please," Kinsman said, "it's the finest."

"Maybe I will," I said.

"Please," Kinsman said, "sit."

I sat in a chair, away from the five.

Remnick handed me a tall glass.

"I could use the whole bottle," I said.

Kinsman laughed.

I sipped the champagne. It was bubbly and good.

"You've met Paul and Clarissa," Kinsman began. He gestured to the tall blonde. "This is Laura Henderson," and to the pink and plump man, "Edward Sayers."

I exchanged hellos.

"Laura and Sayers complete my inner circle," Kinsman said. "I trust all these people with my affairs, my life, and the mission of The Excellence Group."

"I used to be in investment banking," Edward Sayers told me. "I had billions of dollars at the command of my chubby little fingers here." He laughed, and shook his head. "But my life had no meaning, and then I met Cyrano."

"And you?" I asked Laura Henderson.

"Madison Avenue," she replied. "Advertising."

"Advertisers," I said flatly, "put the food on the table."

She raised a brow. "Indeed they do."

"And was your life empty until you met Mr. Kinsman?" I asked her.

"Only my soul," she said.

"I'm glad you're with us," Kinsman said. "I'm sorry that it took strife to get you here; I was hoping you'd come to us before it happened."

I put the champagne glass down. "I want to know what's going on, Kinsman. Why do I keep dreaming about you, and what happened to my girlfriend?"

Everyone laughed. Kinsman held up his hands and said, "I am beginning to appear in people's dreams!"

I didn't find this amusing.

"You must excuse my moment of self-indulgence," Kinsman said. "The first words that came out of my mouth when this all started—when I realized that I could communicate with certain people through their

dreams. Everyone here has had dreams about me."

"We still do," Laura Henderson said.

"It works on a subconscious level," Kinsman said. "When I sleep, I go into the dreams of others. I don't know what I'm telling them—they tell me, later, what I said." He smiled and leaned forward. "So, out of great curiosity, what did I say?"

"A lot of bullshit."

Silence.

"Listen," I said, "my girlfriend was pregnant yesterday, and today she isn't. The doctor claims it's like she never was, but there's medical records saying she was definitely going to have a child. I have this terrible feeling that you may know something, and that's the *only* reason I'm here right now. So—out of great curiosity—do you or don't you? Know?"

"We might," Kinsman said.

"Mr. Bender," Remnick said, "have you had certain unexplainable encounters?"

"With the bogeymen?" I said. "With monsters?"

"With anything."

I nodded. I told them about the tall people with the robes and eyes, and how they were interested in Kelly.

The five appeared perplexed. They all looked at one another.

"What is it?" I said.

"A new race," Clarissa Gregory said to her companions.

"I've heard of them," Kinsman said. "I didn't suspect they were involved. I was thinking—"

"What?" I said. "*What* were you thinking? Talk to me, Cyrano, not your pals."

Kinsman nodded to Remnick; Remnick moved to refill both our glasses.

I said, "I have to tell you guys, this is all...." All what?

"I know," Kinsman said. "Unfortunately, it gets worse."

"Cyrano," said Clarissa.

He held up his hand. "Nolan, you heard my story, what happened to me, the family I lost."

I nodded.

"Like yourself, the woman I loved was carrying my child, and I thought: 'I am the most blessed man on this world.'" He cleared his throat and stood; he paced as he spoke; the others were solemn. "What I didn't give, that evening I told my story, are *details*. I said intruders were in my home. I never said these intruders were human, because they were not. But they didn't look like the ones you have encountered. These—beings— were about five feet tall, round and reptilian. The best way I can describe them—they were like upright frogs. Their skin was smooth and oozed this—I don't know what—a slime. They said they were there for the child my wife was carrying, needed for a future war, they said. I wasn't going to let them do this. I put up a fight. I grabbed a lamp and hit one in the face—I must have killed it, because its face went completely to mush. They overtook me. Not physically; they got into my mind with their minds. They immobilized me. They

also transferred information to me: who they were and what they felt. Who were they? Alien beings, as I'm sure you have now surmised. From somewhere else. What did they feel? Hate. Pure hate. They did not care for the human race and they hated us for a reason—the feeling was akin to jealousy, envy—we had something they wanted. I didn't know what it was then; today, I believe it is our planet they want. When they were in my mind, I saw their planet and it wasn't pretty: devastated by war and industry, their offspring born from their eggs deformed. What they wanted with my unborn child, that I didn't know. And this is when everything went black. When I came to, my home was on fire, my wife was dead, and I was being pulled out of harm's way. These frog creatures wanted me dead, but that was not in my destiny."

"I'm sorry you lost your family," I said to him, feeling for him. The emotions were pouring from him in waves, filling the enclosure of the five-million-dollar boat.

"When I tell my story, I usually leave out the details of my wife's death. People assume it was smoke inhalation or by burning. She was nearly charred by the fire, but I was told she died before the flames engulfed her flesh; I was told by the police that she'd been cut open and the baby was torn from her innards; I was told she did not survive this disgusting mutilation. And what *could* I tell the cops? Was I going to say giant frogs from outer space did this? How could I? I questioned my own memory, my sanity. I told the police

that the intruders were wearing ski masks and dark clothes and I didn't get a good look at any of them. The police asked if I had any enemies; I did have a few, you make them on the path to success on Wall Street. Some of my adversaries were questioned. Of course, I knew nothing would come of it; I knew the police would never solve the case because the case was out of their scope and reach. I fell out of life, Nolan; I could not go back to work and I could not...there were times I was suicidal. But that would be too easy. My goal was to find out the truth, to get to the bottom of this conundrum. I searched everywhere for answers—I read all the alien abduction books, I went to UFO symposiums, I sought the advise of mediums and Tarot card readers. I found nothing. Oh, there were glimpses here and now, but there were no answers. I believed that I was losing my mind; I started to believe that perhaps the intruders were simply gang members out to have sick fun, or hit men from some banker I had pissed off; and that as a defense mechanism, my mind had me believe the intruders were alien creatures. So I opened the Yellow Pages looking for help, and the first name I saw was Paul Remnick. This was, as we know now, divine providence. Paul and I were meant to meet each other."

"When Cyrano told me his story," Remnick said, "the walls of *my* reality came down. I saw the truth. Because I, too, had encountered these beings. I had been in denial of it for years. When I was twelve, I witnessed them murder my mother. I believe this experience made me choose psychoanalysis as my profes-

sion."

Kinsman said, "Paul and I then began to search for others like us. We knew they were out there."

"So the rest of you…," I started to say.

"…Have had 'dealings' with these aliens," Laura said. "In one form or another, always negative."

"Not just the frog-looking ones," Clarissa said, "but others as well."

"They come in all flavors," Edward said, "insectoid, lizard, giant slugs."

"We have heard about the ones you've encountered," Paul told me, "but you're the first person we've known who—"

I cut him off: "Who are *they?* Aliens, yes, but—"

"*They* are the coming darkness," Kinsman said, gravely. "They are working together. They do not have mankind's best interests on their agenda. We do not know what the end game is."

"What did they want with my child?" I asked. "And yours?"

"I don't know," Kinsman said. "We have theories and guesses, but no certain answer. We seek that answer; moreover, we wish to stop their plans. As a collective, I believe we can do this. I could never do it by myself; Paul and I could not do it. So we formed The Group."

"The Group, then, is a front?"

"Not at all. We stand by what we preach; finding your personal excellence, your inner power, makes you a stronger human being. Not only to succeed, and to make money, but to put yourself in a position

to fight the coming darkness. Money puts a person in certain circles, allows a person to move among those in government and religion who may have answers or assets to help our cause."

"I don't have money or power," I said. "Why would The Group be interested in me?"

"Money, wealth, status; it's all energy. What we seek is that energy, an energy that can be transmutated. I believe some are born with it, some have the spark that must be cultivated like a fine garden. *You* have this energy, Nolan; you are probably unaware of it, and yet it is there. Perhaps you have seen glimpses of it in your life—easily swaying people to your side, causing events to happen in your favor, flashes of genius ideas. I saw this in you the night at the Marriott; I was drawn to your energy and I directed my focus to you during my talk."

"I noticed Cyrano singling you out," Clarissa said. "I talked to you to see if I could feel the energy, and I did."

"I saw it too," Paul said.

"As did others in The Group, others who are not here," Kinsman said. "I knew right away that you had to join us. I knew there was something about you—that you had either contact with the aliens or soon would. So, I began to appear in your dreams."

"What could I do to help?"

"Blend your energy with ours."

"And how would we go about stopping these aliens?" I asked.

"We won't have that answer until they make a bold move. Our collective energy will be strong; our influence on the world is excellence. It is my contention that these beings have underestimated the human will to survive and to fight."

"It's an ancient struggle," Clarissa said, "light against the dark."

* * * * * *

I had to get back to Kelly—I *needed* to return to her. I needed to know she was all right. I needed to talk to her about all this; she was the only one who would understand; we were experiencing this together.

She sat on the couch. "Nolan," she said weakly, holding out her arms.

I held her. We both cried.

"Where were you?" she asked. "I was scared."

I told her everything, about Kinsman and The Group and how they knew about the tall beings that took our child.

"So join them," Kelly said.

"Just like that?"

"You have to," she said. "You *have* to find our baby. You have to get our baby *back*. You can't let these *goddamn* aliens have our child!"

An hour later, I called Kinsman on his cell and said, "I'm in. Let me know what I have to do."

"Thank you, Nolan."

"Don't get me wrong: I have a personal agenda. I want to know why they wanted my child; and I want

my child *back*. If that's possible."

"Everyone in The Group is here for a personal reason," Kinsman told me. "It's what binds us together."

Three days later, the alien invasion began....

CHAPTER FIVE
SUBMIT, MANKIND, OR DIE!

These fucking alien invaders are all the same; they chant the same rant no matter where they are from: "Surrender! Submit! Bow down before Us as Gods! Do this or else face doom and die!"

Blah blah blah, yada yada yada, blah.

And, of course, this is what the new invaders demanded. They referred to themselves as The Consortium, the combined forces of half a dozen races. To make a long speech by them (via internet, TV, and radio) short, apparently at some point in earth's long past, they were inhabitants of the earth, and each time they were kicked out by a race of divine light beings who punished them for having mistreated the planet and depleted earth's resources. These races—reptilian lizards and frogs, slugs, beetles, birds, and giant multi-tentacle creatures straight from a Lovecraftian wetdream—were incensed that mankind had not yet been evicted for its crimes against nature, so the Consortium was created to remove the human pests and reclaim the beloved homeworld...the humans could perish, or become slaves of the new governors

and gods.

"What a croc," said Kelly.

"Tell me about it," I said.

The cameras were on them all: the giant oval ships hovering over all major cities of every nation; the smaller ships engaging in dogfights with military aircraft; delegates of each member race of The Consortium entering the hallowed halls of the United Nations and making demands; naval vessels obliterated by bombs or smashed by the giant squids.

"Not again," I said to myself. Always the monsters; always the ghastly homicidal kaiju.

* * * * * * *

Next: The Excellence Group's reaction to The Consortium. They were not in their best, calm, cool, excellent form; they were aghast and terrified. "We were not ready for this to happen so soon," they said. They were thinking another five or ten years before an invasion.

I met them on Kinsman's yacht.

They were all drunk on wine and hard booze by the time I got there, each member glancing nervously out at the ocean to see if one of the big squids would emerge.

"So what's the plan?" I asked.

"That's the problem, there is no 'plan,'" said Kinsman, looking at his feet and much forlorn. "And we never thought they would come in such force...we thought it would be a subtle invasion, an invasion of

our hearts and souls, not the destruction of cities and armies."

"Well, if you want to conquer a planet," I said, "take off the kid's gloves."

"Is that supposed to be funny?" snapped Clarissa.

"Pragmatic," I said. "It's what I would do."

"Yes, yes," said Remnick, "you have that monster of yours, you could have, at any time, summoned Goldgotha and made yourself Emperor of the World."

"But I didn't," I said.

"Yet."

"Meaning?"

"You could be working with *them."*

"Fuck off," I said.

"Stop, both of you," Kinsman said, standing between us. "This is no time."

"I don't know why I'm here," I said.

"You joined us."

"In words."

"We must do something."

"Like what?"

They all looked at me expectantly.

"Goldgotha," said Clarissa, and they all said the same, nodding heads.

I think I let out a heavy, dramatic sigh like one would at such a moment. I said, "So it isn't *me* you want, but my nuclear fish."

"Both," said Kinsman. "Are you not one and the same? A team? We targeted you a month ago. Do you think it was by chance that your editor assigned you

the story about us? Your editor wasn't cheap, but he wasn't hesitant to take our money."

"Vern O'Reilly," I muttered, "you crook." I'd have words with him later.

"The only thing that matters right now is this invasion," Kinsman said. "Nolan, will you help?"

What could I say? The minute those ships and squids popped up, I knew I would have to call on Goldgotha at some point, before things got worse....

* * * * * * *

I walked into the newsroom with clear intent. Few people were working, and all TVs were tuned to live coverage at the U.N. or battles on land and sea. Vern O'Reilly hopped up from his desk, happy to me, saying, "Nolan Bender! There you are! You got some copy for me? Some meat? Something better than this shit coming off the news wires?"

I punched him in the nose.

He fell back and landed in a chair.

He touched his broken, bloody nose.

"What the hell," he said.

"That's for taking the bribe."

He looked at me as if to say: what bribe? Which one? How many bribes had he taken lately?

"Oh yes," he said, knowing. "They said they would never tell. Those lying bastards."

"Thanks a lot, *editor*," I said.

"I thought they just wanted the publicity."

"You want copy? You want an *exclusive?*"

"I want something."

"How's this: 'Thirtysomething reporter saves the earth from alien enslavement.'"

"Eh? Well, ha, ha," he said, "give me that headline and you have my job."

"I'll take senior staff reporter."

"So tell me what you have in mind...."

"The biggest monster battle in the past fifty years," I said.

* * * * * * *

I did it: I called forth Goldgotha and the fish emerged as he always did, although I had my doubts, since I had no idea if my kaiju was still alive or not—for that matter, what was Goldgotha's lifespan, being that he was a one-of-a-kind species? Could he die? Did the nuclear aspects of his physiology grant him immortality? What did he do down there in the depths of the oceans, hibernate? What did he eat? Was he lonely? These were questions I once asked as a kaiju ethnographer, but they still lingered in the back of my noggin. I had a special psychic connection to Goldgotha, yet I knew very little about the creature.

* * * * * * *

It was replayed endlessly on the news channels and internet: Goldgotha leaping from the ocean, high into the sky, laser beams flying out of its eyes and destroying half a dozen small Consortium ships, while colliding

and biting in half a mother ship

"The world is weirder than what I ever imagined," Kelly said when we sat and watched this on her laptop.

"Did you ever doubt Goldgotha existed?" I asked her carefully.

"All I had ever seen were old videos, and wild stories," she said. "Now we have alien invaders, our missing baby, and a giant nuclear goldfish as our savior."

I had not told her about my history with Goldgotha; I didn't want that kind of attention and I wasn't sure how she would react.

* * * * * * *

Goldgotha was winning, of course, there was never any doubt in my mind that he would not, although it had been many years since he had to do any fighting— which is probably why he was taken by surprise and nearly killed.

A one-mile cigar-shaped black ship emerged from the clouds and fired hundreds of what seemed to be missiles at the nuclear goldfish. Kelly and I were watching it on TV and she grabbed my arm, fingernails going into my flesh; she let out a small high-pitched cry as the projectiles hit Goldgotha all over his body.

I felt weak, felt pain, felt terror like I was being attacked by those weapons. The cameras from helicopters and planes, capturing all angles, showed pieces of Goldgotha's body fly off—golden and white scales, a piece of a fin, an eyeball.

Goldgotha sank into the ocean.

The headlines soon followed:

GOLDGOTHA DEFEATED
BY THE EVIL CONSORTIUM

and

IS GOLDGOTHA THE GREAT KAIJU DEAD?

"*Is* he, Nolan?" Kelly cried. "Is that wonderful creature *dead?*"

I did not think so; I could still feel him; he was at the bottom of the ocean and hurt badly.

The next day, I could not feel Goldgotha. Something was wrong....

CHAPTER SIX
ENTER: THE SONS OF THE SUN

Things looked glib; governments and hordes of people bent the knee to The Consortium. My link to Goldgotha was nil and I did not want to admit that he was dead.

This made me very sad. And I was sad to see Kelly cry, praying to God for salvation and miracles. I could not believe in God in those final hours. The masses arrived in the hundreds of thousands to Rome, seeking the counsel of the Pope. The Pope appeared on TV and the intent saying The Consortium were agents of Satan, and people had to have faith that Jesus the Savior would come and rid the earth of these minions of evil, these demons from space....

The Consortium responded by sending ships to Rome and obliterating the entire city, and two million people. They leveled it with particle beams and bombs. There was nothing but a crater left.

The world witnessed this on their screens.

The world fell to the knee.

The Consortium began to target churches across the world, destroying the structures and the people

huddled inside, praying and screaming.

The Consortium sent out a message to the people of earth: "Your religions are false, based on lies. We are here to liberate you from these false deities that never existed. Choose them, or choose us. Choose life, or choose death."

Then the invaders offered body upgrades: free of all disease and ailments, free of cancer and the common flu; a reversal of aging; new bodies, new life, immortality.

Slaves that would live longer.

I was coming back from the store, with milk and booze, eggs and cheese, Kelly waiting for me, and I passed a number of what were called Rejuvenation Centers: spaceships parked in various open areas of San Diego, lines of people waiting to go in and have these body upgrades, which I heard took about ninety minutes inside chambers in the ships.

I noticed someone in one of the lines: Vern O'Reilly, his nose bandaged.

He saw me, broke from the line and approached. "Hey, Nolan, good to see. Are you getting in line?"

"Line?" I said. "Hell, no."

"You should see people after they get the upgrades! They look—new. *Younger.* I have seen people with cancer go on in and come out clean."

"To be controlled," I said.

"It's a *new world*, Nolan, like it or not. I want you to do a series of interviews with people who have had the Rejuvenation."

"Is that the slant? The paper becomes propaganda for The Consortium?"

"We must adapt."

"What about Duane...?"

"Duane and Ellen McMasters had the upgrades," Vern told me.

I knew my career as a reporter was over. How could I work for people who were now puppets of these aliens? Right now upgrades were voluntary, to win hearts and minds, but it was only a matter of time when The Consortium would make it mandatory.

"Come in line with me, Nolan." Vern grabbed my arm.

I shrugged him away, stepped back, ready to hit him if necessary; then I looked at the back of the line and saw someone else I knew: Cyrano Kinsman.

What the hell?

I went to Cyrano and said, "What are you doing?"

He wore a long, thick overcoat, which I thought was odd, it wasn't a cold day. He was wild-eyed and sweating.

"Get out of here, Bender," he said.

"What the hell are you doing?" I asked him. "You, Cyrano Kinsman, of all people, are taking the plunge and going for this?"

"Not what you think," he said, his voice low, eyes darting back and forth. "I'm telling you, get lost, get the hell out of here *now*."

I noticed that things were rather bulky and uneven under that overcoat; I wasn't the only one; our little

commotion got the attention of two Consortium guards, ten-foot-tall skinny things that looked like a cross between a robot and a fish, with fish heads and eyes. They moved our way, laser cannons drawn.

"Aw hell," said Kinsman, opening his coat. He had packets of explosive devices strapped around his waist, and he held up a detonator in his left hand. "Stop right there!" he yelled at the guards. "Stop or everything blows to hell!"

The guards stopped, seeing and comprehending the explosives. People in line looked on in confusion.

"Say, pal," someone said, "must you ruin a good day?"

"Everyone run, now, or die!" Cyrano yelled.

Half the people got the message and took off, screaming; others stared, dumbfounded, scared, or apathetic.

Cyrano bolted toward the guards and the ship. The alien guards pointed their cannons and fired, just as Cyrano pressed on the detonator....

A bright white flash of light blinded my eyes. The light covered my entire body and took me....

* * * * * * *

A voice said in my mind: *With the Sons of the Sun arriving, there is hope....*

That voice. I knew it. How did I know it?

I had heard that term when the fetus was taken from her: Sons of the Sun....

* * * * * * *

I woke up on a hard, cold, metallic floor; the floor was a light gray like the circular wall that surrounded me. I sat up. My head hurt something awful. There was nothing in this room but me. I looked up and could not see a ceiling, just a glare of a white-yellow mist. "Hello?" I called out. "Where am I?"

I wondered if I was in The Consortium upgrade ship. They must have grabbed me, and probably others, before Cyrano blew him and those guards up. What kind of point was he making? What message, and what use was his death in that matter? I knew he probably wanted to get on board, or near as possible, to the Consortium ship.

A door opened and two lithe young women in silver suits stepped in. Asian women. Women I knew, had seen and met before...sexy aliens from Jupiter!

"Sachikos!" I said, moving back as they came toward me. They did not have weapons. They smiled at me.

"We are not the Sachikos you once know," they both said. "We are at the service of the Sons of the Sun, not the Municipality of Startopia. That was destroyed by The Consortium."

"I'm not buying it."

"Come with us."

"I'm not going anywhere with you psycho alien bitches."

"You will want to talk to the Captain."

"Captain who?"

"Your son, of course," they both said. I had no idea

what they were talking about, but I went with them. I had no way of fighting and I wanted to get to the bottom of this death, slavery or not.

* * * * * * *

I was taken to the bridge. I thought I was still on a Consortium ship, but the bridge was occupied by half a dozen humans, or humanoids. They looked as human as the Sachikos, but they were Caucasian or dark-skinned; and there was the tall ones in robes, the ones I had seen take my child. They busied themselves with a variety of computers and consoles, observing about two dozen view screens around the bridge, each monitoring a Consortium ship: in orbit, out by the moon, hovering over cities and parked somewhere—upgrade ships—with lines of people waiting. A frog-like Consortium alien addressed the U.N. about members of The Excellence Group, half a dozen of them who had strapped on bombs and destroyed ships in San Diego and Los Angeles. "A great punishment will be placed on humanity should it happen again," said the frog.

I wondered who was dead. Clarissa Gregory? Laura Henderson?

Sitting in the middle of the bridge, what I assumed was the Captain's chair, was a tall, slender man in his late twenties, blond hair falling over his shoulders, wearing a dark blue, one-piece uniform that had an orange triangular insignia on the left breast. They all were wearing similar uniforms, expect for the Sachikos

and the robed beings.

"This is Captain N," said the Sachikos.

The aliens on the bridge all eyed me with what I guess was shock.

The man turned and smiled warmly at me. Something inside me wanted to cry. I don't know what it was, who he was, but I knew him, I knew him from some-where—another life, a parallel universe, a life I had no yet lived, it all flooded inside me, and these emotions seemed to be triggered in the love present in his bright blue eyes. He looks so much like Kelly, I thought.

He moved toward me. "Hello, Father," he said.

* * * * * * *

They came as unexpected as The Consortium: from the skies, the stars. Later, experts would say a portal opened up between the earth and the moon and from this portal, which was opened on the other side of time, and the Sons of the Sun came to save the people of earth and rid the galaxy of the evil Consortium and their desire to subjugate all sentient life forms to their rules.

The Consortium, we learned, were a group of dying races from seven planets, poisoned by radiation of their solar system's dying sun. They used what they called "upgrade" technology to actually hijack the life force of other races, and feed on that energy to keep them-selves alive. The poor schmucks who thought they were getting longevity were actually passing along such to the Consortium, rather than receiving it.

I had died, or was intended to die, in the explosion set off by Cyrano Kinsman, but the Sons of the Sun— my son, Captain N—had stepped back in time and teleported me out of the situation half a second before the explosion, so I did not "die in this timeline," as Captain N explained.

Yes, he was my offspring, he was the child I had lost but did not lose: he was taken to help a temporal war that was raging across the galaxy.

And not just my progeny, either. Along with their ships came three dozen giant flying goldfish, the children of Goldgotha. Or the clones. The Sons of the Sun had gone back in time and picked Goldgotha up, rescued him from the ocean, healed him, and made clones to fight a war in the past.

I know it's a lot. Took me a while to soak it all in and believe it. It's a funny world that way. Captain N said in one timeline, The Consortium ruled over earth for two centuries, nearly wiping out mankind, before the Sons of the Sun had the forces to attack.

"Time travel was developed," said my adult son. "So we came back now, to change earth's fate."

CHAPTER SEVEN
THE FAMILY OF MANKIND

Kelly had a hard time accepting the concept of what was happening; she could not deny that when meeting Captain N, she too felt the powerful wave of emotions, of recognition in DNA, and she knew that Captain N was from her, and me: our child, a man and an officer in this galactic battle.

Captain N (N for Nolan, of course) sat down with Kelly and I, in a mothership orbiting the moon, and told us what happened.

"I was removed from the womb by the rebels within the Consortium," he said. "They exist two thousand years from now; they have been cured from the radiation poison and they went back in time to offer a cure of the present leadership of the Consortium. But these leaders rejected the cure; they were more interested with imperial expansion across the galaxy, and to other galaxies, sucking the life energy from a billion races and ruling over all. A temporal war began.

"The positive faction became known as the Sons of the Sun, for the dead star that had set out to kill their race was also the origination of the cure. They looked

through time and saw that the last stand against the Consortium had to be earth, just as the invasion began, and that the family of mankind was the key to end the war. Along with Goldgotha. When Goldgotha was badly injured, he was taken into the future where the positive energy of the dying star healed him; Goldgotha agreed to a cloning process so there would be enough to defeat the Consortium squid monsters while we, the Sons of the Sun, took out their war vessels. And looking through time, they knew this battle had to be led by the sons of mankind, the children from the past.

"Do not trouble yourself with the temporal mechanics of such things, dear mother and father. What was done had to be done, and the timelines dictated it. Certain children were chosen, by certain parents. They were taken from the mothers' wombs at ten weeks; taken to the future to gestate, grow, and train for the war. I have seen the timeline where earth, and the galaxy, falls under the foot of The Consortium, and I could not let that happen, even knowing the pain you both felt at what you thought was my demise.

"I am not dead, dear mother and father; I am here to stay on earth for good, and we can be a family at last."

Kelly and I embraced and held our child: the wonderful Captain N, one of the heroes in the great galactic war.

* * * * * * *

The Consortium fell after three days of battle and much destruction on the earth and moon. Goldgotha

bravely led the dozen clones of himself and tore the hell out of the giant squids and any other Consortium kaiju released. Captain N led a battalion of fifty war ships against Consortium reinforcements coming from the base on Jupiter, where they had defeated the Municipality of Startopia.

The person I did not expect to meet on the mothership: Cyrano Kinsman. He too had been lifted out of time, just before the guards had blasted him to pieces, and taken aboard another ship, where his lost daughter was captain. Yes, the child he once saw taken by alien monsters was taken for a coming war....

"My daughter is heading up the ground troop cleanup," he said proudly

Something was not right, however. Didn't Kinsman say he saw the Consortium frogs the night he lost everything in New York?

* * * * * * *

There is hope, with the Sons of the Sun working with mankind to rebuild earth, humans and aliens alike moving forward and back in time to meet in the middle for a projected new dawn in the galaxy.

Goldgotha and his clones patrol the galaxy seeking out and destroying renegade survivors of The Consortium, stopping them from regrouping or attempting time travel to alter this destiny we now experience.

"They have done so, in various timelines," my son explained. "The temporal war ever ends. We keep on fighting, in the past, present, and future."

For now, in this world, Kelly and I have our child. We are getting to know him and he is getting to know us.

It's pretty nice.

Maybe too nice.

I wasn't buying it.

EPILOGUE

Everything around me fell apart, the world as I knew it, my history as I experienced it. I was standing in a white room, a hologram room, I realized. Half a dozen Sachikos were laughing deliriously and calling me a stupid human with a weak mind.

Ethan Lory's headless body lay on the floor by my feet.

"Now we know *exactly* how to defeat Goldgotha," said the Sachikos.

* * * * * * *

I woke up.

Kelly was beside me. She was pregnant. Everything was all right.

* * * * * * *

I woke up.

I was alone. Kelly was not with me. I didn't know where she....

"Nolan!" she cried from the bathroom, where she lay bleeding from her groin.

* * * * * * *

I woke up.

Kelly was beside me. We were surrounded by a dozen Sachikos. They all grinned, looking at us.

* * * * * * *

I woke up.

Kelly was asleep next to me. The Consortium had been defeated. I noticed a giant gold-red kaiju eye peering in through the window: Goldgotha, or one of his clones, checking up on me, making sure his old human friend was all right.

* * * * * * *

I woke up.

Everything was quiet. Kelly was beside me, deeply asleep, and she was pregnant. She told me she was pregnant.

Outside in the world, in the city I lived in, the explosions started. The invasion had begun. I knew I would call on Goldgotha....

I just didn't know what timeline I was in.

* * * * * * *

I was in a large gray metallic room. I was not alone. A man I knew, but could not place his name, sat holding his head in his hands. He was bald and had

dark Haitian skin....

He looked up. "They fooled us all, Nolan," he said.

—September, 2000 – January, 2013
San Diego and Tijuana

ACKNOWLEDGMENTS

Chapter One first appeared as a standalone story in *Delirium Magazine*, 2001. Copyright © 2001, 2013 by Michael Hemmingson.

ABOUT THE AUTHOR

Michael Hemmingson lives in Southern California and Baja California, traveling back and forth like a crazy Ping-Pong ball on chai tea lattes. His first independent film, *The Watermelon*, was released in 2009. He is working on other films, other books, other tales. He is a cultural anthropologist and sociologist, publishing papers on the subject, such as *Zona Norte: An Autoethnography*. He won the the 2009 Norman Z. Denzin Qualitative Research Award from the Carl Couch Center and University of Illinois at Urbana. He is a two-time Everett Helm Fellow at the Lilly Library of Indiana University, where he conducted research into the papers of Gordon Lish/Raymond Carver, and the art books of William Vollmann. He serves as a radio host with a Wednesday show, *The Art of Dreaming*, at Revolution Radio (freedomslips.com), where he focuses on the lunatic fringe and exopolitics. This is his first book of speculative fiction, after publishing many books of crime noir, erotica, and literary fiction, from *The Rose of Heaven* (Prime Books) to *Wild Turkey* (Forge Books) to *Hard Cold Whisper* (Black Mask Books). There will be more SF coming soon.